Betrayed

By Tim Kent

Published by:
Bluewater Publications, LLC
1812 CR 111
Killen, Alabama 35645
www.BluewaterPublications.com

In memory of my Uncle Lawrence Kent who first got me interested in the Civil War.

"Chance makes a plaything of a man's life."

Seneca
First Century, A.D.

CHAPTER ONE

June 14, 1912
Brick, Mississippi

The boy slowly made his way up the dust-covered road toward the shack on top of the hill. He had spent a week trying to work up the courage to visit the old man who lived up here. He paused and looked back at the town below. The view was breathtaking for a ten-year-old boy.

His school teacher, Miss Harman, was the reason he was coming up here today. She'd taught her class about the war that had ravaged this country almost fifty years ago. Until that day, he had never imagined men fighting a war on the very land where he lived. He'd asked around town and no one was able to tell him what had happened here during the war. One name kept coming up though. They called him Old Man Saunders. Everyone said the old recluse had lived here his entire life and would probably be able to tell him anything he'd want to know.

He stood there staring down at the town watching people going about their busy lives. No one seemed to care what had happened here before them. He found that hard to fathom.

He glanced over his shoulder at the dilapidated shack on top of the hill. He dreaded going up there, but he was determined. All the kids in town said the old man was crazy. They said he kept a shotgun at his side at all times, just to shoot trespassers.

He took a deep breath and continued on up the hill. Old Man Saunders sat on the front porch in a rocking chair. He wore an old pair of overalls with nothing underneath. When the boy got close enough, he could see tobacco stains on the old man's bare feet.

The boy eyed the shotgun propped against the wall behind the old man. A shudder hung at an odd angle from the window. The one on the other side had long since disappeared.

"Miss...Mister Saunders," the boy stuttered, betraying his nervousness.

Saunders eyeballed the boy for a long moment. "That shore is some purdy red hair. Almost shines out in that sun. I ain't seen hair that red in years."

"Thank you," the boy didn't quite know how to take him.

"What's your name, boy?" Saunders leaned forward and spat a stream of tobacco juice across the porch. Tiny clouds of dust rose from the impact in the dry soil.

"I'm Charles Rich, sir," the boy kept his head down, hands stuffed into large pockets. "Everybody calls me Charlie."

"Ain't your pa Thomas Rich?" Saunders wiped his mouth. Tobacco juice stained his bare arm.

"Yes sir," Charlie glanced up. He still wasn't sure how to take the old man. He'd heard too many stories about him. The boys at school said he had gone insane because he had lost his entire family during the war.

"I know 'im," the old man managed a small grin. "He come up here and seen about my arthritis."

Charlie saw Saunders grin, and smiled back. He hadn't known his dad tended to Mister Saunders. Strange how he had never mentioned it before. He said, "Yeah, his daddy was a doctor also. They say he fought in the Civil War."

"Hmmph," the old man replied. He stopped grinning. Charlie wondered what he'd said. Saunders looked down at his feet. His face now wore a sad expression.

Charlie quickly added, "I hope I'm not bothering you, sir. I came up here to see if you could tell me about the war."

"The war?" Saunders's eyebrows shot up. "I figured a boy your age would be more interested in that boat that sunk a couple months ago. What's the name of it?"

"The Titanic," Charlie replied. He was surprised the old man had even heard of it.

"I hear'd about it in the journals," Saunders shot another stream of tobacco juice off the porch. "Great loss of life is what it said. It weren't nothing compared to the war though."

Charlie stepped closer to the porch. He figured this was his chance. He would make his play. The old man would either tell him about the war or send him home. He said, "I can't find anyone that can tell me what happened around here during the war. Miss Harman, my teacher, taught us a few things, but she doesn't know a thing about what happened around here. She mostly talked about Gettysburg and Vicksburg and what a great man Abraham Lincoln was."

Saunders grimaced. "This Miss Harman ain't from around these parts, is she?"

"No sir," Charlie smiled. He had expected this kind of reaction from the old man. "I think her family moved here from Indiana."

"Look, boy," Saunders pointed toward the porch, "you better come on in here out of that sun before you blister. Ya'll fair skinned redheads get burned too easy. I used to have a cousin with the same color hair as you. When we was kids and playing out in the sun, he would get so blistered that his ears would peel off. Now, back when we was boys, the Mexican War was a being fought. We marched all over these here hills and hollers. Bet we killed a million Mexicans. That boy always wanted to grow up and be a soldier, but his maw was agin it."

Charlie relaxed. He watched Saunders smile as he reveled in his childhood games. The old man seemed to be warming up to him. He wondered why he stayed up here to himself anyway. He acted as though he just wanted some company. John Tucker had told him that Saunders even had his groceries delivered up here to keep from having to come into town and be around people.

He stepped onto the porch and looked around. Junk was piled everywhere, but there were no more chairs. Saunders stood up and began to dig through a pile of garbage and pulled out an old bucket. He flipped it over and sat it down beside his rocking chair.

Charlie took a seat on the bucket and waited. Saunders stared down the hill toward the town. After a long moment he said, "Don't know much to tell you really."

"Were there any battles fought around here?" Charlie was on the edge of the bucket eagerly waiting.

"If you mean battles like with armies and such," Saunders began to slowly shake his head, "we had one nice skirmish that I can remember. It was right down there in town."

"Oh," Charlie looked down, his face betraying his disappointment. "Dad says my grandpa was a doctor in the war. Do you remember what he did?"

"I reckon he went up to Jackson in sixty-three when Grant was a throwin' his weight around central Mississippi." Saunders spat, sniffed, and wiped at the tobacco juice on his chin. "I hear'd he did some amputatin' and such 'bout that time."

Charlie looked a little let down. He asked, "So we didn't have nobody from here fight in the war?"

Saunders's eyebrows shot up. He laughed and said, "Well, now, I didn't say that, now did I?"

"No sir," Charlie smiled. "Did you fight?"

"Most all of us that was of age fought." Saunders raised his chin. He had a proud look on his face. He said, "The boys from Brick, Mississippi, formed Company H, Sixth Mississippi Infantry. I still remember all the ladies a crying as we marched out of town. You know when they's a war, all young men must go."

Charlie's eyes grew wide. He waited for the old man to continue, but Saunders was deep in thought. Charlie said, "Tell me all about it."

"Ain't much to tell ya," Saunders's expression changed to sadness. He looked down at the ground just in front of the porch. "There was thirty of us went up to Shiloh in sixty-two. The whole regiment attacked this little old bald hill. There was a little over four hunnerd in the regiment. It didn't last five minutes. Anyway, thirty of us in Company H went in and only five came out. The rest were either killed, wounded, or missin'. Just like that and our war service with the Sixth Mississippi was over."

"That's it?" Charlie looked incredulous.

"That's it," Saunders replied. He rubbed the stubble on his chin while he studied the expression on Charlie's face. "I suppose I could tell you 'bout the best soldier I ever knowed. He fought through the whole war. He started out a lieutenant."

"Sure," Charlie was back up on the edge of the bucket.

"Ain't gonna be able to tell it all in one day. You'll have to come by from time to time and visit a spell. I don't get much company up here." Saunders spat another stream of tobacco juice off the porch.

"Sure, I'll come every day if you want," Charlie looked as though he were about to explode with excitement. He watched Saunders's eyes as he continued to rub his chin. The old man was in deep thought now. He had just gone back to 1862.

Saunders said, "Our story starts in Corinth, Mississippi, up in the northeast part of the state...."

****

CHAPTER TWO

April 9, 1862
Corinth, Mississippi

He woke in a strange place. The room was dark and there were no windows that he could see. His mouth was dry, and his head throbbed.

He attempted to rise from the pillow, but pain shot through his head and he fell back onto the bed with a gasp. The pain was excruciating. He squeezed his eyes closed, straining against the torment. There was movement in the next room. He listened patiently to light footsteps moving across the floor.

A gentle voice said, "Mother, come quick; he's waking."

He managed to get his eyes open again. There was a light coming from the hallway through an open door. The light grew brighter as it got nearer. When the lantern entered the doorway, he was forced to close his eyes. The light sent waves of pain through his skull.

He listened to the footsteps approach the bedside and could feel a presence there. He could feel eyes staring at him. He eased his eyes open again to find a short, middle-aged woman with two angels standing on each side of her.

The woman turned to one of the angels and said, "Get him some water."

The angel spun and left the room. The other angel continued staring at him, a look of concern in her eyes. It made him feel uncomfortable. He tried to speak, but his mouth was too dry. The woman said, "Relax now. You can talk after you have a drink."

The other angel soon returned with a pail and dipper. The woman took the dipper and cupped her hand beneath it as she held it to his lips. He drank so fast that he became strangled. When he coughed, bolts of pain shot through his head. He forced his head back into the pillow and clenched his teeth tight.

"What's your name?" the woman asked.

The pain began to subside. He ignored the question and slowly opened his eyes. To no one in particular, he asked, "Am I in heaven?"

"You're back here in Corinth again," said the dark-haired angel who had brought the pail of water.

Again he thought to himself and wondered if he'd been here before. It was a task just to try and think. He looked at the light-haired angel. She managed a weak smile. He could tell she was attempting to cheer him. Her eyes betrayed the concern for him. She reached down and patted his shoulder and said, "You're safe now."

Her gentle voice, fair skin, and delicate features made him want to reach out and touch her. The dull thud in his head was still there, waiting for any movement to send shock waves through his brain. He looked at her and asked, "Are you an angel?"

"Not quite," the light-haired angel smiled, showing beautiful white teeth.

The woman reached down and patted his hand. "Tell me your name, and I'll contact your family for you."

He suddenly felt very tired. His eyelids were growing heavy, and he fought hard to stay awake.

The dark-haired angel noticed him about to fall asleep and asked, "Please tell us your name."

He struggled to speak. He was beginning to mumble incoherently as he drifted in and out of consciousness. After a long pause, he said, "I don't know."

****

He awoke a few hours later. Light poured into the room from the hallway. The light-haired angel sat in a chair beside him, her soft hand holding his. Her chin rested on her chest, eyes closed. She was sleeping. He watched her for a few minutes as the soft skin just below her throat rose softly with each breath.

It was at this point that he first realized that he was alive and she was no angel. His head still hurt, but it was nothing compared to earlier. He cleared his throat and watched the girl

7

open her eyes. She quickly pulled her hand away. She was embarrassed but managed a coy smile.

She gave him more water. He was careful to not get strangled this time. As he drank, she asked, "Are you feeling better?"

"Yes ma'am," he replied. He stared into her big blue eyes. She smiled at his reply. He noticed how beautiful she was when she smiled. He wondered if he was supposed to know this girl. He asked, "Where am I?"

"You're back here in Corinth, sir," she reached out and gently patted his arm. "I'm Mary Rodes. My family's been caring for you the past few days. Can you tell me your name?"

The question sounded simple enough. He wondered how many times someone gets asked that question in a lifetime. The truth of the matter was he didn't have a clue what his name was, and he found that thought terrifying. He shook his head and asked, "What happened to me?"

"You were wounded at the Battle of Shiloh." She looked concerned.

"Wounded?" he asked. He grimaced trying to remember, but there was nothing there.

"You don't remember any of it?" She watched him shake his head again and added, "You were shot in the head. You've been unconscious for four days. Can you remember any of your family?"

He thought for a moment and shook his head again. He couldn't believe he'd been asleep for four days. All this was just too much to take in at the moment.

She continued, unwilling to give up without some sort of answer. "Do you remember your regiment? What state you're from or what town?"

He shook his head to every question. All this thinking was beginning to make his head throb again. He watched her eyes grow wide with excitement.

"I have an idea." She leaped from the chair, placed the dipper back in the pail and quickly left the room. In a moment, she returned with a small mirror. She held it in front of his face and asked, "Maybe this looking glass will help your memory."

He stared at the image in the mirror and suddenly felt depressed. It was as if he were seeing a boy staring at him for the first time. He had no idea who this face belonged to and suddenly had the strange thought that he was trapped in someone else's body.

The face belonged to a mere boy. He didn't look to be older than sixteen. His face was smooth and soft, and there was a thin layer of peach fuzz on his upper lip. The eyes were small and sleepy looking. His expression betrayed the fear inside. Mary seemed to notice and quickly pulled the mirror away.

"You must be hungry," she said, changing the subject.

"I should be if I've been asleep four days," he managed a weak smile.

She walked to the doorway and turned around. "We'll get you fed before we try and get you up, sir."

He watched her leave the room and raised his hands above his head. They were neat and clean, but they told him nothing. He sighed, closed his eyes, and slept fitfully until she returned with breakfast.

She gently nudged his shoulder, and he opened his eyes. The smell of bacon filled the room. Mary held a plate with bacon, eggs, and biscuits. Steam rose slowly from the plate. The smell made his stomach rumble. He hadn't realized he was so hungry.

She tried to help him sit up, but each time, the pain forced him to crash back into the pillow. She gave up and decided to sit on the edge of the bed and feed him. He began to apologize, but she cut him off.

As he ate, she began to tell him the story of how he'd come to be in her home. He had been wounded early Sunday morning and placed in a wagon with other wounded soldiers. Sometime Sunday night, the wagons had begun to arrive. By morning, there were hundreds of wounded in town and a continuous stream arriving each moment.

Mary, her mother, Martha, and her sister, Fanny, had heard the Corinth Hotel was being used as a hospital. They had gone there and volunteered to help nurse the wounded men. There'd been so many wounded that the doctors decided that the ones

9

they deemed mortal were to be left outside on the ground across the tracks from the hotel. She told him how she'd been giving these poor men water when she'd found him. He had looked so young, so innocent, that she had begged her mother to let her bring him home and care for him. They'd brought him home expecting him to die at any time. The surgeons had insisted there was no hope for head wounds.

After he'd finished eating, she helped him sit up in bed. The room began to spin, and he felt as though he was about to lose his breakfast. It seemed to ease up when he closed his eyes. She volunteered to help him get dressed, but he was too modest. She stood outside the door within shouting distance in case he needed her. He struggled to get dressed. The clothes didn't quite fit.

She shouted toward the door, "Those clothes belong to my father. I hope you don't mind; I'm having yours cleaned."

When he'd finished, she came back into the room and helped him to his feet. They struggled out the door and to the stairway. He paused at the top of the stairs and leaned heavily against the plaster wall. Every time he looked down the stairs, his head would begin to spin and he felt as though he were about to fall.

"Just take your time," she encouraged him.

"I'm just going to close my eyes and feel my way down." He grasped the railing with both hands and began to feel for the step below him. It was a slow process, but he finally managed to reach the ground floor. He was exhausted by the time he got there.

She helped him to a horse-hair sofa in the parlor. She placed a pillow on one end and helped him lie down. She went to a closet and took out a blanket and covered him. He watched her pull a stool over and sit down beside him.

"You shouldn't worry over me so," he protested. "I'm keeping you from caring for the wounded at the hotel."

"I can leave you alone if you'd like," she began to rise from the stool. "I don't mean to be a bother."

"No," he said quickly. "I don't want you to go. I just feel selfish keeping you all to myself."

10

Mary sat back down on the stool and said, "Don't feel bad, sir."

She reached down and gently moved his hair across his forehead with one finger.

He stared into the gentle eyes and asked, "How old are you, Mary?"

"I'll be sixteen next month. Why do you ask?"

"I can't help but believe we've got to be close to the same age." His face betrayed a look of puzzlement. "Why do you insist on calling me 'sir' all the time?"

"Oh, I forgot to tell you," she smiled as if she held a dear secret that would truly impress him. "Your uniform is an officers uniform. Mother says you look awful young to be giving orders to grown men. Nevertheless, your coat has two gold bars. Someone at the hotel told us that meant you were a first lieutenant."

He looked a bit shocked, not sure if this was good news or not. He said, "It doesn't feel right, ma'am."

"I tell you what," she nudged his shoulder, "If you'll stop calling me ma'am, I'll stop calling you sir. Although, I'm not sure what to call you."

He thought a long moment, but couldn't seem to come up with a good answer. Mary could tell it was troubling him, so she changed the subject. "Please don't tell Fanny, but I used you as an excuse not to return to the hotel today. The truth is I didn't want to go down there."

He raised his eyebrows and waited.

Mary's voice sounded troubled as she spoke. "Fanny and I have gotten quite attached to a couple of the badly wounded men there."

He felt a twinge of jealousy burn through his heart at the thought. For a moment, he'd felt as if Mary belonged just to him. He could easily fall in love with this beautiful young girl. He wondered if the feeling was mutual.

It was as if she were reading his thoughts when she continued. "There are three men there who are officers from Alabama. They're not like you; they're old enough to remind me of my father. They're not recovering from their wounds like the younger men do."

He could feel the sigh of relief and then felt bad for being so selfish. At the moment, this girl was so soft, so gentle; he wanted to believe that someday she would be his wife.

She lowered her head and said, "The surgeon there yesterday afternoon told me they may not make it through the night. I just couldn't make myself go back there this morning. I don't want to know."

He reached over and held her soft hand. Tears began to roll down her pink cheeks. He tried to justify everything for her. "Those men did their duty. They knew before going to battle there was danger involved. Every warrior prays for a noble death, and there is no nobler death than dying for those you love."

She covered her eyes with her hand as if she were embarrassed. She asked, "Why do men do such things to each other? I hate war. Before the war started, I saw girls practically begging boys to join the army and kill a Yankee for them. I'm proud to say I never did that. I don't want that on my conscience."

"You're a good person, Mary, but you can't stop what's happening, no matter how sickening it becomes."

She fell silent, the soft sobs barely audible. He watched her wipe the tears on her sleeve and shake her head as if shaking off the ugly thoughts. He began to grow tired again and tried to fight sleep. His eyes grew heavy, and he listened to her sniffing lightly as he dropped back off to sleep.

****

He awoke to the sound of a door being slammed. He looked up and saw Mary waking in the chair by his side. The dark-haired angel named Fanny was at the front door. Her back was to him, but he could tell her hands were covering her face. Mary looked up and saw Fanny. She immediately understood what was happening.

"Fanny?" she asked.

Fanny continued to stand facing the door. She said, "They're gone."

12

"Who?" Mary asked.

"The Alabama officers," Fanny's shoulders began to shake as she sobbed.

"All of them?" Mary began to rise from the chair.

"All of them," Fanny continued sobbing into her hands. "Captain Thomas died just after we left last evening. Captain Martin and Lieutenant Tucker died just before light this morning."

He could see tears running down Mary's cheeks as she began to tremble. He thought of trying to rise and hold her, but his head pounded every time he attempted to move.

Mary moved to where Fanny stood and they held each other, sobbing for a long time. He felt helpless and melancholy. He wished he was anywhere but at this place at this moment.

After what seemed like an eternity, they both came and sat near him. Fanny said, "Mother asked Doctor Evans to come check on our soldier on the way home tonight."

"Will he come?" Mary asked. She had a gleam of hope in her eyes.

"I'm not so sure." Fanny was shaking her head, staring at the floor. "The man is way past exhausted; he looks like he will drop any second now. He has been busy ever since the casualties began to arrive, and there seems to be no let up. Perhaps, when our soldier is able to travel, you can take him down to the hospital."

"Perhaps," Mary seemed a little disgusted that Doctor Evans wouldn't be stopping by. The man was exhausted, but he only lived two houses away.

"Oh, I almost forgot," Fanny perked up and began to dig in the pocket of her dress. "I have something for you."

She pulled out a small book and handed it to the young lieutenant. He looked at the title and frowned. The cover said *Rifle and Light Infantry Tactics, by William Joseph Hardee.* He asked, "Why does that name mean something to me?"

Mary smiled. "He's one of the generals here. He commands one of the wings of the army, I believe."

Fanny added, "It was Captain Martin's copy. They were just going to throw it away when he died. I thought with you being an officer, you may find it useful."

"Thank you," he said. He opened the book and scanned a few blood-stained pages. "It will mean more to me knowing that it belonged to such a great man."

"The news is not good, Mary," Fanny looked toward the door.

"What news?" Mary asked.

"The word at the hospital is that the Federal army is going to come take the town," Fanny began to shake her head. "What is to become of us?"

It was several days before he was able to move about without becoming dizzy. He used this time to read the book and learn how to drill a regiment. After he'd finished reading the two hundred and twenty-four page book, he began to study what he'd read.

A few days later, Mary decided the time was right to get him out and attempt to find his company. She hoped they would run into someone who recognized the young officer.

They took the wagon and started west toward town. The roads were rough, and every jolt would send shock waves through his skull. Mary held onto his arm as he held the reins. Other than the pain, he was happier than he'd been since waking. She'd gone through the trouble of cleaning his uniform, which looked sharp, other than the blood stains on his left shoulder and collar. He had a beautiful girl on his arm. What more could he ask for at the moment?

As they rode toward town, Mary began to describe what had happened in the Battle of Shiloh according to what she'd been told. The Confederates had attacked the first day and almost pushed Grant's army into the river. General Beauregard had faltered at the last moment and pulled back. General Grant had reformed his army and received reinforcements during the night and drove the Confederate army from the field.

"So," the young officer was squinting against the pain, "General Beauregard is responsible for losing this battle."

"Yes, but don't tell Fanny I said that," Mary smiled. "She loves General Beauregard."

"I see," he said, but his expression told her he didn't really understand.

"General Beauregard is greatly admired by the ladies." The wagon hit a pothole and Mary watched the look of pain spread across the young officer's face. "When he first arrived here in Corinth, he kissed Fanny's hand and made a big fuss over her beauty."

The young officer shook the reins to remind the horse to continue moving. He said, "Flattery will get you everywhere."

"Exactly," Mary laughed. "I tend to think the man is overrated. If he was such a genius, why did he lose the battle?"

They began to enter town. Mary pointed out a white house to their right. "That's the Curlee House. Some people call it the Verandah House because of the porch going all the way around it. It's the headquarters of General Bragg."

"Bragg?" the lieutenant asked.

"He's a corps commander or something." Mary was shaking her head. "He's a grouchy man. He has this big bushy eyebrow that goes all the way across his head. They say he's a cruel man. On the retreat from Shiloh, he had a man shot for killing a chicken."

The young officer began to shake his head. "Who would put a man like that in command?"

"The Confederate president," Mary frowned. "They say they're good friends." She pointed toward a pink brick house across the street. "That's the Rose Cottage. It was the headquarters of General Johnston. Had he lived, we would have won the battle. When he died, Beauregard took command and ordered the army to halt while on the verge of victory."

"General Johnston," the young officer repeated as he looked at the house. None of these names seemed to ring a bell.

"I liked him far better than General Beauregard," Mary smiled. "He was a great man, a true leader. He cared about his men. He was a likable man. Beauregard is all ego, but Johnston was nothing like that. I remember when they brought the body back. It was so sad."

They rode on past and began to pass several buildings. They rode past a small store with two armed guards standing in front of the door. He motioned that way and asked Mary, "Whose headquarters is that?"

Mary burst into laughter. "That's no headquarters, silly. That's a tavern. One good thing that General Bragg did was close down all the taverns to keep the soldiers sober and out of trouble."

They were soon approaching the Tishomingo Hotel. The long two-story hotel stood next to the railroad depot. Two rail lines crossed just beyond the depot. Wounded soldiers littered the long verandah in front of the hotel. The second-story verandah was also covered with the wounded.

"That's the Tishomingo Hotel. They're famous for being the only place in town that serves iced tea," Mary pointed toward the building. She motioned to a grassy spot just north of the tracks across from the hotel. "That's where I found you. They'd just left you outside to die."

He looked around the area, but nothing seemed to shake his memory. Mary insisted they go inside the hotel and see her mother. He helped her dismount and tied the horse to a post.

He stepped inside the open door of the hotel and almost gagged. The smell was horrible. He wondered how these poor men could stay inside here. *I bet they'll have a hard time getting that odor out when they try to get back in business, he thought.* He found a bench and took a seat while Mary went in search of her mother.

He noticed Mary and her mother returning with a tall, balding man following close behind. His attire suggested that he was a doctor. Martha asked, "So how is our young soldier feeling?"

"Tolerable, ma'am," he shifted, betraying his nervousness.

"This is Doctor Evans," Martha introduced the older gentleman. "He's gonna have a look at you."

Doctor Evans stepped forward and looked hard into the young man's eyes. He moved the young man's head roughly to the side and dug through the hair as he eyed the bullet wound. "That's healing up nicely. You still have no memory?"

"No, sir," the lieutenant replied, "nothing."

The doctor stepped back and thought a moment. He turned to Mary and said, "I read of a man that was mugged and beaten on the docks in New Orleans. He didn't remember who he was either. This is not the first time this sort of thing has happened. It's quite common, actually, with head wounds."

The young lieutenant felt very uncomfortable. He wondered why the doctor couldn't just talk to him; he was sitting right here. After a moment, he said, "Doc, just level with me. I can handle the truth."

Doctor Evans looked hard at the wounded soldier. He said, "Look, son, I'm just gonna be honest with you. You may get your memory back in a week, a month, a year, or maybe never. You're gonna have to learn to get on with your life either way. You may think it's not much of a life, but it's far better than what a lot of these boys got. It's been one continuous funeral around here since the battle."

The young officer didn't know what to say. He staggered out onto the verandah with Mary. She asked him if he felt like searching for his regiment, but he was suddenly not in the mood anymore. He wanted to ask her what good it would do him to locate people who knew him, if he would never remember them.

****

She'd spent a week trying to cheer the young officer's spirits. She had tried everything. She explained to him that life is like painting a picture. You've got to paint it the way you want it. You can't just wait for it to come to you. He'd finally come out of his slump and began to search for his company.

He spent several days looking for someone that may recognize him, but so far he'd found no one. This particular morning, he borrowed the family horse and rode north of town. The Confederate army was busy digging entrenchments all the way around Corinth, and the north side of town was the only area he had yet to visit.

He rode north up the Hamburg Corinth Road until he reached the main line. There he found Confederate troops

17

sweating as they dug entrenchments in the spring heat. Shovels threw earth into the air. Men were cursing at having to do what they called 'slave labor.'

He saw a commotion in a field behind the main line and rode the horse that way. Before him was an entire regiment drawn up in what appeared to be a hollow square, except one end of the square was open. There was a young boy sitting in the back of a wagon on top of what appeared to be a coffin.

The young lieutenant climbed from the horse and stood beside a gray-bearded sergeant. He casually asked, "What's going on?"

"They's fixen to shoot that poor boy," the sergeant spat a stream of tobacco juice. He turned and noticed he was talking with an officer and snapped to attention. "Sorry, sir. Didn't know you was no officer."

It shocked him the way the man apologized. It just didn't feel right. This old soldier looked old enough to be his father and he was apologizing. "It's quite all right."

"That's the Twenty-third Tennessee Infantry," the old sergeant continued. "That boy there was a member, but he deserted to the Yankees and was captured at Shiloh. They's gonna shoot him for desertion."

The young lieutenant watched the proceedings with interest. Something told him to turn and walk away. He really didn't want to see the poor boy killed, but something about the scene wouldn't allow him to turn away. The poor boy in the wagon looked to be about sixteen. *Surely they're just trying to scare the boy, he thought. How can men become so cruel to kill a poor scared boy?*

They pulled him from the wagon and began to tie him to the post. There was a freshly dug grave beside the post. The grave was filled with water from the fresh rains. Several men pulled the coffin from the wagon and laid it beside the grave.

The colonel of the regiment stepped forward when they had finished tying the condemned boy. He asked, "Any last words, son?"

The boy looked toward the grave. He kept his head bent low near his chest and spoke in a low tone. "Can I have a drink of water out of my grave?"

The colonel looked confused. "What in hell for?"

"They tell me that water is scarce in hell," the poor boy closed his eyes. "This may be the last drink I ever have."

The colonel granted the boys wish and ordered one of the guards to dip the boy some water from his grave. After he'd finished drinking, the colonel offered him a blindfold. The boy refused. Six men were brought forward with rifles. They took a knee and prepared for the order to fire.

The colonel read the order. "Because you have deserted your comrades and gone and joined the enemy, you are hereby sentenced to die."

The boy said nothing, but continued staring at the ground.

The old sergeant began to shake his head. "They's only one of them rifles loaded. That way them boys don't know who actually done the shootin'."

The young officer wanted to turn his head, but was drawn to the scene before him. He couldn't seem to believe what was about to happen. It seemed a tragedy unfolding before his eyes. He heard the colonel give the commands, "Ready, aim..."

He paused and seemed to wait an eternity before he shouted, "Fire!"

Several bullets ripped into the man's chest and he sagged against the ropes holding him to the post. The sergeant had been wrong. Five of the rifles had been loaded and only one was firing a blank round.

The boy was still alive. Incredibly, he screamed out in pain. It was a horrible sound. The young lieutenant was about to turn from the sight when the colonel stepped forward and drew his pistol. He placed the barrel about six inches from the boys head and pulled the trigger.

"God almighty!" The old sergeant spat a stream of tobacco in the dirt. "That's about the sorriest thing I've ever seen."

The young lieutenant couldn't believe what he had just witnessed. He wondered how men could be so cruel to one another. It was a sickening sight. The scene would cause him to have nightmares for weeks to come.

He understood he was an officer. It would be his responsibility to do the same thing, but he was sure that he could never do something so horrible. He made a promise to himself to never let the war make him so callus inside.

CHAPTER THREE

Old Man Saunders sat on the front porch of his dilapidated little shack watching the rain fall. The weather was nice and cool and he was actually enjoying the rain.

He caught a glance of someone racing up the road. It was Charles Rich running through the rain to hear his daily war story. He raced onto the porch and bent over, hands on his knees breathless from the run.

Saunders pointed toward the bucket. "Didn't spect to see you up here today with it rainin' and all."

"Sorry," the boy was panting. He paused to catch his breath, after a long moment, he said, "Told you I would come every day."

"Charlie, you ain't got to do that. Least not in bad weather." Saunders reached into a bag and pulled out a plug of tobacco.

"I wanted to," Charlie sat down on the bucket. "I want to know if the lieutenant ever finds out who he is."

"Patience, boy," Saunders smiled. "Mary had been reading the Bible to him when she'd found a verse he really liked. It was in the book of Samuel. So that's how she had come up with a name for him. They called him Samuel you see. He took Mary's last name, and during the war, he was known as Samuel Rodes. Now don't ask me no more what his original name was. He didn't know his original name. Now where were we in the story?"

"He's in Corinth with that nice girl, Mary," Charlie was on the edge of the bucket, eagerly waiting. "He was trying to find someone who could tell him who he was."

"That's right," Saunders raised an eyebrow in thought. "The Yanks were advancing, you see. He done been all over town looking, but didn't find nobody. The Rodes family was gonna evacuate town, like all the other families before them blue bellies got there. The young lieutenant was just gonna join a unit and fight as a private. He didn't have no other idea of what to do."

Charlie was shaking his head. Saunders paused a moment, and asked, "What's wrong, boy?"

"That's sad," Charlie didn't want to wait for Saunders to finish the story. He wanted answers now. "So, he ever find out where he was from?"

"Charlie," Saunders couldn't suppress the smile, "you not gonna wheedle the story out of me before I'm done telling it."

"Sorry," Charlie smiled back.

"That Martha Rodes insisted that the young officer help them move their belongings in the wagon to her sister's house in Alabama. She told him it was the least he could do to repay them for all the nursing they'd done on him." Saunders waited to see if Charlie was catching on. "You see, they didn't want to doctor that boy up to just see him get shot up again, and that Mary girl was getting attached to him."

He watched the light come on in Charlie's brain. Charlie said, "Oh, I see. Did it work?"

"Yeah, how can a man say no to women in distress?" Saunders spat a stream of tobacco off the porch into the rain. "So's anyway, it took him most of a week to get 'em to a place called Ford City, Alabama, where her sister lived. Once there, he wasn't sure what to do with himself. That Martha's sister's husband was friends with Alabama governor John Gill Shorter. She wrote the governor and told him about the young officers plight. Well, just so happens that the governor had a newly recruited regiment in Montgomery. He'd made his first cousin, Robert Franklin Shorter the colonel, but that weren't working out too well. See, Robert Shorter was no officer and knowed nothing 'bout no military. So when the governor heard 'bout the young wounded hero of Shiloh, he jumped at the chance to have him help Robert run that outfit."

"Wow," Charlie was hanging on every word. "So he had to go to Montgomery?"

Saunders smiled at Charlie. "You always trying to stay a step ahead of me, boy."

****

22

He'd been going by the name Samuel Rodes for a week now. Mary was flattered that he had taken her advice for a name and honored that he had taken her last name as his own.

She packed him various sundries for his long trip to Montgomery. She walked him to the nearest depot on the Memphis and Charleston Railway alone. He held her in his arms before boarding the train. It was all he could do to keep from bursting into tears. He avoided eye contact with her. She was already crying. He could feel her shaking inside his arms, and he squeezed her tighter.

Sitting inside the passenger car, he stared at the beautiful young lady who had grown so attached to him. She seemed to worship him as if he was her own personal war hero. Mary was extremely proud of what he'd become and the fact that she had saved his life. She actually felt good that she had cheated death by taking this boy home. Every inch of him was a soldier; and to her, he looked like one, although to others he appeared a mere boy.

The young officer thought of Mary most of the journey. He hated to leave her, but what choice did he have. His heart was full of torment, and he knew she felt the same. He concentrated on the image of her beautiful smile and soft face in his memory. *Someday, when this war is over, he thought, I'll marry that girl.* He imagined what the wedding would be like. It would be perfect; he would make sure of that. One thing that was certain during this trip was how lost he felt without her. The trip was a long and miserable journey. There were only three people he knew in the world, and he was leaving them behind to enter the unknown. He couldn't help but wonder what was ahead of him, what was to become of him.

Samuel spent most of the week-long journey keeping his head situated on a small pillow. The severe headaches still plagued him daily. The train moved slowly across Northern Alabama and into Tennessee. It was in Chattanooga that he would change trains and begin the long, arduous trip through the Georgia mountains to Atlanta. From Atlanta he took a train to Montgomery, Alabama. It was a roundabout journey of four hundred and fifty miles to reach a town just two hundred miles from where he'd began.

The train reached Montgomery on a cool, rainy Thursday. He grabbed his few belongings and climbed from the railcar. Lieutenant Samuel Rodes walked through the lobby of the Montgomery depot. Heads were turning, staring at the officer who looked to be no more than fifteen years old. He never bothered to look back.

There were two officers standing near the exit, waiting for someone. As he came close, the one in the colonel's uniform stepped forward and extended his hand.

"Are you the lieutenant from Shiloh?" The colonel looked a little shocked as the young man extended his hand. Sam was the only person to step from the train in a uniform and that's the reason the colonel had approached him.

"That's right," Samuel nodded. He tried to hide his nervousness. "I'm supposed to report to the capital, I think."

"I'm Robert Franklin Shorter," the colonel nodded and pointed to the officer standing next to him. "This is my second in command, Major Randall Martin. We're glad to have you, but we expected someone a little older."

Samuel introduced himself while he shook the major's hand. He said, "I'm sorry, but I have no idea how old I am. I have no memory prior to three weeks ago."

"You got a horse?" Colonel Shorter asked.

"No, sir," Samuel replied. "If I did, I lost it at Shiloh."

"No problem," Colonel Shorter opened the door and started out onto the platform. "I brought an extra just in case. I have quite a horse farm. You can use one of mine."

Samuel thanked him. They climbed into the saddle, and he rode along with them toward the state capital. Along the way, Samuel found Colonel Shorter to be a friendly, talkative man. Major Martin was reserved, but overall a nice guy. Samuel was nervous, speaking only when spoken to. Reaching the state capital, Colonel Shorter rode onto the front lawn and up to the front steps.

As they climbed from the saddle, Colonel Shorter said, "I have something to show you."

Samuel and Major Martin followed the colonel up the steps and onto the verandah. Colonel Shorter gently took Samuel's arm and moved him to a spot near one of the columns. Samuel looked confused.

"You're standing on the spot where President Jefferson Davis gave his inaugural address." Colonel Shorter smiled as he saw the impressed look on Samuel's face. "They're gonna place a marker of some kind there to commemorate the event."

He then followed the two officers inside the capital and to the governor's office. They were immediately shown into his office. Governor John Gill Shorter was clean-shaven with bright blue eyes. He wore a black suit, neatly pressed. His hair was receding, exposing a large forehead, and he was beginning to show signs of the pressure he was under to protect his state from invasion.

"Welcome to the capital," Governor Shorter stood and extended his hand. His face betrayed the shock of seeing such a young man before him. "I wasn't expecting someone quite so young."

"Sorry, sir," Samuel said.

"He doesn't know how old he is," Colonel Shorter said as he reached over and patted him on the back. "He'll be fine, cousin. He has seen the elephant."

It was the term used during that time to describe someone who had been in combat. Governor Shorter motioned for the three men to sit. He looked at Major Martin and asked, "How are you, Randall?"

"Tolerable, sir," Major Martin nodded.

"So you were at Shiloh?" Governor Shorter watched as Samuel nodded. "That was a horrible battle is what I'm told."

"I think so," Samuel shifted uncomfortably in his chair. He didn't want to come right out and say he didn't remember for sure.

"Son, I'm just gonna level with you," Governor Shorter reached into a drawer and pulled out a cigar. He offered each officer one, but only his cousin accepted. "You see, I've given my cousin command of our newest regiment, and he has no military experience whatsoever. Major Martin is a friend of the family, and he has no experience either. That's the reason I asked the Rodes family to send you here. I need a man with experience. But that's just the point—I need a man. I didn't expect you to be a young boy."

He lit the cigar and blew out a cloud of smoke. After a long pause, he asked, "Do you think you can prepare these men for battle?"

"Yes, sir, I do," Samuel replied. "I've been studying Hardee's tactics and almost know the book by heart. I also took quite a bit of time in Corinth to visit various regiments and see how their commanders handle their troops."

Governor Shorter didn't look very convinced. There was a look of worry in his eyes. He asked, "Would you excuse us a moment?"

"Yes, sir," Samuel replied and left the room, being sure to close the door behind him.

Once the door was shut, Governor Shorter asked, "Are you comfortable with that boy running the regiment?"

Colonel Shorter was glad to have someone help him take responsibility of the troops. He replied, "I say we give him a chance. He's the only man here with combat experience, regardless of his age."

Governor Shorter looked at Major Martin and asked, "Randall, you're the one giving up the rank; are you all right with this?"

"Sir," Major Martin sat up in his chair, "like I said before, I'll do what is best for the regiment."

"Fine then," Governor Shorter felt relieved now. "Would you two excuse yourselves and send the young man back in?"

The three men shook hands before parting. Outside, they told Samuel the governor would like to see him alone. He went back into the governor's office and closed the door.

Governor Shorter motioned toward a chair. As he watched Samuel take a seat, he said, "Young man, I'm giving you a commission as Lieutenant Colonel of the 64th Alabama Infantry regiment. That position was Randall Martin's, but he took a lesser rank to allow someone with experience to come in and shape the unit up. You're now Lieutenant Colonel Samuel Rodes."

"Thank you, sir," Samuel relaxed in the chair.

"Don't thank me," the governor ran his hand through his short, brown hair. "You're in charge. Although my cousin outranks you, he hasn't a clue what he's doing. You're to do whatever you think is necessary to get these men combat ready. They're nothing but an armed mob at the moment. There's been very little discipline with my friends and family as officers. That will be your job; whatever you say goes. Now, you have your work cut out for you, and it's a big responsibility, but that's what I had you brought here for. Are you sure you're up to this?"

"Yes, sir," Samuel lowered his head in thought. "There is just one question."

The governor eyeballed the boy and waited.

Samuel cleared his throat. "What will Colonel Shorter think about me running his regiment?"

"Don't worry about that," Governor Shorter replied. "I've had a long talk with cousin before your arrival. He understands that you are in charge of getting this regiment ready for battle. He will give you no trouble, and if he does, you report to me."

The meeting was over. Samuel was having a little trouble taking all of this in. He left Northern Alabama to come to Montgomery to receive a commission in a new regiment only to learn that he was in charge. He felt the weight of all that responsibility crashing on his shoulders at once. He wondered what Mary would think when she received the letter he would write her tonight. *She'll be proud, he thought. I'm just not sure how proud I am of this sudden responsibility.*

Not just Mary, but I bet if my family knew where I was and what I was doing at this moment, they'd be extremely proud also. If he had a girl back home, he figured she would be just as proud as Mary.

On the verandah of the capital, he found Colonel Shorter and Major Martin waiting. Colonel Shorter asked, "What would you like to do first? How about going with me to a dinner party tonight? There will be quite a few Southern belles present."

27

Samuel wasn't in the mood. The responsibility was already heavy on his shoulders. He wanted to get right to work. He replied, "I'd like to see the regiment. Get a feel for what kind of men we have."

"Right," Colonel Shorter replied with a smile. "I must attend this little dinner party, but I'll have Randall here give you the grand tour."

Major Martin took the newly commissioned lieutenant colonel to the army camp. He found the men camped on a vacant block in downtown Montgomery.

He called a dress parade for the next morning. It was interrupted by town citizens coming out to see what was going on. Colonel Shorter arrived in the middle of the event with several dignitaries and their wives. It was almost hopeless. Samuel realized immediately what must be done. He had Major Martin locate a piece of land they could use about five miles north of town. The major wrote the orders up and gave them to Colonel Shorter to approve. Colonel Shorter wasn't very happy. He walked over to where Samuel was watching the proceedings of the regiment, extended his hand, and smiled to break the ice.

"Randall tells me you want to move the regiment out to an isolated location." Colonel Shorter finished shaking Samuel's hand and reached over and patted him on the arm. The man was obviously a politician and very good at it. "That's gonna place these men at a severe disadvantage, Samuel. They'll be far from their families and friends, not to mention the fact that the officers will be far removed from the social life of Montgomery."

"That's what this regiment needs, sir," Samuel wasn't backing down. "These men can't learn to be soldiers with all these distractions. We need a remote location so the men can learn to drill. They need to work like a well-oiled machine when they go into battle or we'll lose most of them."

Colonel Shorter rubbed his forehead and looked at the ground as if trying to come up with another reason the regiment shouldn't be moved. He asked, "Is that the final word?"

"That's the final word," Samuel replied almost apologetically. "I know it's inconvenient, but we have a responsibility to the men."

"Right," Colonel Shorter turned and began to walk away. "I'll sign the order, Samuel. Keep up the good work."

Samuel couldn't help but like the man. He didn't respect him as a military leader just yet, but he respected that he could understand what was best for the regiment.

The next morning was sheer chaos. Men were racing around trying to get all their gear together. He couldn't believe how much gear these men were trying to take with them. They'd finally all gotten into the road and into marching formation.

Samuel turned to Major Martin. "Give the order to move out, Major."

"Yes, sir," Randall Martin turned and shouted, "Sixty-Fourth Alabama, forward, march."

The line of men lurched into motion. Men were shouting; there was no organization to them. Some carried trunks of clothes on their backs. Others had wads of clothes under their arms. It was mass pandemonium.

Samuel shook his head and smiled. "I could have given them an order to leave that stuff behind, but I figured they'll learn more this way."

Randall Martin laughed. "We may need an ambulance to pick up the stragglers. They're not going far with all that junk."

"We have a lot of work to do." Samuel spurred the horse to keep pace with his major. "I haven't seen two men in step yet."

"I'm sorry." Major Martin lowered his head. "I'm partly responsible for that. I haven't been doing anything to train them. I've just been waiting in vain for Robert to lead."

Samuel held up a hand. He could find no fault in Major Martin. At least the man was trying, which was more than could be said for Colonel Shorter. The commander had found an excuse to remain in Montgomery a few more days. "Don't worry about that. We'll have them looking like soldiers in about two weeks. I haven't seen a man with a uniform. Can you send a request to the governor about uniforms and equipment?"

"I'll take care of that as soon as we reach camp, sir."

Crowds began to gather along the sides of the streets. Old men, women, and children were jostling to see the regiment march out of town. One lady saw the stars on the officers' collars and shouted, "Is one of you the captain of this outfit?"

Samuel thought about ignoring her but decided that wouldn't be proper manners for a Southern gentleman. He rode over to the side of the street and replied, "Ma'am, I'm the lieutenant colonel of this regiment."

"They a mighty fine looking set of soldiers," she replied. "I bet you sure are proud."

"Yes, ma'am, I am," Samuel smiled. He was in fact proud to be leading these men, even if they were rough around the edges. It wasn't anything he couldn't fix. He was sure of that.

Before they'd gone a mile, men began to throw away their excess baggage. Trunks littered the sides of the road. Some men were broken down already; some sat on their trunks, sweat running into their eyes. Still the march continued.

It took them most of the day to march just five miles. When they reached the large field where camp would be, men were complaining about aching legs and feet. Samuel began to wonder if two weeks would make much of a dent in these men. It appeared there wasn't a one of them that had done a day's labor in their entire life.

The first night he called a meeting with his officers and set up a schedule for drill. They would drill the men off and on all day long. At night, while the men rested, the officers would come to Samuel's tent and learn how to lead. Randall Martin was growing extremely excited with the new leadership arrangement. This boy was telling the truth when he'd told the governor he knew how to run a regiment.

****

They'd been camped there for two weeks, when summer was introduced. Samuel was extremely proud of the progress he'd made. The work had been slow and painstaking, but it was actually beginning to pay off. The men were beginning to look and act like soldiers. The request for uniforms and equipment had been answered.

30

Samuel wrote a letter to Mary every night after the officer's meetings. He was beginning to worry that he would never hear from her again, when a letter finally arrived from her just a few days earlier. The Federal army was laying siege to Corinth, and she was worried about what would become of their home. She confessed to him that she had cried all afternoon the day he had left and hadn't slept a wink that night. She missed him terribly.

He wrote her back that night and thanked her for saving his life. Everything he had become was because she had cared for him. He confessed to her that he had fought back tears the day he departed. It was a long and miserable trip to Montgomery without her. He told her he couldn't wait for a furlough to get back up there to see her.

Samuel often took long walks at night. He would walk just beyond the campfires and listen to his men telling various anecdotes. He would migrate from tent to tent, checking on the condition of his men. Most of the time, they didn't even notice he was there. He tried to arrange things in his mind, but it wasn't easy. The headaches were still a curse, and he had trouble ignoring them long enough to oversee the daily drills.

The next day, Samuel called Randall to his tent. Randall walked in and saluted. Randall Martin was in his late thirties. It seemed strange to have a man so much older salute him and call him "sir." Samuel motioned for him to take a seat.

"I have a surprise for the men tomorrow." Samuel gave a wide grin. "The men look like soldiers now, but they need more than just drilling."

Randall was confused. "Like what, Sammy?"

Samuel liked the way the officers had all nicknamed him "Sammy." It meant they liked him and respected him for all he'd done for them. He replied, "I wasn't gonna tell you, but I've decided you need to be in on the lark also. At about three in the morning, you're going to receive a false report that Yankees are approaching Selma. We're gonna get the regiment up and on the road, hopefully within an hour. We'll make a forced march to Selma and return."

31

"Sir," Randall was shaking his head. "That's about fifty miles."

"That's right," Samuel looked at a crude map he'd had someone draw for him on his table. "We join an army somewhere and they'll need to be able to march. Hell, coming out here from Montgomery, I thought we were gonna kill them all."

"True," Randall agreed. "So you want this secret between the two of us, right?"

"Yeah," Samuel smiled. "Let's let them think this is for real and see how well they do."

Samuel sent word to Colonel Shorter back in Montgomery what they planned to do. He asked the colonel if he would like to lead the men on the march. Robert Shorter sent word back that he had pressing business to attend to in Montgomery and appreciated the work Samuel was doing with the regiment. Samuel was having a difficult time understanding his commander. The man hadn't been out to the camp but twice and hadn't spent a night in the field with his men. Samuel wondered how the commander would ever be respected by the men he led if he refused to share their hardships.

The march began as a nightmare. Getting the men up and ready to move was like herding snails. On the road, the men were ready for action and bragging about what all they would do when they caught them Yankees in Selma. After a mile, the big talk disappeared, and it appeared as though half the regiment wouldn't make Selma.

The officers encouraged, cursed, and pleaded for the men to stay in line. Most men truly tried to keep up but just weren't in shape for it. Out of the seven hundred and fifty men in the regiment, only three hundred arrived in Selma the next night. He had pushed them harder than he meant to. He had the men camp in Selma until the rest of the regiment caught up. He then gave them all a few days rest and started them back. He didn't march them as hard this time, giving them three days to march the fifty miles back to camp. When they all got back to camp, the men's spirits were soaring. They truly believed they had gone after the enemy and scared him away. Sammy realized that he needed to keep these marches up. It was important for the men to remain in shape and be prepared for when they had to march for real.

The next afternoon, Colonel Shorter arrived to take command of the regiment. He brought along enough wagons and baggage to support an entire brigade. He had tents set up for his political hacks and also for his lady friends. There was nothing he left behind to spare his comfort. During the afternoon drill, he asked Samuel for a few minutes alone in his tent.

Samuel followed the solid-built man into his large wall tent. He hadn't known they made tents this big. Inside, he found a large desk, a dining table, and a bed. Where the other officers had a small table for writing orders and a cot, Robert had a full size bed. He wondered if the man planned to take it on campaigns with him.

Robert motioned for his subordinate to sit. He pulled a cigar from his pocket and offered it to Samuel. The boy declined. Robert lit the cigar and said, "I don't know how to go about telling you this, Sammy."

Samuel was taken aback. "I guess just spit it out."

"Right," Robert was trying to be as diplomatic as possible. "You see, Sammy, I've gotten quite a few complaints about you drilling too much. This forced march thing has worn the men out. Several men are threatening to shoot you. Were you aware of that?"

Samuel's face quickly turned into a scowl. "Are these men officers?"

"Oh no," Robert quickly held up a hand. "There hasn't been a single complaint from an officer. These are the soldiers themselves."

"I see," Sammy said.

Robert took a couple of puffs on the cigar. "Sammy, don't you want the men to like you?"

"I haven't given it much thought actually," Sammy's eyes met Robert's. The look told Robert that whatever Samuel Rodes had been before the war, he was no politician. He didn't seem to plan ahead. Some day he may need these men's votes. Sammy continued, "I have a responsibility to get these men ready for battle. If we don't drill these men and teach them to endure long

33

marches, we'll lose at least half of them in the first battle. You see, the war could be lost because of the little things. You and I both have a responsibility to get these men ready, and whether they like us or not shouldn't be important."

"I understand," Robert was beginning to learn that his new subordinate was more than just an innocent boy. This boy had seen war and knew how to ready other men for the fray. "Enough of all that. How's the horse holding up?"

"Very well, thanks," Sammy smiled. *Robert may not understand how to command, but he's very likable, he thought.* "How do you like camp life so far?"

"Not very well," Robert began to frown. "I hate mosquitoes, gnats, and flies. So you understand how I feel about camp life. I'll stay the night, but I'll be leaving for town tomorrow. I have important business to take care of for my cousin."

Sammy couldn't help but notice how Robert always seemed to use his cousin as an excuse to avoid his responsibilities here. Sammy said, "Not a problem, sir. I'll continue with the training, and I do appreciate you talking to me about the men."

"We've got to work together and remain on the same page," Robert extended his hand. "I hope you'd do the same for me."

****

They continued to drill all summer, with no prospects of being sent to an army. Sammy began to wonder if the governor planned to keep them here to guard Montgomery for the duration of the war. He grew antsy as he read of the battles around the capital of Richmond, Virginia. The new commander there had just defeated a larger Federal army under a general named George McClellan and then turned north to face another large army under John Pope near Manassas.

The battles had resulted in large numbers of casualties, and the *Planter's Gazette*, Montgomery's newspaper, had a column stating that President Davis was begging for more troops to replace the losses there.

34

It was past dark, and most of the troops had already turned in for the night. Sammy got dressed and walked to Randall Martin's tent.

Randall had just lay down on his cot for the night. He heard footsteps outside and hushed voices. One of his aides stuck his head inside and said, "Sir, Colonel Rodes is here to see you."

"By all means, send him in." Randall rose from the cot and quickly put on his shirt and boots.

Sammy walked into the tent and held the journal up for his subordinate to see. He asked, "Have you read this, Randall?"

"No, sir," Randall looked a little shocked. He thought he'd done something wrong. "Is there something the matter?"

Sammy tossed the paper on Randall's camp desk. "General Lee's army in Virginia has just defeated McClellan's army, resulting in thousands of casualties. Now they've turned north to face another army under General Pope. President Davis is practically begging for troops. They say if Richmond falls, the war will be over."

"I see," Randall still looked perplexed. He wondered what this had to do with him. He waited patiently, not sure what else to say.

"We've got to do something," Sammy sat on Randall's camp stool. He motioned for Randall to take a seat on his cot.

Randall sat down and shook his head. "I'm not sure what you're saying."

"We've got to go see the governor," Sammy said. "We've got to get him to send this regiment to Richmond. What good is it doing us sitting here?"

"He'll never go for it, Sammy." Randall looked at the ground and shook his head. "He thinks that President Davis has abandoned the western theater of operations. He said he'll send no more regiments to Virginia."

"Look, Randall, I need your help here." Sammy was practically pleading. "What will it matter if Richmond falls? The game is up, and we lose the war. We'll be sitting out here doing nothing in the meantime, benefiting no one. I'll do the talking if you'll just back me."

Randall took a deep breath and sighed. He was a friend of the governor and understood how he felt about sending troops out of state. Still, Sammy was right about the matter. What good was it doing them if the war was lost because the capital fell? After a long pause, he said, "All right, Sammy, when do we go?"

Sammy couldn't suppress a large grin. "First thing in the morning."

They both knew better than to ask Robert to attend. The man would side with his cousin, regardless of how he truly felt.

The next morning the two officers dressed in their best uniforms and mounted for the ride to the state capital. Randall was nervous. He dreaded this conversation with the governor. Sammy was determined to press his case. The governor had been nice enough to him before.

To make matters worse, they arrived to find Governor John Gill Shorter in a foul mood. Davis had just sent him a letter begging for more troops. North Alabama was now open to invasion and the Confederate president wanted the governor to send troops to Virginia. It just didn't make any sense. He'd just spent the past hour with his staff, arguing about how to respond to the Confederate commander in chief. The meeting broke up without the group settling the problem.

Governor Shorter's secretary stepped in the door and announced, "Sir, a couple officers of the 64th Alabama are waiting to see you."

"Show them in," Governor Shorter's voice betrayed his agitation with the state of current affairs.

Randall followed Sammy inside and immediately understood they had come at a bad time. Both men shook the governor's hand and took a seat. Governor Shorter said, "Jefferson Davis is gonna be the death of me. He is begging every governor to send more troops to Virginia. How can we defend the heartland of the Confederacy if we send all our troops to Richmond?"

Randall lowered his head. He hoped that Sammy would understand that it wasn't the time to bring up his proposal. Sammy said, "Governor, sir, I've come here to discuss that very proposal."

36

Governor Shorter had a blank expression on his face. He wondered what a mere regimental commander could know about sending troops to Richmond. He said, "What the hell are you talking about?"

"Sir," Sammy had rehearsed in his mind what he would say at this moment, "the president is right, however that may appear. If the capital falls, the Confederacy falls. We must do whatever it takes to save the capital."

Governor Shorter shook his head. "Is that what the two of you came here to discuss?"

Sammy wasn't about to back down now. "Sir, we've come here to ask if you would send the 64th to Richmond. The capital must be saved."

Governor Shorter looked from Sammy to Randall. "Are you in agreement with this?"

"Sir," Randall's eyes stared at the governor's desk. He refused to make eye contact. "I know how things appear, but Sammy...I mean, Colonel Rodes is right. It's imperative that we save the capital."

"I beg to differ, sir," the governor shook his head. "We can lose the war just as easily here as there. What difference will your eight hundred men do there?"

"Sir, in battle, one man can make a difference in winning and losing. One straw can break a camel's back." Sammy had begun to argue, when the governor held up a hand, cutting him off.

"You two nerve-wracking sons-of-bitches are going to be the death of me." Governor Shorter stared at them out of hard eyes. Suddenly, he began to smile. *I could kill two birds with one stone, he thought. I can send these two fellows to Richmond and say I did what Davis asked. It'll look like I'm trying to help him, but at the same time, I'll be keeping my best troops back here to defend the state.* He remembered that farcical march out of town over a month before. He said, "So, you fellows want some action. What does Colonel Shorter say about this?"

"He doesn't know we're here, sir," Sammy quickly added. "I asked him to talk about this, but he refused. He's not real excited about leaving the city here. He hasn't spent but two days with the regiment since we left town almost two months ago."

"I'm sorry about that," the governor began to shake his head. He reached into his desk drawer and pulled out a cigar. "He's really no officer, but he wanted a commission; you know, something to tell the grand kids about."

"I'm not complaining, governor," Sammy wanted to make sure the governor understood that he hadn't meant anything by the remark. "He's been a good friend to me. I've prepared the regiment for him, and I'm proud you've entrusted me with that task. Richmond needs our help now more than ever before."

"I'll write up the order," Governor Shorter lit the cigar and blew a puff of smoke toward the ceiling. "You get your regiment prepared to go."

"Yes, sir," Sammy stood and saluted the governor. Randall wasn't sure what to do, so he just stood and saluted as well.

When they had exited the capital, Randall looked at Sammy and asked, "What the hell just happened?"

"What do you mean?" Sammy asked.

"How the hell did you just pull that off?" Randall motioned back toward the door. "That man said he wasn't sending another man to Virginia. You walk in, and within a minute, he agrees to send our regiment."

"Not sure," Sammy smiled. "Maybe I should have been a politician."

CHAPTER FOUR

Charlie looked extremely depressed today. He climbed onto the porch and took his seat on the bucket.

Old Man Saunders eyed the boy up and down. "What in the world happened to you, boy? You lose your best friend or somebody steal your gal?"

"Neither," Charlie continued staring at the cracks in the porch as if he were trying to see what lay beneath. "I can't come up here as much as I used to."

"Why not?" Saunders looked confused.

"My parents," Charlie shook his head. "They think I'm wearing my welcome out is all. They say I'm probably getting on your nerves."

"Well, is that all?" Saunders smiled through tobacco-stained teeth. "I thought it might be somethin' bad."

"It's bad enough to me." Charlie stared at Saunders and wondered why he thought this was nothing. He thought perhaps he was getting on the old man's nerves, but he'd never acted that way before. "I told them you were happy for the company, but if I've gotten on your nerves, I apologize."

"Oh, hush boy," Saunders reached over and scuffed up Charlie's red hair. "Your daddy's coming up here in the morning for my arthritis checkup. I'll have it all straightened out tomorrow soon's you out of school. You just plan on coming on back up here like you been doin'."

Charlie's face lit up. "You mean I'm not getting on your nerves, sir?"

"If'n you were, I'd a told ya," Saunders spat tobacco juice into the yard. "I ain't got no family left, and you the closest thing I got. Now stop calling me 'sir.' You can just call me 'Uncle Sol'."

"Sol? Why's that?" Charlie frowned up.

"Cause, that's what ever body used to call me." Saunders smiled again as he wiped tobacco juice off his chin with his sleeve. "You didn't know that, now did you, boy?"

"No, sir," Charlie was a little embarrassed that he didn't even know Mister Saunders's first name. He assumed Sol was short for Solomon.

"There you go calling me 'sir' again," Saunders was about to give up. "Now where were we in our story?"

"Sorry, Uncle Sol," Charlie gave a sheepish grin. "We're about to leave Montgomery for Richmond."

"That's right," Saunders was nodding, "but, things don't always work out the way they seem."

Charlie asked, "So they don't go to Richmond?"

"Now, I didn't say that," Saunders shook his head in disbelief. "I said things don't always work out the way we plan them..." Saunders noticed Charlie was holding his hand up as if he were in school. "What in the world you doin', boy?"

"I have a question," Charlie lowered the hand.

"Well, we ain't in that Yankee woman's school up here," Saunders snorted. "What you want?"

Charlie lowered his head. He had a difficult time understanding when Mister Saunders was being serious or not. He had come to the conclusion that, nine times out of ten, he just liked hacking on him.

"What ever happened to that beautiful young girl back in Corinth? Don't they get married or something?"

"Oh her," Saunders spat again. "What in the world made you think they would get married?"

"Just the way they seemed to be in love. You know, writing every day." Charlie leaned forward on the bucket and rubbed his back. "They wrote every day is what you said."

"Hell, I go to the outhouse ever day, but don't mean I'm gonna marry it," Saunders tried to stifle the smile but couldn't. He saw Charlie smile also. The boy seemed relieved that the old man was just making sport of him. "That old bucket ain't too very comfortable, is it, boy?"

"No, sir," Charlie was still rubbing his back. "It gets pretty rough on my skinny butt."

He watched the old man stand up and push open the door to his rickety shack. It was the first time he had seen the inside

40

before. Junk lay cluttered everywhere. It was the biggest mess he'd ever seen inside someone's home. The old man walked in and banged around just out of sight for a few moments. When he returned to the door, he was carrying a nice padded chair. He said, "Here you go, young man. No sense in sitting here a hurtin'."

"Thanks," Charlie sprung from the bucket and grabbed the chair. He sat it down next to Saunders and took a seat. *I could sit here all day in this chair, he thought.*

"Now, he loved that Mary—ain't no doubt about that." Saunders eased back into his rocking chair. "It's pretty hard to court a woman when you off fightin' a war. He was down in Montgomery a training troops, and then he was off to Virginia to do some fightin'. He still wrote her ever day he got a chance, and she wrote him at least twice a week."

Charlie's eyelids narrowed as he thought. "So they never got married?"

"Boy," Saunders cocked his head to the side and gave Charlie a glare, "how many times I done told you, you ain't gonna wheedle none of the story out of me before it's time."

Charlie couldn't help but laugh. The story so intrigued him that he couldn't help but try to find out what was gonna happen. It was the same way for him when he read a book. He could never keep from skipping over and reading the last page.

"During those days, there was a sword over the land. All of the country was ablaze with the flames of war at this point. It seemed to me that we was living in the last days. I thought every day I would awake to the coming of the glory." Saunders scratched his head and took a moment to remember where he'd left off with his story. "They marched back to Montgomery and to the train station. The ladies in Montgomery presented them boys with a nice battle flag. Of course, Colonel Robert Shorter weren't so happy about leaving town. He had lots of belles for friends, tea's to attend, and in Montgomery, he was someone. In Richmond, he'd be just another army officer in a tent. After he gave a long speech at the depot, they climbed on the train and left for the war. Them boys didn't have no idea how long they'd be gone. It took 'em a week just to get to Richmond."

****

They arrived in Richmond just after General Lee had fought the Battle of Second Manassas. Again, he had defeated a larger army and pushed them back toward Washington. Federal General Pope was immediately fired, and McClellan was placed back in command.

They were then placed on a train and sent to Fredericksburg to try and catch up with Lee's army that had begun an invasion of Maryland. He marched the regiment pretty hard until they reached the Potomac River and then moved them carefully across the river to a town called Berlin. They'd been listening to artillery fire somewhere to the north all afternoon.

They made camp there that night. With Colonel Shorter's permission, Samuel decided to try and find out where Lee's army was located before moving on into the state and possibly behind enemy lines.

They'd just set up camp on the town's small square, when a young girl approached the group of officers. She seemed to be especially attracted to Sammy as she attempted to disarm these soldiers with a smile.

"Ma'am," Sammy nodded. He couldn't help but notice how cute she was. Her dark hair was curled inside a white snood. Her long, sharp nose was the only flaw he could find on her small face, but it too was attractive in its own way. He admired the flowers on her light blue dress.

"Excuse me," she curtsied politely, "are you gentlemen going to make demands on the town."

"Demands?" Sammy asked.

"Yes, sir," the girl fabricated a smile. It was easy to tell the smile was a forced one; the girl was nervous. "We've been told that the Confederates were going from town to town demanding money, clothing, and food."

"We're not here making demands, ma'am." Sammy smiled back. She had to be brave to come out and talk to enemy soldiers all alone. He hadn't seen a man since they'd arrived here. "We're attempting to catch up to the main army. We've heard firing north of here all afternoon and have no idea what's happening or which direction we should go."

"Would you care to take dinner with me tonight?" Her smile was coy. She seemed to be interested in the young officer, hardly even noticing the other gentlemen around him. "We can discuss things that I would rather not talk about out here in the street. There are many loyal citizens here, although we are just across the river from Virginia. My brothers are serving in the Confederate army under Lee."

Colonel Shorter slapped Sammy on the back rather harshly and laughed. "Ma'am, he'd be happy to join you."

Sammy gave Colonel Shorter a glare for the rather rough treatment. His face began to turn red from embarrassment. For some reason, he was having trouble talking to this beautiful young girl. He said, "I'd be honored to. I'm Lieutenant Colonel Samuel Rodes, second in command of the 64th Alabama Infantry, at your service."

"I'm Rose Thompson," she turned and pointed toward a house just across the street. "I live in that white house yonder. I'll start on dinner right away. Give me about an hour."

"Yes, ma'am," Sammy gave the girl a bow and watched her curtsy before moving away.

When she was out of earshot, Colonel Shorter turned to Randall and said, "Damned, Randall, if he's not the luckiest boy I've ever seen. She's a keeper, Sammy."

Sammy blushed. He was shy around women, and Colonel Shorter was making him more nervous by the minute. "Maybe you should go, sir. I mean, you are in command of the regiment. She has valuable information."

"Hell, boy," Colonel Shorter gave him another rough pat on the back, "she's not interested in this regiment or this war. It's you she come to see."

Sammy was becoming more nervous as the hour passed. He wanted to go eat with the beautiful girl and her family, but he was also wary. He didn't know what he would say when he arrived.

He soon began to worry that he would stutter in front of her. Randall noticed Sammy beginning to fidget.

"Sammy," Randall patted him on the shoulder and smiled, "she can kill you, but she can't eat you. We won't let her."

"Thanks a lot," Sammy shook his head. "Makes me feel so much better."

"Relax," Randall took out his pocket watch, "it's about time for you to be going. Don't want to make the young lady wait."

"Guess so," Sammy began walking toward the house at a very slow pace. He acted like a man headed to the gallows.

Randall shouted at his back. "Just try and enjoy yourself. I would much rather be eating with her than this damned bunch here."

He knocked on the door, and when it opened, he couldn't hide the surprise on his face. The snood was gone, and the dark hair reached almost to her shoulder blades. She looked prettier than before. She smiled as she flicked her head to the side, making her hair fly wildly, and then asked him inside.

Sammy removed his kepi and followed her. In the dining room, the table was covered with food. He asked, "Where's your family?"

She smiled over her shoulder as she led him to the table. "My mother's in Baltimore visiting my sister. I'm here alone for another week."

This information made Sammy's tension build even more. He swallowed hard and asked, "What about your father?"

"Dead," she replied plainly.

"I'm sorry," Sammy lowered his head.

"Don't be," she pointed to his seat. She sat uncomfortably close to him. "He died when I was a baby. I don't remember him at all. I hope you're hungry."

As they ate, she would appear to accidentally brush her elbow against his arm. He was already nervous, but now he was practically shaking. When they finished eating, she offered to take him to the parlor where she could play piano. He listened to several songs and then she insisted they sit in the garden before darkness came.

He'd finally begun to relax. He was actually enjoying himself, but he had to admit that nothing here seemed real. Why would she be remotely interested in this stranger who looked to be about fourteen years old?

As they took seats in the garden, she said, "I sit out here in the afternoons and read."

"This is nice," Sammy admitted. He suddenly remembered why he was here. "You said you had information for us."

"That's right," she smiled. He looked at her mouth, the smile was extremely attractive. She gave him a look that told him that he may have to tickle the information out of her. After a long, awkward pause, she asked, "How old are you?"

"I have no idea," Sammy lowered his head. "I think about eighteen."

"You think?" Rose fought hard not to laugh, but her smile told him she thought the statement was funny. He felt his face going flush again.

"Yes ma'am," he nodded. He told her about the Battle of Shiloh and waking up in Corinth. The smile quickly left her face.

"I'm sorry," she whispered as she lowered her head. "This war is nothing to laugh about. How did you get to be an officer?"

Sammy told her about the trip to Montgomery and how he'd been made lieutenant colonel. He explained how he had trained these men and was now trying to reach Lee's army where he hoped they could help end this war.

He began to wonder why it was so difficult to get information out of this girl. She had seemed so eager to share what she knew an hour ago. He thought he would try again. "Have you heard anything about the location of Lee's army?"

"My, you're impatient," she smiled and gave him another coy glance.

"I suppose," Sammy waited. He watched her reach out and take his hands in hers and fought the instinctive reflex to pull away. He could feel his face turning red and hated the fact that he couldn't talk to a girl without embarrassing himself. A red face was nothing you could hide.

"The rumor today was that the Federal army is trying to press across South Mountain." She caressed his hands with her fingers. "If that's true, and you continue north from here, you'll move in behind the Federal army of about ninety thousand men. Part of Lee's army has taken Harper's Ferry to the west of here. If I were you, I would move west along the tracks of the Baltimore and Ohio Railroad to the town of Weverton and then continue northwest along the Potomac River until reaching a part of Lee's army."

"I appreciate everything you've done," Sammy lowered his head. "I hope you're not bothered by your neighbors after we've gone."

"I won't be bothered by them," the smile on her face disappeared, "but I do have a problem."

"What's that?"

"I'm just gonna be honest with you," she looked away as if she were embarrassed at what she was about to say.

He waited patiently. "Just say it; it can't be that bad."

"I'm afraid to stay here alone tonight," She glanced at his face and then quickly turned away. "Could you stay with me? You know, just as a guardian. I don't mean to imply that we'd be together."

Sammy was taken aback. She quickly added, "I've heard stories about soldiers far from home raping defenseless women."

"I suppose I could," he replied. He began to worry about what the other officers would say in the morning. Then he realized that Colonel Shorter would just be hacking on him all day long.

"Thank you," she said and smiled, "It won't cause you any problems will it?"

"Not at all," he lied. *I'm never going to live this down, he thought.*

Rose seemed genuinely relieved. She began to relax. The sun was getting low in the sky. She said, "I suppose I should go inside and light candles."

"Right," Sammy said, "and I've got to let my command know where I can be reached tonight."

He dreaded the walk back to tell Colonel Shorter as much as he'd dreaded the walk here. After informing the colonel, he hurried back to stay with Rose. It hadn't been as bad as he'd expected. Colonel Shorter had just given him a sly wink.

Returning, he found Rose to be a completely different person. She had been nervous all along also. He hadn't noticed because he had been so worried about his own emotional state.

He took a seat on a sofa in the parlor, but this time, she sat across from him on a Victorian ladies chair. She said, "I witnessed a large part of Lee's army passing through Frederick over a week ago. They were the dirtiest men I've ever laid eyes upon. They reminded me of wild animals, wolves maybe. I bet the entire Potomac River couldn't wash them clean. Your men look nothing like them. How did you keep your men so neat and clean?"

"My men have never seen combat. They're a raw regiment. I've trained them well, but they're still green behind the ears."

"I hadn't thought of that," she shook her head. "Although Lee's men are filthy and their uniforms are ragged, there is something about them that the Federal troops lack. It's difficult to place a finger on. I guess you would say they have a dash about them that the Northern troops lack. I can't look at the Confederate army without admiration."

Sammy worked up his courage and cleared this throat. "Why me?" he asked.

"Pardon?" A look of confusion appeared on her face.

"Out of everyone on the street today, why did you pick me?"

"Honestly?" She watched the young officer nod. "You looked the most innocent. I figured if I wanted to be safe tonight, I'd best find the most innocent-looking officer and befriend him. I'm sorry if that hurts your feelings."

"Not at all," Sammy relaxed. He couldn't blame her for using him as protection. Deep down, he could feel a sting of pain, having thought this girl was actually attracted to him.

"I lied," she added.

He looked confused and started to say something, but she interrupted him. "My brothers aren't in the Confederate army. I don't even have brothers. Both my parents are dead. I live here with my aunt. My cousin lives in York, Pennsylvania, and she's about to have her first child. My aunt traveled there to be with her. I promised to stay behind and look after the house. I'm sorry."

"No need to apologize, ma'am." Sammy realized that most people in this war were just trying to survive until it's over. "Not everything in this war can be labeled black or white. There are a lot of gray areas, you know."

"I know," she lowered her head in shame, "and I could care less about either side's cause. I think wars are stupid. Why do men try to solve everything with violence?"

"That's a good question." Sammy didn't have the answer. "The only reason I'm here is to do my duty for my country."

She frowned, stared hard into his eyes, and asked, "Is dying your duty?"

He tried to think of the proper answer to her question. After a long, awkward pause, he said, "If that's what happens, then yes, dying is my duty. I mean I'm not afraid to die. Those men I'm leading out there have joined of their own free will, and they're willing to die. I think that, as a leader, I should be just as willing to give that up for the betterment of my country."

She shook her head. "I find that sad."

She was asleep when he crept out of the house just before daylight the next morning. Staying with her had depressed him dearly. He wondered how there could be people that cared less about the country where they live. She didn't seem to understand why men would fight and die for a piece of ground they call home, and he didn't quite know how to explain that to her.

They marched west along the railroad all morning. When they reached Weverton, they turned northwest, following the winding course of the Potomac River. By dark they had reached a small town called Sharpsburg.

****

The 64th Alabama Infantry found Lee's army there just before dark that afternoon. All except for part of Jackson's Corps, A.P. Hill's division was still in Harper's Ferry paroling prisoners.

48

The regiment was exhausted, having marched all day in rather warm temperatures. Nearing Sharpsburg, Sammy recommended that Colonel Shorter allow the regiment to fall out in a vacant field while someone reported to headquarters. Shorter agreed but suggested that Sammy report for assignment. Sammy couldn't help but notice that the closer to combat the regiment got, the less interested Colonel Shorter seemed.

Sammy rode into town and asked a sentry where he might find army headquarters. The man told him that he'd find headquarters just west of town. He rode west, and just outside town he located a group of tents with lots of officers. There were several thousand men camped on both sides of the road. At the tent with all the officers, Sammy noticed a large flag, similar to the 'stars and bars,' flying overhead. The star pattern was extremely odd. With that many officers busy, it seemed the logical place to search for instructions.

Beneath a tent fly, Sammy noticed an important-looking young officer sitting at a table. The man wore a thin mustache and goatee. He was scribbling furiously on a piece of paper. Sammy dismounted and cleared his throat. The young officer glanced up, noticed he was being watched, and slowly rose from the table.

"Sir," Sammy leaned his head to the left, dodging his horse's muzzle, "can you point me in the direction of headquarters?"

"Whose headquarters?" The officer looked confused. "Whose command do you belong to?"

"That's the problem," Sammy pushed the muzzle of his horse away. "We've just arrived from Richmond. I'm Lieutenant Colonel Samuel Rodes of the 64th Alabama Infantry. We've marched hard to catch ya'll."

"I see," the young officer paused in thought. "I'm Walter Taylor, adjutant general of the Army of Northern Virginia. Wait here, and I'll ask General Lee where he wants you fellows assigned."

Sammy couldn't believe he'd found Lee's headquarters this easily. He waited as Taylor disappeared into the tent. He attempted to catch a glimpse of the commanding general as the tent flap flew open, but it happened too quickly.

Taylor bounded back through the fly and said, "General Lee says for you to report to McLaws for the meantime. He'll give you final assignments as soon as possible. We are on the verge of some serious fighting here, and we need every man you've got."

"Right, sir," Sammy saluted. He turned to mount the horse and then paused in thought. He looked back at Walter Taylor and asked, "Any idea where we can find this McLaws?"

Walter Taylor smiled. He motioned over his shoulder toward the field behind Lee's tent. "General McLaws's division is camped right here. I'm assuming your regiment is one of the more verdant. Is that correct?"

"That's correct, sir," Sammy replied. He couldn't believe he'd made it that obvious that they were green.

"Don't worry," Taylor assured him. "McLaws is one of the more laid back generals in the army. You'll like the man. How many men ya'll got?"

"Seven hundred and one," Sammy replied. He felt foolish for saying the one. Taylor didn't smile at the remark the way Sammy had expected he would.

"Good," Taylor nodded as he peered down at the table. "That's the best news we've gotten in a while, Colonel. We need every man. The enemy army outnumbers us at least two to one."

Sammy started to salute and noticed that Taylor had sat back down at the table. He mounted his horse and rode around General Lee's tent toward the men camped in the field beyond.

****

Major General Lafayette McLaws was a large man with a thick, dark beard and dark hair. He sent the 64th Alabama Infantry to Brigadier General William Barksdale's brigade of Mississippi infantry. It was dark by the time Sammy got his men to Barksdale's position, and his men collapsed on the ground from exhaustion without supper.

The next morning at dawn, skirmish fire could be heard to the north. Many of Sammy's men stood and stared in that direction but could see nothing but a patch of trees full of Confederate troops. General Barksdale soon ordered his brigade to form in line of battle. He had the 64th Alabama placed in reserve just back of his main line. The man was in his forties but appeared much older. His hair had turned white, and for some reason, he'd stopped cutting it. It was down below his collar now. Once he got the men on line, he had them stack arms and told them to rest in the vicinity in case they were needed.

A young lieutenant from Barksdale's brigade walked up to Sammy and saluted. He said, "Mornin', Sir."

"Morning," Sammy replied as he returned the salute.

"Name's Basil Manly," the man extended his hand.

Sammy shook the man's hand and replied, "I'm Samuel Rodes; nice to make your acquaintance."

The lieutenant rubbed at his thin goatee and asked, "You didn't happen to attend Jefferson Military College in Mississippi, did ya?"

"Not sure," Sammy gave a slight frown. He would have to go through the entire story of what he knew of his own life again. When he'd finished, he asked, "Do you think you know me?"

"You look familiar. That bothers me when I see someone that looks familiar but I can't remember where I saw them before," Basil replied.

"Try hard," Sammy was almost desperate. "You may be my only hope of finding my family."

Basil removed his kepi and ran his hand through his sandy hair. "Well, I only saw this fellow a couple of times. He had just started, you see, and I was about to graduate. I think it was probably another boy. That's been almost two years ago."

Sammy lowered his head. A cannon fired from the Federal lines almost a mile away. The scream of a shell passed overhead and exploded in the empty field beyond. Sammy noticed everyone ducking in unison, as if you could actually dodge a cannonball.

"That was a Hotchkiss," Basil said calmly. He hadn't even flinched. "They make a horrible sound."

"I see," Sammy tried to appear calm.

More artillery opened fire from both sides. Soon the air was filled with the screams of shells and explosions. Shrapnel began to rain down around the men. Most were flat on the ground. Sammy would have been flat on the ground also if he weren't standing next to Basil, who stood erect as if nothing unusual was happening. Sammy heard a commotion and turned to see Colonel Shorter grabbing his thigh as if he'd been hit.

As Sammy began to move that way, he noticed there was no blood. Shorter yelled, "My ulcerated leg is acting up!"

Sammy stopped, unsure of what was happening to his commander. Another shell whistled past overhead. Colonel Shorter screamed. The look of terror was evident on his face. He looked at Sammy and said, "My bad leg is aching. I've got to get to the rear."

Before Sammy could reply, Shorter raced away at a sprint. Some of the men were about to follow him, when Sammy shouted for them to remain still. He'd just become the ranking officer of the regiment. He forced himself to remain calm. Sammy shouted, "Remain calm and stay on the ground. I will not leave you. I'll stay here and die with the last man if I must."

Randall forced himself off the ground and walked along the line urging the men to remain calm. Once Sammy was sure the men weren't going to break, he returned to Basil Manly. Basil was the most affable man he'd met since awakening in Corinth. He wasn't sure what it was about the man that made him so likable.

"What unit you with?" Sammy asked.

"Seventeenth Mississippi," Basil replied. The artillery shells continued to pass overhead like messengers of death. Basil acted as if it was just an ordinary day. "I'm from Tippah County, Mississippi, near a small town called Blue Mountain."

Sammy noticed that his entire regiment was lying flat on the ground, every man watching his every move. This was the point where he would set an example. He too would remain calm, as if nothing were happening, even if it got him killed.

Sammy said, "We're the 64th Alabama Infantry from Montgomery, Alabama. Like I said, I have no idea where I'm really from."

The roar of musketry erupted just beyond the trees to the north of their position. Both officers spun that way, but again neither man could see what was happening.

Basil pointed toward the trees and said, "That's what they call the West Woods. See that building to the right of them?"

Sammy looked at the small, white, one-room building and nodded.

Basil said, "That's the Dunker Church. It's called that because the congregation that meets there believes in full immersion for baptism. About a mile beyond the church is Antietam Creek. Lee chose this position because it is very defensible."

They listened to the roar of battle for two hours and wondered if they'd even be called into action. Many stragglers and wounded wandered past toward the rear, their blank faces staring off into the distance.

In the distance, Sammy saw General McLaws racing his horse from the West Woods, trailed by his staff. He galloped up to General Barksdale and shouted for him to move his brigade forward through the woods. In moments, the entire brigade was in motion. Barksdale rode up to Sammy, and his eyes flashed. The man seemed transformed. He seemed like he was born for this moment.

Barksdale shouted, "Bring your regiment on line on the right of my brigade. We're gonna have to hit them with all we got to stop 'em. It's a full division moving toward our left."

"Right," Sammy shouted and turned to his men. He shouted, "By the right oblique, march! Once you reach the main line, guide left and form on the right of the line!"

He watched the men he'd drilled so often perform the maneuver perfectly, despite the shells passing overhead. It was a beautiful thing to see. They operated like a well-oiled machine just as he had planned.

His men broke ranks as they passed through the trees and reformed as best they could. Ahead, coming across the field from the right, Sammy saw double lines of blue infantrymen moving forward with their bayonets advanced. The sun reflected off their polished rifles. The scene was entrancing, drawing every man's attention to them. Sammy noticed that not one of his men wavered but continued moving forward.

The long lines of Federal soldiers struck the tree line just ahead of the 64th Alabama and were halted there by a line of Confederates in the trees. Sammy immediately realized what was about to happen—Barksdale's brigade was about to crash right into their exposed flank. Within forty yards of the Federal line, Sammy screamed, "Fire!"

The regiment unleashed a volley that tore down the line. Enfilade fire was devastating. The angle at which they were firing meant they couldn't miss. If a man missed his mark, the bullet would travel on down the line until it struck someone. The left flank of the Federal division seemed to melt away. Men fell in piles. Sammy estimated they'd hit a couple hundred men with that one fire. The Federals never had a chance.

Barksdale rode down the line screaming for his brigade to charge. Sammy rushed forward to his line and screamed above the din, "Charge, men! For God's sake, charge!"

The line surged forward toward their bewildered enemy. The blue soldiers sank back from the rush. They had their bayonets fixed but wanted no part of hand-to-hand combat. They were being hit in the front and on the flank at the same time. There was nothing they could do. Sammy wondered what kind of officer would send his division across the field alone without support.

As they rushed at the Federal soldiers, Sammy knew they would break before contact. Just twenty yards from the line the blue coats turned and raced north away from the threat and across the field. Sammy ordered his men to fire at will and saw many men shot in the back as they attempted to escape.

He walked across the ground where his men had fired into the flank. Many men were wounded, and the cries perturbed him. They were in such a pile that he could hardly walk among them. One boy, who appeared to be about sixteen, looked up at the young colonel and begged, "Please don't kill us."

Sammy looked at the wound in the boy's calf. The bullet had gone completely through, but he was bleeding profusely. He said, "We don't shoot the wounded. I'll have you carried back to the surgeon as soon as I can."

Sammy walked back and reformed his men in the woods. He paused behind the line alone and took a knee. Reaching up to rub his forehead, he noticed how his hands were shaking. The combat hadn't scared him at all. He hadn't given a thought to being harmed while he had been so engrossed in doing his duty. What bothered him were the bodies. His own losses had been slight, but the sight of all the blood and gore unnerved him.

Lieutenant Basil Manly walked over and placed a hand on his shoulder. He bent over and said, "You'll get used to it."

"I'm not so sure," Sammy covered his eyes with his hand. "It's not what I imagined."

"Never is," Basil took a knee and laid his arm across Sammy's shoulders. "Next battle it'll get easier and easier until you think no more about it than you would of someone slaughtering hogs. Hell, at Second Manassas, I sat down and ate my rations among the dead bodies."

"I hope I never become that callous." Sammy shook his head, but deep down he understood how a man could become used to such sights.

He rose from the ground and rubbed his knee. He wondered if he'd marched all this way for a ten minute fight. That would be quite ironic. But he'd also helped to break a Federal division that was intent on breaking Lee's left flank. That counted for something at least.

Musket fire soon broke out to the right beyond the Dunker Church. An officer galloped down the line, trailed by his staff. Basil said, "That's Stonewall Jackson."

Sammy watched the man gallop past. He wore a faded blue uniform and was covered with dust. The man was nothing to look at; there was nothing there to make one believe he was a great leader. Basil could read Sammy's mind. He said, "Don't look like much, but the man is a genius."

"So I've heard," Sammy continued to stare after the group.

The noise of the firing to the right continued to grow. A rider galloped up to General Barksdale and said, "General Lee wants one of your larger regiments to reinforce the Sunken Road in the center. We're being pressed there."

"Take the Alabama bunch," Barksdale pointed toward Sammy. "They almost outnumber my entire brigade."

Sammy soon had the regiment following the staff officer past the white church and through the artillery beyond. He could see high ground a few hundred yards further with lots of gray-clad soldiers. They approached the sunken farm lane and crowded in with the men already there.

Sammy saw a general standing on the high ground behind the road. He walked over and saluted. "Lieutenant Colonel Samuel Rodes of the 64th Alabama Infantry reporting for duty, sir."

"George Anderson," the general replied. The man was young but had a beard that almost reached his belly. "You can't see them now; they're in that gully right ahead. But there's a division of Federal infantry coming straight at us. When they top that rise, give them hell."

"Yes, sir," Sammy turned and entered the sunken road with his men. The North Carolina boys in the road with his regiment fidgeted with their rifles. They had seen the Federal division disappear into the hollow ahead, and they understood how large of a force was moving against them.

A North Carolina captain turned his face to the sky and said, "This is the longest day of my life. Will the sun ever set?"

It reminded Sammy of a story Mary had read to him in the Bible, where Moses made the sun stand still so the Israelites could win a battle. It made Sammy wonder if the Federal army had a Moses on their side.

At the crest of the hill in their front appeared something that resembled a spear slowly moving upward. Soon it became apparent that it was a flag staff. The stars and stripes finally came into view followed by the heads of the Federal soldiers. Slowly their bodies continued to appear on the horizon just thirty yards away. Sammy moved down his line, saying, "Hold your fire, men. Remain calm, let them get up close, and present a big target."

The waiting for the order seemed to grate on the men's nerves. They wanted to open fire before the enemy could get any closer, but still Sammy waited. His men had the protection of the ditch and a split-rail fence in front. The Federal troops were out in the open field marching ahead to their doom.

At twenty yards, Sammy yelled, "Fire!"

The Federal division seemed to be swept from the earth. They lay in one continuous line. A few scattered shots were returned, but most of the line turned and ran back over the horizon and into the hollow beyond. Sammy's men joined the North Carolina and Alabama troops already in the road with the rebel yell.

A lull in the action then occurred. Sammy checked on his men. Most were running low on water but hadn't fired enough to need ammunition. He called for water details to carry the canteens back for refills. After he'd seen to his men, he sat down against the split-rail fence and began to write Mary a letter.

He'd just begun to write when he heard someone yell, "Here they come again. Twice as many as before."

He stood and watched the Union soldiers moving across the field toward his position. They moved over the rolling hills, reminding him of boats in the ocean. It seemed to be an entire corps this time. Sammy looked up and down the sunken farm lane. There were barely two thousand Confederates left against what appeared to be about fifteen thousand Federals advancing toward them. He turned in time to see the blue line disappear into the gully. The next time they would be seen would be just thirty yards away.

Randall was at his side shaking his head. Sammy held up a hand and said, "I know, I know. This is gonna be short and desperate."

"Suicide," Randall stated. Sammy wasn't sure what he meant by the word.

"Maybe we can blast them full in the face again and drive them back. You know, catch them off guard." Sammy patted Randall on the arm.

Again the flag staff appeared first. The Federal line approached at the half step, keeping their lines perfectly aligned. The slow trudge of the enemy perturbed him. He wished they would just come on. The waiting and wondering for the outcome was testing his patience.

At twenty yards, North Carolina General George Anderson shouted, "Fire! Pour it into them, boys!"

The entire line along the sunken road erupted like thunder. Federal soldiers again fell in heaps, but this time there were plenty of them. They stood there and returned the fire. It wasn't going to be as easy this time. The slaughter became enormous as men fell on both sides. The lines stood there just yards apart and seemed to melt away like wax over a fire.

Sammy moved along his line and shouted encouragement to his men. They had managed to stop the Federal advance, which made Sammy optimistic they may push them back again. The enemy resolutely stood his ground, trading shots with the Confederates. The Southern boys had the fence for cover, but they couldn't afford to lose men against such a large force.

Sammy heard someone screaming behind him. It was George Anderson rolling on the ground holding his ankle. The bullet had bounced off the bone, and the man was in obvious torment. Sammy moved that way. The sight told him the foot may have to be amputated. George Anderson gritted his teeth against the pain. Sammy ordered a couple North Carolina troops to carry their general to the rear.

He watched them leave with their tender load and turned back to his men. There was movement to his right. The Alabama troops under General Robert Emmet Rodes were breaking for the rear. They'd stood all they could take. Sammy immediately understood that to remain any longer would be suicide. He reluctantly gave the order for the regiment to retreat.

The North Carolina brigade raced along with them, many slowing down to turn and run backwards for fear of being shot in the back. Sammy was looking for Randall, but the man was nowhere to be found. A man told Sammy that Randall had gone down, shot through the thigh. There was little he could do about that now.

They raced on past the Piper Farm, which had served as General Longstreet's headquarters. There was a line of artillery parked hub to hub on the hill beyond. That was the only defense available to stop the Federal corps from pushing Lee's army into the Potomac River on the other side of town.

Sammy began to reform his regiment in a peach orchard just beyond the artillery pieces. The Federals continued to advance, aiming to press their advantage. Just a hundred yards away, the Confederate artillery opened fire with canister. Thousands of small round balls ripped through the enemy line. Sammy saw a man's arm fly thirty feet through the air. He watched the cannons reload and unleash another canister barrage as the Federal line closed to within sixty yards. He could actually hear the small iron balls ripping through bones.

The Federals stopped advancing and broke for the rear. They'd had enough. Sammy wiped sweat from his eyes. He dropped down on both knees. The strain had become more than he could bear. His eyes began to well with tears. He swallowed the lump that appeared in his throat and forced himself to rise.

His regiment was just a shadow of its former self. He walked among them, quietly counting heads. Of the seven hundred and one he'd brought on the field this morning, he could only count three hundred and sixty three. Sammy looked at his men's faces. They were all blank and filled with despair. They'd seen their friends shot to pieces and were asking themselves why they'd been allowed to live.

Sammy collapsed against a peach tree. He pulled out the letter he'd begun earlier and wondered how to describe what he'd seen here today. He would write about the enormous battle, but there was no way he could tell the horrible sights he'd witnessed here. Finally he decided to just refer to it as a great tumbling together of heaven and earth.

Luckily the fighting on the left and center had come to an end. The battle moved to the right, where it continued to rage until almost dark. He began to reorganize his men, shift men to their respective companies, and send some sergeants to the rear to bring up any stragglers that had been lost along the way. By sunset, he'd gotten his strength back up to four hundred and eighty-three men.

He began to take stock of his situation. Colonel Shorter had run off the field at the first sign of danger. Major Martin had been shot in the thigh, and six of his ten captains were either killed, wounded, or missing. There would be little he could do about that tonight, but at the first opportunity, he would have to sit down and promote some men.

It had been an exhausting day, not physically but mentally. Sammy collapsed on the ground among his men and slept hard until midnight. He awoke to the sounds of the groans and cries of the wounded spread across the field. It was heart-wrenching, but there was nothing that could be done. The men were lying between the opposing lines, and to move out there would bring gunfire from both sides. He placed his fingers in his ears and attempted to go back to sleep.

He lay there half an hour and finally gave up on getting anymore rest. Sammy sat up and noticed a group of men talking quietly in a circle. He got to his feet and made his way to the edge of the group. He lay on the ground nearby to just listen to what his men were saying. Their words shocked him.

"He's got no life left, no family. I'm telling you boys, he wants to die, and he'll get us all killed doing it," one of the men was saying.

Another man cleared his throat and said, "I thought we was gonna be all right until Major Martin went down. Now who's gonna watch out for us?"

The man sitting closest to Sammy said, "I don't know boys, but I think you're wrong. I mean, when that artillery opened fire this morning and Colonel Shorter ran off, I wanted to go with him. I've never been so afraid in my life. But I saw Colonel Sammy, and I wouldn't feel right running away after watching such a young boy be so brave. I like him. He stayed with us through the fight, brave as hell. He's a natural leader no matter whether you boys like him or not. I've made up my mind. I'll follow that boy if he charges the gates of hell."

"I agree," said another dark figure nearby. "When we charged them boys this morning in the woods, we went through them like shit through a goose. I complained about all that drilling, but now I see how it paid off. The boy knows what he's doing even if he don't know who he is."

The first man who'd started the conversation added, "Well, I'll have to admit, he did handle the regiment with ease. He could make a general someday if'n he don't get killed first, which is highly likely the way he leads."

Sammy got to his feet and moved away. He was shocked that they'd thought he wanted to die. His greatest fear was dying without having any idea who he was. He moved down his line until he came to Company E. There he found Captain Patrick South smoking his pipe.

"Mind if I sit a spell?" Sammy asked.

"Not at all," Captain South spoke up. It was so dark that he hadn't known it was his colonel. "You all right, sir?"

"I'm fine," Sammy replied as he sat on the ground beside his captain. "Your men asleep?"

"Most of 'em," Patrick said as he blew out a puff of tobacco smoke. "What's on your mind?"

Sammy lowered his voice to nearly a whisper. "We've got a mess to straighten out tomorrow."

"Right," Patrick lowered the pipe. "Any word from Major Martin?"

"Nothing," Sammy replied. "But if he was hit in the thigh, he's out of action awhile, and of course there's the problem with Colonel Shorter."

"The man should be shot," Patrick said louder than he meant to.

"Easy," Sammy whispered, "I like the man. It could have happened to any of us—first engagement and all."

"But it didn't happen to any of us," Patrick wasn't as forgiving as Sammy. "It happened to the damned colonel commanding the regiment. What kind of message are we sending the troops if we allow him to command again?"

"You're right," Sammy shook his head. He dreaded having to deal with the situation tomorrow. He truly liked Colonel Shorter. He was a nice man, but Sammy understood there had to be consequences for the colonel abandoning his regiment at the first

61

sign of danger. Sammy mumbled to himself, "Maybe he's halfway to Montgomery by now."

"Perhaps," Patrick wasn't in the mood to joke about the matter. He was angry with his commander for what he'd done. He changed the subject. "Sammy, how'd you remain so calm today? I know you were at Shiloh, but you say you don't remember a thing."

"To be honest with you, I was so absorbed in doing my duty that I didn't have time to think about my own personal safety." Sammy chuckled under his breath. "I was so afraid I would let you fellows down, and I couldn't have that. How about yourself?"

"I was as scared as the next man," Patrick puffed on the pipe a moment. "Then I saw you standing there as if nothing out of the ordinary was happening. I told myself you'd been right about everything else you'd done with this regiment—you know, the training and all. I decided I would just do as you were doing."

Sammy hadn't realized he'd made such an impression on his men until now. "Well, I have more good news for you, Captain."

"Can hardly wait to hear it," Patrick took another drag on the pipe.

"In the morning, when I find out who's dead or not..." Sammy paused a long moment for effect. "Well, Captain South, you're getting a promotion."

"What if I don't want it?" Patrick asked in his normal voice.

Sammy patted him on the arm and rose to his feet. "I don't remember asking you if you did."

As Sammy moved back down his line, he heard Patrick whisper, "Thank you, sir."

As dawn broke, the sounds of the wounded had finally died down. Sammy stood and breathed the cool, crisp air. Winter was approaching. He could see men milling about. Soon a truce was called between the two armies, and men were sent forward to recover the wounded. There was nothing left for him to do but await word from these men.

He sat back and watched the recovery operations across the field. Blue and gray-clad soldiers worked to recover their comrades, often stopping to talk and trade tobacco for coffee. It amazed Sammy that just yesterday these men were attempting to kill each other without mercy, and now they were like friends.

There was a steady stream of wounded men being taken to the rear. Soon word came back that Major Martin had been found. He was lying on the side of the sunken road. A bullet had clipped his femoral artery, and he'd bled to death soon after. Sammy lowered his head. Randall had been a good man, a good officer. He would be difficult to replace.

Sammy decided to walk back toward the Dunker Church and try to locate General Barksdale. He passed back across the field in front of the church, where the line of artillery had stood yesterday. There were several Confederate artillerymen lying where they'd fallen. One man had been struck in the side by a cannonball that had passed all the way through his body. The man was cut in half. Sammy tried to look away, but for some reason, he couldn't take his eyes off the sight. He'd never seen the insides of a man before today.

He searched the trees beyond the church and found the dead there as thick as harvest sheaves. Some of the dead were stiff with rigor mortis, and their arms were stretched in the air above their heads. Some of the mangled bodies appalled him.

He was finally told that Barksdale's brigade was back in the field where they'd camped before the battle. Sammy located Barksdale in a tent back there and was invited inside. The Mississippi general was sitting at a small desk, writing. When he turned, Sammy saluted.

"How are you, Colonel?" Barksdale ignored the salute.

"Tolerable," Sammy replied. He removed his hat and rubbed his eyes. "I've lost a lot of good men, and my major is dead."

"Sorry to hear it," Barksdale motioned for Sammy to sit on his cot. "Listen, your colonel was here earlier. He came to resign his commission. He's gone home, but he did say for you to keep the horse."

"Yes, sir," Sammy replied. He continued to stare at the ground just beyond his feet.

"You sure you're feeling all right?" Barksdale asked.

"Yes, sir, just exhausted is all." Sammy's eyes met Barksdale's briefly.

Barksdale extended his hand. "I need to know you're all right because I'm promoting you to colonel of your regiment. Congratulations."

Sammy looked up and took Barksdale's hand. Barksdale continued, "I watched you yesterday. I know your regiment is green, but you handled them like a veteran commander, and they followed you where you led. Your action was extremely commendable. That tells me all I need to know about you. Now you've got to promote you a lieutenant colonel and a major. Can you handle that, or should I do it for you?"

"I can handle it, sir, no offense," Sammy had already been thinking about replacements. "I have several captains that deserve the positions."

"Well, get to it," Barksdale smiled. "We have a truce today, but we may be back in action by tomorrow."

Barksdale was dismissing him. Sammy had enough sense to know it. He rose and saluted. This time Barksdale returned the salute. He said, "Once you've finished reorganizing your regiment and promoting officers, move your men back here with the rest of my brigade."

"Yes, sir," Sammy stepped from the tent and took a deep breath. Just like that, and the dead are forgotten. Another man is chosen and put in their places. He thought about what Rose had said the night before. War is extremely sad.

He walked to the area where the 17th Mississippi was camped and found Lieutenant Basil Manly taking a nap. He nudged the lieutenant with the toe of his boot. Manly attempted to open his eyes, but the sun forced him to squint. He asked, "What the hell?"

Sammy said, "Get up, Lieutenant."

Manly rose slowly from the ground. He stood and noticed it was the lieutenant colonel he'd been speaking with yesterday. He saluted and wondered if he were in some kind of trouble.

"How would you like a promotion?" Sammy asked.

"Promotion?" Basil asked. A confused look appeared on his face. "What kind of promotion?"

"How about captain to start with?" Sammy squinted into Basil's eyes. "Are you awake enough to comprehend anything, Lieutenant?"

"I'm getting there," Basil replied. "How you gonna give me a promotion? You're not even in my regiment."

"You'll have to transfer to the 64th Alabama Infantry," Sammy liked Basil Manly for some reason. The man had seemed carefree from the moment he'd met him yesterday.

"Which company would I command?" Basil asked. He understood that a captain normally commanded a company. At the moment, Basil was in Company A, 17th Mississippi Infantry, and had a captain and another lieutenant ranking him.

"Regimental staff," Sammy said. "You'll be my adjutant for starters. Maybe get a promotion to major before long if you do a good enough job."

"Regimental staff," Basil repeated. "Damned if I don't like the sound of that."

"Come on," Sammy motioned for Basil to follow him. He found the colonel commanding the regiment and asked for him to transfer Basil Manly to the 64th Alabama Infantry Regiment. Just like that, and Sammy had an adjutant.

Returning to the peach orchard, Sammy found Captain Patrick South and informed him he was the new lieutenant colonel of the regiment. South nodded without saying a word. Sammy found Captain Jeremiah Burnett and informed him that he was the regiment's major. He then had the regiment formed and moving back past the Dunker Church to rejoin Barksdale's brigade.

They passed smashed caissons, abandoned muskets, blankets, and canteens. It appeared as though a tornado had struck the army and had strewn debris everywhere. Sammy reported to General Barksdale upon arrival and was told to have his troops ready to move at dark. Lee was pulling back to Virginia. The news saddened Sammy as much as the death of Major Martin.

It was about nine that night that he received orders to move his regiment back through town and across the Potomac River. As they marched past the field hospitals, Sammy could see surgeons busy and covered with blood. Amputated arms and legs lay in piles almost four foot high. The stench was dreadful.

He heard a commotion behind him as they neared the river. Sammy turned and approached a group of his men beneath a tree. They were holding a lantern over something on the ground. Sammy asked, "What are ya'll doing out of ranks?"

"Sorry, sir," one of the young men replied. "It's William Parsons, sir. We all grew up together. He's been hit in the chest, been unconscious since yesterday. We was a goin' to carry him back with us, but he's dying."

Sammy noticed all the men gathered around the boy, tears filled every eye present. The poor boy's chest was rising in irregular heaves. It was obvious he was dying. He'd have to be left behind. Each man took turns kissing the boy on the cheek. It was the saddest thing Sammy had seen yet. All this poor boy's dreams—his entire life—all erased by a couple ounces of lead.

As soon as they'd finished saying their goodbyes, they rose and stood, waiting for someone to tell them it was all right to leave him behind. Sammy stepped into the group and kneeled by the boy. He held his hand and lowered his head in prayer. It didn't take a genius to understand this was a fine man. All these men wouldn't be here making such a scene if he wasn't.

Sammy rose and said, "Only our Heavenly Father knows why he wanted to take this boy so young. It's not for us to ask why."

Sammy returned to the front of his regiment and led the march across the waist-deep river. He had been serious about what he said and did back there. He wasn't setting out to gain more respect from the men, but they naturally respected him more for his understanding of their loss. He wished it had been him back there dead instead of that innocent young boy. He began to worry about his mental status. There was genuine fear that this war would put him in an asylum if he continued to let things affect him so. He marched on into Virginia, wet, cold, and miserable.

CHAPTER FIVE

Charlie didn't show up as soon as school let out, and this caused Sol some concern. He took out his pocket watch and noted the time. Normally, Charlie would have been there thirty minutes earlier, eager for his daily war story. Sol spat a stream of tobacco juice into the yard.

He'd gotten attached to Charlie. No one had taken an interest in visiting him in years. He began to fret that Charlie was growing bored with the stories. *Boys got other things to do besides sit and listen to an old man every day, he thought. Couldn't blame him if he stopped coming.*

Sol eased his head back in the rocker and closed his eyes. He was soon asleep. How long he'd been asleep he didn't know, but he was awakened by someone clearing their throat. Sol looked up and noticed Charlie at the edge of the porch with a sack in his hand.

Charlie asked, "Not disturbing you am I?"

"You're late today." Sol looked at the sack and asked, "What's in the bag?"

"Sorry," Charlie stepped onto the porch. "I'm late because my maw wanted me to bring you supper, and I had to run home and wait for her to finish."

"Say she did now," Sol's eyes lit up as he watched Charlie pass the sack to him. He pulled the plug of tobacco from his mouth and hurled it into the yard. "That's mighty nice of her. I ain't had no woman cook for me in thirty years or so."

Sol dug into the sack and began to eat like a man who'd gone a week without eating. Charlie eased into the chair. It had tried his patience waiting for the food to cook so he could get up here and hear his daily war story. He patiently waited for Sol to finish eating.

Sol spoke while he chewed, bits of food spraying from his mouth. "You be sure and tell your maw how much I appreciate the grub. Shore is good."

"Yes, sir," Charlie propped his chin on his hand and rested his elbow on his knee. Patience wasn't one of his virtues. Luckily for him, Sol ate extremely fast.

When Sol had finished, he rose from the chair and went inside with the plate. Charlie wondered where he was going. In a few moments Sol returned, wiping the plate with a dish towel. He'd washed the plate before sending it back.

"Now," Sol said as he sat back in his rocker, "where were we?"

"Just finished the Battle of Antietam," Charlie replied.

"No, it was the Battle of Sharpsburg," Sol gave Charlie a scowl.

"I know that's what we called it," Charlie held up his hand, "but Miss Harman calls it Antietam. She corrected me today when I called it Sharpsburg."

"She's a damned old Yankee, Charlie," Sol was shaking his head. "Don't listen to her. She come down here to try and make you think we was the ones in the wrong in that war."

"She says the war was fought to free the slaves and make all people equal," Charlie shrugged.

"She trying to sell you a load of manure," Sol dug in his pocket and reloaded his mouth with tobacco. "Answer me this. If'n all they fought for was to take care of the black man, how come they ain't made sure he has equal rights with the white man? It's been fifty years since that war, and the black man is still treated like a slave down here. Bet she won't be able to answer that question."

Charlie smiled. He hadn't thought about it that way.

Sol wasn't finished with his rant. "I get so tired of them damned Yankees with their "holier than thou" attitude. You ever hear of Pat Cleburne?"

"No, sir," Charlie replied.

"He was one of the greatest Confederate generals ever," Sol wiped his mouth on the back of his arm. "Born in Ireland. He said, 'If we lose this war, we'll be taught from Yankee textbooks that what we did was wrong.' He was right about that part. I can assure you I didn't fight for no slaves."

68

"What was the war about, Uncle Sol?" Charlie was on the edge of his seat. He was so inquisitive and eager for knowledge, desperate to know everything he could about the war.

"Money," Sol said. "Plain old dirty money. Ever war been fought been fought over money, or maybe religion. You think them Northern boys came down here and lost 450,000 men to free slaves who was a gonna be taking their jobs for less pay?"

"I suppose not," Charlie smiled.

"Damn right they weren't," Sol was enjoying educating Charlie on something that he'd had no idea about. "Ever one of them boys would tell you they was a fightin' for the Union."

"Yes, sir," Charlie agreed. He was fascinated that Sol knew all this, but he wanted to learn what happened to the young officer. He asked, "Now, did that Colonel learn his real name yet?"

Sol shook his head again. The boy just wouldn't give up. He said, "Alright, boy, hold your pants on...we'll get back to the story now...they thought they was a going into winter quarters and wouldn't be no more fighting until spring, but Lincoln had other plans. He replaced McClellan with an old boy named Burnside. That's where sideburns got their name from. Burnside had the biggest bushiest sideburns you ever did see."

"Really?" Charlie was amazed.

"Yep," Sol replied. "And he might have had fancy facial hair, but he didn't have not one lick of sense in his head."

****

Barksdale's brigade had been placed in the town of Fredericksburg to stop the Federals from crossing the river until all of Lee's men arrived. He had detached Sammy's regiment and placed them under Brigadier General Thomas Cobb of Georgia. The man placed his brigade behind a stone wall just west of town halfway up Marye's Heights.

Cobb wasn't nearly as likable as Barksdale, but the man was just as aggressive. He hated Yankees with a passion and hated most of his own commanders equally. He continuously carped about how General Lee despised him. The man was almost paranoid. He'd managed to alienate almost everyone around him. The man obviously felt inferior in some way, but Sammy just couldn't place his finger on what that was.

Sammy's men were on the left of Cobb's brigade. He loved their position. There was a sunken road behind a chest-high stone wall that would provide his men with excellent protection. He arranged his troops in such a way that there was one man for every foot of wall in their front, while two men would stand behind him loading and passing up their muskets. If the Federal troops were stupid enough to attack this position, they would be annihilated.

Basil was ever present by Sammy's side, and he'd been a God-send to the young Colonel. Where Sammy had been depressed since awakening in Corinth, Basil seemed to have the ability to lift his spirits. The man took nothing seriously and could always be counted on to get Sammy out of a slump. He was garrulous and kept Sammy on his guard with his humor.

"It's incomprehensible," Basil mumbled behind Sammy's back.

Sammy turned with a look of confusion. He saw Basil staring across the river to the mass of blue troops on the heights beyond and asked, "What's that?"

"It just doesn't make sense," Basil was shaking his head. "I can't believe they've just been sitting over there idle, allowing us to fortify our position. We command the field now. There is no way they can take this position. You know, Sammy, I'm afraid they are up to something."

"Maybe," Sammy agreed. "I can't imagine them trying to cross that river and attack these heights with us entrenched so."

They soon heard firing down near the river's edge. Barksdale's brigade was firing at the pontoon builders, making life difficult for those men in blue. A rumor floated down the line that Lee had ordered Barksdale to allow the Federals to cross the river. There was nothing he would enjoy more than to have them assault him here with their own backs against a river. Barksdale soon fell back, which gave credence to the rumor. He marched his brigade up the road and settled into a reserve position in the rear. *He won't be very happy about that, Sammy thought.*

The Federal army was soon across the Rappahannock River and began looting the town. Federal soldiers put on women's dresses and paraded in the streets. They cut gashes in family portraits and even tossed a couple of pianos in the streets.

Basil leaned on the stone wall and lowered his head. "This is not warfare. What's wrong with those people?"

"A lack of leadership for one thing," Sammy placed his arms on the stone wall and spoke to Basil in a low voice. "They're different people than we are. I haven't been able to put my finger on what it is just yet, but they weren't raised the way we were. When we were in Maryland, we acted nothing like them. We treated all the citizens with the utmost respect. Those men are not gentlemen."

"What can we do?" Basil shrugged.

Sammy looked at Basil through hard eyes. He whispered, "Kill them all."

The statement shocked Basil. This was the same innocent boy who said he wouldn't allow war to change him just two months earlier. Now that he'd seen the true face of war, he was realizing that it changes everyone. Basil understood that deep down, no matter what they'd been before this thing started, they could never return. They were boys no more, but men scarred by warfare, and they'd carry those scars to the grave.

December thirteenth dawned cold, and fog hung close to the ground. A man couldn't see twenty yards. The men shook inside their blankets. Colonel Samuel Rodes walked down his lines, checking on the welfare of his men. He encouraged the ones he thought needed it and told them all the Federals would probably be coming today. He wanted them to keep a sharp eye, take steady aim when firing, and keep it hot on the Yankees.

The ground was frozen, and Sammy listened to the Federal artillery moving somewhere in the fog below. Basil walked up to Sammy, saluted, and said, "If they come, this will be beautiful. That Federal army is the largest and best equipped on the planet, and we're gonna mow them down like wheat before a scythe."

71

"It's beautiful as long as we're not the ones attacking entrenchments," Sammy mumbled.

Firing broke out a couple miles to their right. Basil spun that way. It soon grew into a continuous roar. They followed the battle there with their ears. The Federals were hitting Stonewall Jackson's corps on the extreme right flank. They could hear the firing moving forward, moving toward their right rear.

"They're pushing Jackson. If he breaks..." Basil left the rest unsaid.

"If he breaks, we're cut off from Richmond," Sammy finished the statement for him. "But that's Stonewall, and he never breaks."

"True," Basil felt reassured by Sammy's statement.

It was after one before the Federals attempted to assault Marye's Heights. The sun had long since burned the fog away, and every movement made by the enemy troops was observed by the Confederates. Sammy watched a division move out of town and make its way across a drainage ditch below their position. They reformed and began moving up the open field against the stone wall.

Confederate artillery soon opened fire on the advancing enemy troops, tearing great gaps in their lines. Sammy admired the way they would close up their lines and continue forward. Regardless of how he felt about them, they were definitely brave.

When they'd advanced to within a hundred yards of the stone wall, General Cobb shouted the order to open fire. The results were just what Sammy had predicted. The slaughter was terrific. Hundreds of men in a straight line on the ground. The others paused and attempted to fire back. The only visible targets were the heads of the Confederates, and very few were hit. The rear rank passed up rifles, and the firing became a continuous roar.

The Federals stood the firing as long as they possibly could and then broke for the cover of the canal. Sammy almost felt sorry for those brave men. The wounded were begging for help; the dead lay piled across each other.

Basil was screaming the rebel yell along with the men. He looked at Sammy and said, "Sir, they could place the entire Yankee nation in front of our wall and we'd kill every one of 'em."

The men didn't have long to celebrate. Another division was marching out of town and headed toward the canal. Sammy had to admit it was a beautiful sight—the long blue lines, the sun reflecting off the bright bayonets. It was difficult to imagine that in a few moments, most of those brave men were going to be a dying mass of humanity.

They cleared the ditch, and the Confederate artillery raked their lines with shot and shell. Still they moved toward the wall. They looked as though they'd walk right over the position. The slow pace at which they advanced was a shock tactic from the Napoleonic days. *It works pretty well, Sammy thought, but they won't march over us. They'll never reach us.*

When General Cobb gave the order to fire, the Federal line was within fifty yards of the wall. The survivors immediately stopped and returned fire. The air seemed to be alive with the flashes of the rifles. Shells screamed past overhead. Another volley from the Confederate lines forced them to fall back a few paces. Then they collapsed on the ground among the dead and wounded. Men were using the dead bodies as breastworks against the terrific gunfire coming from the wall.

Sammy walked down his line shouting encouragement to his men. They seemed to quicken the pace of reloading and firing when they realized he was near. The entire regiment was eager to please their brave young commander now that they understood he loved each and every one of them.

He watched a Federal officer ride across the canal on horseback and ride to the prostrate men. Incredibly, he made it all the way to the position just fifty yards from the wall without being hit. The officer seemed oblivious to the missiles of death flying past him each second. The man was fearless. Sammy had to admire such courage in the face of death. The man ordered his troops up and forward again, but it was useless. Men stood only to be mowed down by the continuous fire. They began to break. The officer's horse was hit and crashed to the ground on his leg. He was trapped, and his men were fleeing the field. There was no one there to save him. Luckily, he fell on the side opposite the Confederate fire, and although his horse was hit multiple times, he was unharmed.

Sammy saw Basil walking toward him as if he were just out for an afternoon stroll. His nonchalance was amazing.

"Where you been?" Sammy asked as he smiled and shook his head.

"Other end of the line watching those idiots down there commit suicide," Basil replied as he jerked his thumb over his shoulder. "Gotta admire their determination. They're so frivolous it's ridiculous. How long you think it would take someone to learn what they're attempting is impossible?"

"As long as they continue to send a division at a time, we're in good shape," Sammy replied. He stepped to the wall and looked down toward town. Another division was preparing to move out. He nodded his head toward them. "Here comes another. The mistake they're making is in stopping in front of our position to return our fire. They need to charge when they get here. Someone should be hanged for getting all those men killed here today. Killed for nothing at that."

"Damned Yankees," Basil shook his head. "What else would you expect?"

Sammy looked back toward the division now moving out of town toward the canal. He attempted to count the number of killed and wounded in front of the wall but soon gave up. There were just too many. The ground was covered in blood near the bodies. As the enemy line neared the canal, Confederate artillery opened fire from the heights behind the stone wall.

The gunners had gotten their range now and every shot seemed to strike a portion of the line. Sammy saw bodies blown through the air. Most were dismembered by the heavy iron shells. Still they closed the gaps and continued forward.

Sammy looked to his right and saw Brigadier General Thomas Cobb motioning to him. He walked down the line and saluted his commander. Cobb said, "Damned Longstreet has given me orders to fall back up the hill to the main line."

"What for?" Sammy asked.

"The idiot thinks we're about to be overrun. He tells me I can't possibly hold this position." Cobb was in a rage. He disliked his superiors under normal conditions, but at moments under stress, Cobb loathed his commanders.

Sammy shook his head. "As long as we have ammunition, there's no one gonna overrun us. What are you gonna do?"

"Make a stand right here," Cobb's eyes were flashing. "I take it as an insult to me and my men that he doesn't have more faith in us than that. If they wait for me to give the order to fall back, they'll be waiting for hell to freeze over."

"Right, sir," Sammy saluted and moved back to his regiment. The division had just crossed the canal, and they were moving out into the open field. There was nothing to do now but wait for Cobb to give the order to fire.

Sammy walked along his line instructing his men to wait for the order. Every man along the wall had his rifle resting on top, aiming down the barrel and waiting. There was never any doubt in Sammy's mind what was about to occur. It would be nothing more than murder from this point forward. The murder would be the fault of the Federal commander who continued to send these men to their deaths knowing what had occurred here before.

The division marched to the point where the other two divisions had been destroyed, when Cobb gave the order. The gunfire opened at almost the same instant down the line. The volley was devastating to the Federal infantry. The front line melted away, but the second line pressed forward. The ground had become slick with the blood of the fallen. Men were slipping as they passed through the bodies. A few more paces and the loaded rifles were passed forward and another devastating volley was delivered. Still, the survivors pressed forward to within twenty-five yards of the stone wall. Sammy thought they would extirpate them all. Another volley was unleashed, and it was over. The survivors again crashed on the ground and sought protection behind dead comrades. Sammy noticed the sound of the bullets striking the dead bodies, and it reminded him of someone thumping a ripe watermelon. He turned his head from the scene.

He heard a shout to his left where General Cobb had been standing. A group of men were gathered around someone on the ground. Sammy moved that way. He arrived to find a stream of blood flowing beyond the circle of men. Easing a man aside, Sammy saw that Cobb had been hit in the thigh. Obviously, he'd been struck in the femoral artery the same way Randall Martin had at Sharpsburg two months earlier. A tourniquet would have saved the man's life, but it was too late now. He was already unconscious and had lost too much blood. Colonel Robert McMillan took command of the brigade.

Sammy returned to his line and saw another division of Federal infantry preparing to leave town. He called in his officers and asked for a casualty and ammunition report. The news was good. The regiment still had over fifty rounds per man, and there were less than twenty casualties because the wall had offered so much protection. The casualties they suffered were mostly due to head shots. A couple had been wounded in the arm or shoulder.

He had his men return to their posts and prepare for the next charge. The butchery in front of his position had been horrendous, and it seemed it would just get worse. The Federal division left town and headed for the canal. There seemed to be some confusion when the line reached the canal, for no man seemed to want to leave the safety the position afforded them. There was nothing but open field between the canal and the stone wall. After some agonizing moments, the line left the canal. It soon became apparent that this assault was going to be to the right of Sammy's regiment. There would be some enfilade fire he could place on them as they got into range, but otherwise he would be a spectator to this assault.

The assault ended as all the previous ones had. Sammy stepped up to the wall and looked at the slaughter before his position. He'd been as responsible for those deaths as the men he commanded. In a way, it actually felt good. Those were the same men who'd been down there in town looting and destroying innocent people's property for no reason. They'd gotten what they deserved in his eyes. He turned and sat on the ground, back to the wall. Night was fast approaching, and he dreaded listening to the wounded again. It brought back memories of Sharpsburg, but this time it was only the enemy wounded he would have to hear. Sammy pretended it didn't bother him.

A man cleared his throat. Sammy looked up to see Basil Manly standing over him. Sammy motioned toward the wall. "Come sit a spell, Basil. You're the man I need to talk to just now."

"Right," Basil said as he plopped on the ground by Sammy's side. "I think it's over. At least for today. You all right, Colonel?"

"Exhausted is all," Sammy wiped his eyes. "Just now realized I haven't had a thing to eat all day."

"Shall I round us up some rations?" Basil inquired.

"Please," Sammy replied. He removed his hat and ran his hand through his hair.

After dark, the dreaded sound of the Federal wounded began to haunt the night. Several men approached Sammy and asked permission to cross the stone wall and give such aide as they could to the poor men beyond.

Sammy was disinclined to allow them. He said, "You will be crossing into no-man's land, subject to enemy and friendly fire out there. Although all is quiet, we don't have a truce. I believe it would be imprudent for you to risk your lives for men who were trying to kill you just a few hours ago."

One of the men replied, "Sir, all I'm asking is if you will arrest us if we go out there. I'd hope if it were me out there, someone would assist me."

"I have no intention of arresting anyone," Sammy shook his head. "I understand what you want to do, but I leave it in your hands. I want to do something as much as you fellows, but I can't give you orders. You'll just have to make up your own minds what you should do."

Sammy lay back against the stone wall and attempted to get some rest. He'd finally nodded off around midnight when Basil jostled him awake. Sammy spun his head thinking they were being assaulted at night.

Basil said, "You got to see this, Colonel."

Sammy rose from the ground and peered over the wall into the darkness.

Basil said, "Not out there. Look at the sky. It's beautiful ain't it?"

Sammy looked into the sky and saw beautiful images of green lights. The sight was the most ethereal thing these men from Alabama had ever seen. A private who was standing beside the two officers asked, "What is it?"

Basil spoke quickly, "I think it's the transmigration of the souls slain here today."

The man asked, "What the hell is a transmigration of souls?"

"It's the souls of the slain leaving their bodies for heaven," Basil replied.

A man just beyond the private said, "Hell no, it ain't. We blew them sons-of-bitches to hell. Ain't a one of 'em going to heaven."

"Actually, it's the aurora borealis," Sammy said as he continued to stare at the beautiful spectra.

"The what?" Basil asked.

"The Northern Lights," Sammy replied. "It's rare for them to be seen this far south, but that's definitely what it is."

"How do you know that?" Basil asked. His colonel couldn't remember where he was six months ago but was full of all kinds of information. It perturbed him.

"I have no idea, but that's exactly what it is," Sammy smiled into the darkness. He loved it when he got Basil worked up.

He continued to watch the show in the night sky, while listening to the wretched moans and cries of the wounded. It was too dark to see them; it was almost like listening to ghosts. He heard one man begging over and over for his mother and it depressed him.

The next day a truce was called and Sammy ventured out among the work parties. Men tried to dig in the frozen ground but couldn't get far. He watched men unceremoniously toss the bodies in the shallow graves and attempt to cover them with dirt. He heard an argument to his left and moved that way. Basil Manly had two Federal greatcoats in his hand, and a Federal officer was berating him for stealing from the dead.

Basil said, "It's cold out here, and you think these two dead men need these coats?"

"That is U.S. Government property you're taking there, Captain," the Federal officer replied.

"Well, I captured it fair and square," Basil wasn't about to back down.

"You'll give me those coats, Captain, or else," the Federal officer tried to sound forceful.

Basil walked around the Federal officer and stared at his boots. He said, "What size shoe you wear? I need me a good pair of boots."

The officer realized he was getting nowhere with this Confederate officer and quickly moved back toward his lines.

Sammy asked, "Basil, why do I have to keep you out of trouble so much?"

Basil gave a sheepish grin. "Yeah, but when you're warm tonight because I got us a couple nice coats, you'll be thanking me."

Sammy understood he could always count on Basil looking out for his welfare.

****

Sammy had been careful to make sure his appearance had not changed. He'd kept the peach fuzz on his upper lip and shaved the rest of his face daily. He often stood in front of the mirror and wondered who this young boy actually was. There was always the chance someone would recognize him some day. He stared hard into the mirror, and the reflection stared back at him just as intently. He remembered a saying he'd heard somewhere before about being careful when staring into the abyss because at the same time, the abyss stares into you.

Basil Manly opened the door to his crude cabin that his men had helped to build and peered inside. He said, "Oh good, you're shaving. I have plans for us tonight."

Sammy paused and cut his eyes toward Basil. He asked, "Who's in command here anyway?"

"You, of course, but sometimes I have to take matters into my own hands to ensure you have a little fun," Basil strolled into the shanty—it could hardly be called a cabin—and took a seat on Sammy's cot. The place was small and built from logs, with room for a desk, cot, and little else. "We're in winter quarters now. There'll be no action until spring. You might as well enjoy life a little."

"What the hell are you talking about?" Sammy asked as he turned back to the mirror and continued to shave.

"We have an engagement this fine evening—the two of us." Basil lay down on Sammy's cot and began to smile.

"Engagement?" Sammy asked.

"That's right, young Colonel," Basil crossed his legs and stared at the top of the cabin. "Two young ladies request our company tonight, and I've volunteered you to attend with me."

"Ladies," Sammy repeated. He shook his head. "I don't think so."

"Don't even start, sir," Basil grew serious. "The girl I'm going to see is Susannah, and her sister is in love with Confederate officers. The higher the rank the more she admires. So, I don't have an engagement tonight unless you come along. And I know you're not gonna knock me out of it after all I've done for you. Besides, she hasn't had an officer call on her who was ranked higher than captain."

Sammy cut his eyes toward Basil as he finished shaving his neck. "What does this girl look like?"

"Well, to be honest, she's the prettier of the two, but she has no interest in me at all." Basil realized he'd peaked Sammy's interest and leapt from the cot to press his case. "She's shorter than you. Long dark hair and the most gorgeous eyes you've ever seen. I believe she's nineteen years old. Susannah is sixteen, which is just right. You know what my pa used to say. If she's old enough to go to the store, she's old enough to get bred."

"Damn," Sammy shook his head. He couldn't believe Basil was being so profligate. "At least I won't have to worry about the Yankees killing you. Her pa will take care of that soon enough for 'em."

80

Basil eased over and gave Sammy a rough pat on the back. "Hot damned, Sammy. I bet I get in her dress before daylight."

"You'd look good in a dress I bet," Sammy burst into laughter at the thought. "What will you say when I tell those ladies you're my amanuensis?"

Basil looked hurt. "You wouldn't refer to me as your personal secretary, would you?"

Sammy smiled. "It's according to how this girl looks. Now what's her name?"

"I knew you'd go," Basil clapped his hands together. "Her name's Lillian. Lillian Duncan—and you're gonna love her."

"I better," Sammy warned.

They rode west together away from the town of Fredericksburg. They entered a deep, thick wilderness. The night was dark as pitch. Sammy began to fear his captain had been set up. He wondered how anyone could live in this mess.

"They call this place the wilderness," Basil mumbled. The night was so quiet that every sound seemed to magnify into the darkness. "All the way to Chancellorsville, this is nothing but cut over. Would be one hell of a mess to fight in."

"You sure you know where you're going?" Sammy asked.

"Have faith, Colonel, sir," Basil was shaking his head in the darkness. "It's not much farther; I promise."

Ahead, Sammy could see lights in the forest. The road soon came to a small opening where a nice two story house stood. Basil chuckled, "Told you I knew the way. Now don't embarrass me, sir."

Sammy shook his head. If anything, he'd embarrass himself. He'd had problems talking to the ladies ever since he'd awoken. He could almost feel guilty coming here, but he'd received no word from Mary in over a month. Her letters had arrived further and further apart, as if she were no longer interested in him. Sammy had written her four letters since he'd heard a word. The last letter he'd received mentioned her meeting a young lieutenant in the Fourth Alabama Cavalry who'd been calling on her. Sammy had felt guilty, but he could understand it had been six months since he'd gotten on that train and left her.

81

They tied their horses to the hitching post near the front porch. Basil could hardly wait to get inside. Sammy was nervous and took his time. Basil almost leapt onto the veranda and turned to wait for Sammy. "Come on, Colonel. Those ladies will die of old age before you get inside."

Sammy took his time tying the reins. He dreaded going inside. The scene was already playing out in his mind. Basil would keep the girls in stitches, and he would just sit there like a knot on a log, red-faced every time he was spoken to.

As Sammy started up the steps, Basil gave a firm knock on the door. Sammy had just reached the top step when a young girl opened the door. She saw Basil and said, "Oh, you did come."

"A Southern gentleman always keeps his word," Basil bowed formally. He nodded toward Sammy and said, "This here is my colonel. Sammy, meet Susannah."

Sammy bowed and mumbled, "Nice to meet you, ma'am."

"A pleasure," Susannah replied. "Please come in and make yourself at home."

Sammy began to get more nervous than before. If Basil was correct, and Lillian was more beautiful than Susannah, he would be speechless in her presence. He worried that he would stutter when he spoke to her. Sammy followed Basil inside and together they followed Susannah into the parlor. She asked them to sit and excused herself to go upstairs and get Lillian.

As soon as she'd left, Basil turned to Sammy, slapped him on the knee, and said, "Told you they were beautiful girls."

Sammy nodded. He wondered if Basil was aware how nervous he'd become. Sammy cut his eyes toward Basil and noticed that he was being stared at. Basil said, "Would you relax? We came here to have a good time. You look as though you're about to pass out. You're gonna embarrass me to death."

Sammy shook his head. "You're not helping."

Both grew silent at the sound of tender footsteps falling on the stairs leading to the foyer. Sammy tried to relax, but he'd gotten himself too worked up. He began to think he was going to be sick.

82

Susannah led the way into the parlor followed by a beautiful girl with dark hair. Lillian wore a peach-colored evening dress with a hoop skirt. Sammy and Basil rose from their chairs at the same time. Susannah introduced Lillian to Basil. Basil bowed and kissed the back of her hand. He said, "Allow me to introduce you to my Colonel. Lillian, this is Sammy, I mean Samuel Rodes, commander of the 64th Alabama Infantry."

Lillian curtsied before the young officer. Sammy bowed formally and took Lillian's extended hand. He gave a nervous peck to the back and quickly let go. He mumbled, "A pleasure to make your acquaintance, ma'am."

"The pleasure is all mine, Colonel," Lillian smiled broadly, revealing pearly white teeth. "I see you're a full colonel. Three stars on the collar. One more grade and you'll be a general."

Sammy was taken aback. It was rare for a lady to be interested in military matters. "And I see you know your stuff."

"I don't want to talk about the war," Susannah interrupted as she grabbed Basil by the arm and led him across the room. She called back over her shoulder, "Bring your colonel to the piano, Lillian."

Lillian took Sammy by the arm and led him across the room. Susannah had sat down in a mahogany rocking chair next to the piano. Basil sat in a horsehair chair beside her. Lillian perched herself on the end of the bench in front of the piano and motioned for Sammy to sit beside her.

The bench was so short that his arm rested against hers. He could feel his face growing redder by the moment, yet he was beginning to enjoy himself. Basil hadn't lied about Lillian's beauty.

Lillian began to play a nocturne on the piano as Susannah crooned along to the music. The song was slow, dreamy, and almost depressed Sammy, although he couldn't understand why. When she'd finished, Susannah demanded her play something that she could sing aloud.

Lillian began to play the song "Lorena," and Susannah began to sing. Her voice was beautiful. Basil sat with his hands gripped across his knee. Sammy's captain was captivated by Susannah.

Lillian continued to brush against Sammy as her fingers moved across the piano. Sammy was also captivated. He forced himself to sit erect, holding his chin high. The girl was enamored with soldiers, especially officers, and he decided he would give this girl what she wanted.

Lillian played the piano as Susannah continued to sing for half an hour. Sammy was beginning to hope this night would never end. After they'd tired of the music, Lillian asked Sammy if he'd like to walk out onto the veranda with her. Sammy agreed and rose from the stool. Lillian playfully placed her arm through his and said, "Escort me out, Colonel Rodes."

Sammy blushed again as Basil laughed. He led Lillian through the foyer and onto the veranda. Lillian sat on a rocker there and listened to the sounds of a cool night. Sammy sat on the top step and leaned back against a column.

"I thought we'd give those two lovebirds some time alone," Lillian gave Sammy a coy smile. "Can I ask you something?"

Here we go, Sammy thought. "Sure, anything."

"How old are you?" Lillian's expression changed to one of curiosity. "I mean, you look awful young for a colonel."

"I have no idea, ma'am," Sammy replied. He'd been expecting this question ever since his arrival. He was forced to again repeat the story of his awakening and how he remembered nothing.

Lillian lowered her head. "I'm so sorry. That is truly a sad story."

"Could have been worse," Sammy tried to lighten the mood, "I could be dead right now."

"True," Lillian smiled, "and I wouldn't have you here on my veranda. I didn't mean anything when I mentioned your age. I'm only nineteen myself. I may be older than you, but who can know for sure."

Sammy leaned his head back against the pillar and closed his eyes. This was the happiest moment he'd had since being with Mary.

Lillian said, "It's always nice when you first meet someone. You know, before you know each other very well and there's the

84

mystery of the other person. It's rare for the person to turn out the way you have them imagined, but it's different with you. You truly are an enigma. I don't mean that in a bad way."

Sammy shook his head and smiled. "I'm an enigma to myself."

"Each time you smile, it brings me cheer. I can't say why." Lillian turned her head. She'd embarrassed herself. She'd never been quite so formal with someone of the opposite sex. It just wasn't proper manners. She mumbled, "I'm sorry."

"No apologies, ma'am," Sammy held up a hand.

"Stop calling me ma'am," Lillian attempted to give him a hard look but couldn't restrain her smile. "It's Lillian. Do you want me to call you Colonel?"

"No, Lillian," Sammy loved to see her smile. She was already beautiful, but smiling seemed to do something to him. "I have to admit something to you. While I was waiting for you to come down those stairs, I thought my heart would come out of my throat. I was forced to swallow it back down a few times."

"You're silly. I bet you got a dozen girls back home." Lillian regretted it as soon as it left her mouth. The last thing this young officer wanted to be reminded of was the fact that he knows nothing of his home. She thought of apologizing but remembered what Sammy had said about apologies. She quickly asked, "Have you been in combat yet?"

"Of course there was Shiloh, but honestly, I have no recollection of it," Sammy looked down at his hands. He'd finally stopped trembling and began to relax. "I took seven hundred men into the Battle of Sharpsburg and only brought four hundred and sixty men back to Virginia with me. I fought at Fredericksburg behind the stone wall there and only lost twelve men. I imagine every man in my regiment killed somewhere between eighty and a hundred men that day. It was nothing but murder."

"If they would let me, I'd join the army and fight." The way Lillian made the statement convinced Sammy that she was serious. "I know that sounds horrible, but I would love to fight for my country. I'd love to be a soldier."

The door swung open and Basil stepped outside, followed by Susannah and an older gentleman. Basil had a disgusted look on his face. He said, "Sammy, I'd like to introduce you to Parson Lucius Duncan."

Sammy got to his feet and bowed to the man. The man asked, "You're a colonel, son?"

"Yes, sir; 64th Alabama Infantry, sir." Sammy stepped forward and shook the man's hand.

"You boys are doing a good service for our country," the man spoke in a firm voice. "I'm the reverend of Salem Church, just north of here on the Plank Road. We're Baptists, and I'm sure you're aware that Baptists are early to bed and early risers. I mean no disrespect in dismissing you two fine young gentlemen."

"No, sir, it's our fault for wearing out our welcome," Sammy quickly accepted the blame for the situation. "I apologize to you and your family."

"Oh, Father," Lillian smiled as she rose from the chair. She curtseyed before Sammy and asked, "Will I be seeing you again?"

"If it's all right with your father, I would love to call on you," Sammy looked from Lillian to Parson Duncan."

Duncan took the two young officers and turned them toward their horses. "Oh yes, you are welcome back here. Just try and come earlier in the future."

"Thank you, sir," Sammy replied. He again shook the man's hand and climbed on his horse. Before reining the horse away, he stole one last glimpse of Lillian. She was standing in the doorway watching him intently. He wondered if she truly liked him or was just pretending to be interested.

They rode back out into the road and headed east back to camp. Basil didn't say a word until they were out of earshot of the house. He was furious when he spoke. "How in the hell are you supposed to court Baptist women? Hell, it's only seven. You reckon they really going to bed, or is that old man just running us off."

Sammy began to laugh. Basil stared hard at him through the darkness, although he could barely make out his commander's profile. Basil asked, "What's so damned funny?"

Sammy continued giggling. He asked, "Don't you mean 'what's so damned funny, *sir*?'"

Basil liked the way Sammy emphasized the word 'sir.' He said, "Yeah, that's what I meant."

"You're funny," Sammy said. "By the way, how did it go with Susannah? Are you calling on her again?"

"Sure am," Basil said louder than he meant to. He corrected his volume and said, "You are too. I've gotten word from Susannah that Lillian is impressed with you. I hadn't realized you were such an inamorato."

"Don't start," Sammy held up a hand.

"I'm serious as hell, Sammy," Basil began to make his argument. "I wouldn't lie to you about something like that. You know me."

Sammy felt good knowing that he could call on Lillian again and knowing that she wanted him to call on her. He couldn't get the smile off his face as he continued to ride eastward through the darkness.

****

He'd been calling on Lillian for two weeks thus far. It was a bitter winter, yet it felt like spring to Sammy. He was never happy until he'd heard from her each day. The better days were when he actually was able to see her. Most days he found a way to see her at some point. He could never get enough of her.

Lillian had a hard time understanding why the young colonel was so enamored with her. He could have any lady in the Confederacy in her eyes, but he wanted her. That made her feel special.

They would spend most evenings riding down near the Rappahannock River waiting for the sun to set. Occasionally, they would happen upon Brigadier General Dorsey Pender and his wife. The general's wife would always go out of her way to speak with the young couple. Pender was a well-known disciplinarian, yet he'd taken an interest in the young colonel and had mentioned that he would approach General Lee with the request that he allow

Sammy's regiment to join his North Carolina brigade. Sammy couldn't have been more pleased at the kind words from one of Lee's best generals.

Sammy had been out seeing to the condition of his men all afternoon. He'd visited with almost every man of his regiment and made sure everything was all right with them. They'd learned to love Sammy since Sharpsburg, when they realized he truly cared about their welfare.

He returned to his cabin that afternoon in a melancholy mood. It was another weekday that he would not get to see Lillian, and it hurt him. He'd become attached to the beautiful young girl who seemed so stricken with him. Approaching his cabin, he saw Basil standing near his own cabin across the way. He began to approach Basil, when the boy disappeared inside as if avoiding his commander.

Sammy shook his head and wondered what he'd done to offend his favorite subordinate. He turned and headed for his own cabin. Stepping inside, he was shocked at what he saw. There was Lillian sitting on his cot, patiently waiting for his return.

Sammy was speechless for a long moment. Finally, he managed to say, "Lillian, is everything all right?"

"Everything is perfect," she gave him a coy smile.

It was the most enchanted moment of Sammy's life. He was captivated with the beautiful young girl. She seemed so delicate, so soft and frail. He situated himself on the cot a good two feet from her. Sammy found everything about her ingratiating. She pleased him, and he'd missed her today.

He said, "I was down near the river today. I couldn't help but think about how much you love to walk along the edge of the river and watch the sun go down."

"I couldn't go on without seeing you, Sammy," Lillian said as she reached up and touched his cheek.

Sammy couldn't help but think about how his life had turned out. How badly he'd been done wrong, not knowing where he'd come from or anything else, yet he understood that he was lucky. He was sitting in his cabin in the presence of the most beautiful woman he'd ever seen. They'd spent a lot of time together.

They talked until the sun had set and darkness was introduced. She seemed genuinely happy to be here with him. Sammy wondered what her father would think. Would he be upset that she was alone in his quarters although nothing was happening? He pushed the thought out of his mind. He was happy for the time alone with such a perfect lady.

Although it had grown dark, there was still quite a bit of light out. Sammy walked to the door and peered into the night sky. There was a full moon. He turned and caught sight of Lillian's soft white neck. The expression on her face told him that she wanted to be kissed. He knew, but she never admitted this to him. Sammy wanted to walk back to the cot and hold her, maybe even kiss her, but he was afraid. He wished the night could last forever and began to try and convince himself that it would. She'd stay here with him for the rest of the winter. Perhaps she'd go with him everywhere he went until this bloody war was over. Deep down, he understood he was just pretending. She couldn't possibly stay. Her reputation would be ruined.

Sammy returned to the cot and sat down. He stared into her beautiful blue eyes, and they stared back. Lillian would be the belle of any ball. There could never be anyone more attractive. He could imagine himself going to a dance with Lillian on his arm and how everyone present would be jealous of him. Somehow he knew that had never happened before.

Sammy worked up the courage and said, "You're so lovely, darlin'. I can't help but wonder why you're interested in me."

She smiled. That same smile that had mesmerized him the first moment they'd met. She asked, "Why me?"

"What?" he was confused.

"Why me?" she repeated and lowered her head. "I mean, I feel like you could have anyone in the Confederacy, so why did you choose me?"

Sammy smiled and shook his head. "You're so innocent. Pure like driven snow. Everything you do makes me happy. As long as I can make you happy, I feel the greatest pleasure. Does that make sense?"

"Of course it makes sense," she replied. "It's the same way I feel about you."

He stared into her beautiful blue eyes and found himself speechless. Anticipation for what would happen next ran through him like a bolt of lightning. Sammy leaned forward, and her lips moved to meet his. He reached around her and pulled her close to him so that their chests touched. He could feel her breath, and he could feel his heartbeat quicken. Their lips touched, and he could begin to taste her. It was as if their souls were becoming one.

After a long moment's kiss, Sammy lowered his head, and their foreheads met. He said, "I don't want you to ever leave."

"Me either," she whispered.

Both of their eyes were closed in the heat of the moment. Sammy said, "The hardest part of this war is having to sleep alone. Do you know how lonely I've been, not knowing who I am? I have nightmares that I'll die without ever knowing. Now that the cold has arrived with winter, my melancholy deepens."

The moment went against everything they'd learned in the South. A lady could never be alone with a gentleman and especially not touching. Yet, Lillian was determined. She admired the officer here with her. She loved him more than anyone before. It was selfish of her, but she wanted him and meant to have him.

"I now realize," she whispered softly, "I've been lonely all my life. All my life I've been dreaming and waiting for someone, and now I understand that someone was you."

"Lillian," Sammy started to protest. He wanted to protect her reputation, but she quickly kissed his lips again, cutting him off.

They kissed a long moment. She whispered, "Don't you want someone to care about you?"

"Yes," he replied.

She smiled. There was no way he could turn her down. She asked, "Do you want to go to heaven?"

"I'm in heaven," Sammy replied as he kissed her neck softly. It was the best he'd felt yet, but he still worried about how she'd feel about this tomorrow. He asked, "Are you sure?"

"It's what I want, what I came here for," she whispered in his ear. He felt chill bumps rising on his arms. "I've been planning this for three days."

He took her in his arms and together they collapsed onto the cot. Things began to happen fast. The most anticipation came as she sat up and slowly removed her corset, which seemed to take an eternity. They were again kissing, and to Sammy, the unthinkable had happened. They were conjugated.

Sammy lay on the cot drenched in sweat. He could never imagine having lived through such an erotic moment. Lillian lay sideways next to him, her head lying across his chest. She could feel his heart still pounding fast beneath his breast.

He asked, "How long can you stay?"

"Until the morning's light," Lillian whispered. "I've taken care of things with my family. They believe Susannah and I are going to a ball in Fredericksburg and then staying with friends there."

Sammy smiled toward the roof of the cabin. He couldn't believe he was going to be able to stay in this room all night with Lillian. He asked, "Do you have any idea how many nights I've spent alone in this cabin just dreaming of a night like this?"

"Plenty, I'm sure," she whispered.

It then dawned on Sammy what she'd said a moment earlier. He raised his head and attempted to peer down at Lillian. "You told your family you and Susannah were going to a ball?"

Lillian giggled and tried to cover her mouth with her hand. She was afraid of being heard by someone camped nearby. "I hope you don't need your adjutant tonight. He's as preoccupied as you are."

Sammy's head collapsed back onto the cot. So that was why Basil had avoided him like the plague earlier.

****

The days passed and they became more in peril of being caught. It was just before Christmas when she appeared at his cabin, seemingly agitated. Sammy couldn't for the life of him understand what was wrong with Lillian.

91

She sat at his desk when he entered the cabin, staring forlornly toward the plain wood top.

Sammy cleared his throat, but Lillian never acknowledged his presence. He asked, "Everything all right, dear?"

Lillian ignored the question, choosing to continue staring at the grains in the wood top of the desk. Sammy took a step closer. He took a knee beside her and placed an arm gently across her shoulders. The move seemed to catch her off guard, almost as if she wasn't expecting this very movement.

Sammy asked, "What's wrong?"

His mind began to race. Could they have been found out? Maybe her father had heard something. They'd been extremely secretive about the affair, if that's how one would refer to their relationship. Sammy tried not to think of it in that light. He studied her downcast face a long moment. He began to worry that she may be pregnant and fought back the urge to vomit. That would have been the worst thing he could think about just now. Nothing else came to him.

After a pause that seemed to last an eternity, Lillian raised her head and said, "Sammy, I've been waiting for you to propose for two weeks now. I thought sure each day I arrived here, you'd ask me to marry you."

"Propose," Sammy repeated to himself.

"Yes, propose," Lillian said the word more forceful this time. "You insult me by thinking that I have done the things I've done with you before."

Sammy lowered his head. He struggled for the right words. Never in his lifetime would he ever suggest she had done anything like this before. He wanted to tell her how much he loved her, and he wouldn't be lying. He wanted her to know that she was the only thing that made any sense to him since he'd awakened in Corinth, Mississippi. Sammy couldn't lie either. He worried about who he really was, who he had waiting on him back home. He struggled to understand what he could say just now to make her understand his dilemma.

After a long, awkward pause, Sammy said, "It's as if my life just began less than a year ago when I woke in Corinth,

Mississippi. I have no life beyond that. I've spent my short life not knowing who I am or what I'm supposed to be. Now, I've found who I want to spend my life with, but I'm not sure I can even do that. That's my misery. How do I know I'm not already married to someone? I have no idea who I am."

"It's not fair," Lillian protested. "It's not fair to make me fall for you the way I have and now you inform me that you can't have me."

"I'm sorry," Sammy mumbled. He struggled to find the right words, but there was nothing there.

Tears dripped from Lillian's face onto the desktop. Sammy just stared, not sure what to say. She raised her face, no longer attempting to hide her tears and asked, "Where does that leave me?"

In the days and weeks that followed that miserable winter, Lillian would slowly begin to dissociate herself from Sammy. The happiest time of his recent life was over. There was nothing left to do but brace for the coming year's bitter fighting.

****

It was nearly dark, and Charlie was stifling yawns. Sol looked at the fair-skinned boy and said, "You getting tired on me, boy. Better head on home, and we'll finish tomorrow."

"Sorry," Charlie fought back another yawn.

"How many times I have to tell you, there ain't no sense in apologizing all the time," Sol shook his head.

"Sorry," Charlie repeated and then held up a hand in recognition. "Uncle Sol, my pa says his dad saved a lot of lives while those men you call heroes were taking lives."

"Hmmph," Sol grunted. He ran his hand through his thin, gray hair. He asked, "He don't thank much of the fighting man?"

"I'm not sure what to make of him," Charlie lowered his head in thought. "I think it has a lot to do with the way his pa raised him. You see what I'm saying, Uncle Sol? His dad taught him that war is wrong and the physician's job is difficult enough without men doing horrible things to each other."

93

"I see," Sol stared at Charlie a long moment and then asked, "What do you thank?"

"I think it takes a special kind of man to march onto a field with the air filled with bullets and cannonballs," Charlie's chin rose as he made the statement. "I wouldn't be here listening to you every day if I didn't think those guys were heroes."

"I knowed your grandpa," Sol eased back in his chair and thought carefully about what he was gonna say. There was a huge difference in what he wanted to say and what he could say without causing an uproar. "He didn't go to Shiloh when the rest of us did. Claimed he was too busy doctoring the folks back here. He was made to go to Jackson when Grant was taking Vicksburg and do some amputating and such like. I'm not calling him a coward by no means, Charlie, and I don't want to say anything that would make you mad at Uncle Sol. I think he feels some regret that he didn't do nothing worthwhile in that war. You know how the veterans get treated now, like we some kind of gods or something. He don't get to feel that. Probably feels somewhat left out."

"You're not gonna make me mad, Uncle Sol," Charlie smiled, although what he'd just learned tore at his heart. He didn't want to think of his grandfather as hiding behind his medical profession while men were fighting for him. Deep down, Charlie had never really felt a close bond with his grandfather. "My dad and grandpa never were very close. Seems like he's closer to my dad's sister and her family than us. I've never understood why."

"How's your grandma?" Sol asked. He watched the boy's reaction to his question.

"She's pretty good," Charlie replied. He hadn't been aware that Uncle Sol knew his grandmother. "She complains of arthritis a good bit."

Sol stared off toward the wall of the shack. He said, "She was the prettiest gal in the county back before the war. Ever boy within a hundred miles wanted to court Miss Phoebe."

"You knew her?" Charlie asked. His eyes grew wide.

"I knowed of her," Sol looked down at his hands. "Weren't no way I could get close to the likes of her."

94

Charlie sat there a long moment, not quite sure what to say. He felt depressed. He wasn't sure if it was the story or the way Uncle Sol had made him feel about his grandfather. It could have been both.

Uncle Sol said, "Now Charlie, you run on home before it gets dark and your ma and pa stop letting you come see me. I don't want that to happen."

Charlie began to nod in agreement. After a long, awkward moment he said, "Uncle Sol, I need to ask you a question, but I'm not sure if I should."

Sol shook his head. He was growing tired of dealing with a proper kid. He'd tried everything he could think of to just get the kid to relax and treat him like a friend. His mama had obviously raised this boy right. He said, "Just spit it out for goodness sake."

Charlie looked at the floor and asked, "What does conjugated mean?"

Sol's jaw dropped open and his eyes widened. He was speechless for a few seconds, but he finally managed a reply. He said, "Damn, boy!"

****

The new year came in with nothing happening besides listening to his men's teeth chatter when they were on picket. Sammy always made it a point of checking on his pickets at least twice a shift. He'd grown to love his men, and they'd grown to respect him for the leader he was. Many of his men were talking about signing a petition asking President Davis that he promote Sammy to brigadier general, but Sammy discouraged this talk when he heard it mentioned.

He awoke one morning in January, and stepping from his cabin, he found a winter wonderland. It had snowed about four inches during the night. Some of his men were throwing snowballs at each other. His men were from South Alabama and had few opportunities to play in the snow.

Sammy walked out and placed his hands over a fire and shivered. He heard footsteps behind him and a man clearing his throat. Sammy turned to find a staff officer he didn't recognize saluting.

"Sir," the man said, "I'm Lieutenant Adams, Twenty-fourth Georgia Infantry. Colonel Robert McMillan asked me to deliver this message to you with his compliments and to await your reply."

Sammy took the note, unfolded it, and began to read it to himself. It was a very proper challenge, in the way a gentleman would challenge another to a duel, but more friendly. Sammy couldn't believe his eyes for a moment and was disgusted with himself for not being the one to think of the idea first.

He handed the note back to the young man standing before him and said, "Tell Colonel McMillan that Colonel Rodes accepts his challenge, and I take it to be a great honor that he chose me."

"Right, sir," Lieutenant Adams saluted and moved away.

Sammy shook his head and smiled to himself. This was just what his men needed at the moment. He turned back to the fire and asked a young man standing there to go get Captain Manly for him.

Soon Basil was trudging out of his cabin, shivering against the cold. Sammy couldn't help but like the man. Basil was a form of entertainment struggling against the depression Sammy suffered from. There was more to it than that. Sammy also liked the man's company whether he was being humorous or not.

Basil walked up to the fire and gave a sloppy salute. "Colonel, please tell me the Yanks ain't out and moving in this weather. I could have used another hour in the warm cot."

"There's no Yanks moving," Sammy shook his head. "I need you to form the regiment immediately. We have been given an important assignment."

Basil looked at the fire. He placed his outstretched hands beside his lips forming a trumpet and turned toward the cabins. He shouted at the top of his lungs, "Sixty-fourth Alabama, fall in!"

The snowball fights instantly stopped. Men were running for their huts to retrieve their rifles. They were formed within five minutes. Sammy walked down in front of the regiment to the center company. Basil followed along behind his commander wondering what was so important.

96

Sammy stopped and faced the regiment, the color guard just in front of him. He announced in a loud voice. "Gentlemen, we have important work to do here today. When I dismiss ya'll, you need to put your rifles and cartridge boxes away. You won't be needing those things. We've been challenged to a battle by the Twenty-fourth Georgia, our neighbors next door. It is a great honor, them choosing us. It means they want to challenge the best—and that is us. I know I can count on every man to do his duty today and win this battle. Now, when I give the command to fall out, I want each of you to load your haversacks down with snowballs and be prepared for action. We will meet them on the field at one this afternoon, so I want every company formed and ready at twelve-thirty. Dismissed."

Before he'd finished his speech, he noticed all the smiles. His men, especially the younger boys, were elbowing each other and nodding their heads. When he'd dismissed them, there was a rush to get rid of their extra baggage and begin making snowballs.

Sammy turned to make his way back to his cabin and almost ran into Basil. He asked, "What, Basil?"

"You sure are a sneaky one," Basil smiled, the grin going almost to his ears. "It's a good way to drill and have fun at the same time."

"Wasn't my idea, Basil," Sammy brushed past him. Basil turned and walked alongside his colonel. Sammy continued, "It was Colonel McMillan's idea. I just accepted the challenge."

"I still like it," Basil laughed. "Just look at their enthusiasm."

The regiment was formed at the proper time. Sammy noticed the haversacks were packed full. *The first time that has ever happened, he thought.* Sammy gave the order, and the regiment marched out of camp toward the west where there was a small field. They drew up in line of battle directly across from the Twenty-fourth Georgia Infantry, who had already arrived. Colonel McMillan and one of his staff officers marched out to the middle of the field. Sammy motioned for Basil to follow.

They met in the center of the field. Sammy had seen the man during the battle of Fredericksburg but didn't know him personally. He was larger than Sammy and had a huge square head and a bushy brown beard. He reminded Sammy of General Longstreet.

McMillan saluted and extended his hand. Sammy did the same. McMillan said, "It is an honor to meet you on the field of battle today, sir."

"Likewise," Sammy replied. "We appreciate the challenge."

"We should lay some ground rules beforehand, don't you think?" McMillan asked.

"This is your party, Colonel. You make the rules," Sammy nodded.

"Men could get carried away in this. There'll be no fighting except with snowballs," McMillan paused. "Is that fair enough?"

"Right, sir," Sammy smiled. "I couldn't agree more."

McMillan again extended his hand before turning to his command. Sammy and Basil began to walk back to their lines. Sammy addressed the men and voiced his concern. He told them he was sure they wouldn't do anything that would embarrass their commander. Most of all, he told them he wanted them to have fun.

Both lines advanced to within snowball range and opened fire. Sammy stood behind his men exhorting them to throw faster. He yelled for them to give a rebel yell and smiled as it spread up and down his line.

Suddenly, Basil was beside his commander yelling at the top of his lungs. "It's a trap! Look to the right!"

Sammy spun in time to see two companies emerge from the pine trees toward his right rear. He and Basil began to race down the line toward his threatened right flank. Both were in boots, and progress was slow on the slippery surface. Once, Sammy fell and managed to grab Basil by the arm and pull him down with him. They collapsed in a heap, only to struggle to their feet and continue onward.

Sammy was shouting to his right company to refuse the line, but he was too late. He and Basil arrived just in time to be captured by the advancing Georgians. The Georgia troops were proud to be carrying a colonel and his adjutant back as prisoners. There was no shame for Sammy, he gave back as good as he got.

The snowball battle continued to rage as Sammy was brought before Colonel McMillan. The colonel eyed both men and said, "Imagine meeting you two again so soon."

"That was sweet," Sammy admitted. "Excellent move. You've been a step ahead of me all morning."

"What now, sir?" Basil asked.

"Since the Sixty-fourth Alabama is without their colonel and adjutant," McMillan began to smile, "I think it only right that I take my adjutant, turn over command to my Lieutenant Colonel, and retire to my hut with my prisoners for a drink. How does that sound to you, boys?"

Basil gave a sharp salute. "That sounds most excellent to me, sir. I'm also speaking for my commander. Let's go, Sammy."

Sammy was a prisoner now. There was nothing he could truly say in argument. He followed Lieutenant Adams and Colonel McMillan toward his cabin.

Inside, Sammy found the cabin as cozy as his. There was a cot, table, and nice warm fire going. Colonel McMillan introduced his adjutant, Lieutenant Means Adams and insisted that for the rest of the day, his name was Robert, not Colonel.

Sammy introduced Basil and told them to refer to him by his name also. Robert reached into his trunk and took out a bottle of brandy. He looked at his adjutant and said, "Get out the cups, Means."

"Right, sir," Means took four tin cups off a shelf behind his chair and placed them on the table. Colonel McMillan wasn't bashful with his brandy, pouring the cups almost full.

Sammy wasn't sure if he'd ever drank before but decided it would be rude to not have one drink with the man who'd captured him. Basil took a long hard swig and frowned. He said, "That's good stuff, sir."

"Robert," McMillan frowned through his thick mustache and beard. "I've already told you, it's Robert this afternoon."

"Right, Robert," Basil nodded with a smile. He turned to see if Sammy would take a drink. It worried him that his commander might insult the man by not drinking with him. His mind was soon put to rest.

99

Sammy took a small sip and fought the urge to frown. The brandy burned his throat as it went down, and his stomach felt as if someone had started a fire down there.

McMillan eyed him closely. He asked, "So, what do you think?"

"I can honestly say that's the best brandy I've ever tasted," Sammy lifted the cup toward McMillan. He didn't mention the fact that it was probably the only brandy he'd ever tasted, and there was nothing delicious about it.

"Ha," McMillan took a long swig. "It's an old family recipe. It's stout stuff too."

Sammy took another drink, a little more this time. Basil took another long swallow. Adams was sipping his in the chair in the corner.

"Don't be bashful, boys," McMillan took another sip, "there's more in my chest. I keep plenty on hand."

Basil took another drink. He smiled when he finished. "You're talking my language now, Bob."

They continued sipping the brandy. Sammy's head began to feel strange. Basil was talking so fast that Sammy couldn't follow the conversation. McMillan was listening politely, but Sammy wondered if he was even listening to Basil. Lieutenant Adams was smiling at Basil's story. Sammy began to feel detached, as if he were watching the conversation without being seen. He took another hard swallow of brandy, hoping it would clear his mind.

Everything the other men said seemed funny to Sammy. The more he laughed the harder they tried to be humorous. Sammy attempted to stand, but stumbled and landed on his knees. He eased his head and chest onto McMillan's cot. McMillan said, "You're no daisy, Colonel."

Sammy never answered. Every time he attempted to raise his head, the room began to spin and he thought he'd be sick. That was the last thing he remembered. He was unconscious until just after daybreak the next morning.

He woke face down across the cot, his knees still on the ground. His head was aching when he attempted to lift it from the bed. He asked, "Who shot me?"

"Ain't nobody shot you," McMillan laughed. He was sitting at the table, eyes and face as red as a beet. "You're still intoxicated, or at least suffering from the effects. Didn't take much to do you in, neither."

Sammy struggled off the ground and onto the cot. He sat there holding his head in his hands. There was no way he could hold his head that would ease the pain.

McMillan motioned toward the corner near the cot. "Your adjutant made it just a little longer than you did. That boy is some talker."

Sammy looked over and saw Basil curled up in the corner of the hut with his arms hugging his knees. Lieutenant Adams was sitting in the same chair, his head lying across his arms on Colonel McMillan's desk.

Sammy struggled to his feet and fought the urge to vomit. He said, "I appreciate your kindness, Colonel McMillan, but I've got to get back to my regiment."

"Steady there," McMillan said as he watched Sammy swaying and trying to keep his balance. "I'll send your adjutant back when he comes back into the world."

"Thank you," Sammy pushed the door open to the cold wind outside. It helped sober him up for the walk back to his cabin.

As he closed the door behind him, he heard Colonel McMillan call out, "Will you be coming back this afternoon for another round of drinks?"

Sammy eased his head against the closed door and mumbled, "Hell no."

CHAPTER SIX

Charlie walked to the porch and climbed the steps. He smiled at Uncle Sol and took his seat. Saunders asked, "Ever thing all right with you, boy?"

"Everything is fine, sir," Charlie replied, but his eyes remained glued to the floor of the porch.

Sol leaned forward and stared hard at the boy. "Ever thing don't appear to be fine. Something on your mind?"

"I just had a discussion with my teacher, and I think I lost," Charlie looked into the old man's eyes. "She says the South would have been way better off if Lincoln had lived than it would have by Booth killing him."

"I see," Uncle Sol lowered his head in thought. "She might be right. I ain't so sure myself. I mean, Johnson hated anyone from the Southern states that had money or education. The man was a tailor before getting into politics, and he hated everything about the Southern gentleman."

"Really," Charlie sat up on the stool. "She said he was from Tennessee but didn't explain why he sided with the Union."

"Let me explain something about politics to you, Charlie," Sol noticed that the boy was on the edge of his seat waiting. "Politicians will do whatever gets them votes. They condemn prostitutes for the way they make a living, but lawyers and politicians would cut their own mama's throat for a dollar. It's as simple as that."

"I see," Charlie replied, but deep down he didn't understand.

Saunders continued, "You see, a man like Johnson has not the least bit of shame in asking other men to die for him, but he wasn't about to risk his neck for the nation. Hell, the man was drunk at his inauguration as Vice President."

"He was?" Charlie asked. His face betrayed his feelings.

"He was," Saunders replied. "You didn't hear that from that Yankee teacher now, did you?"

"No, sir," Charlie looked at the floor in disbelief.

"Lincoln didn't speak to the man again," Saunders leaned forward and spat a stream of tobacco into the yard. "He died without acknowledging the Vice President. And do you know why he chose Johnson as his running mate?"

"No, sir," Charlie replied.

"For votes," Saunders couldn't believe Charlie knew none of this. "He was about to lose the election to General McClellan, and he needed a contingency plan. He had issued the emancipation proclamation, which freed slaves he couldn't free, but didn't free a single slave held in the Northern states. Are you following me, boy?"

"I think so," Charlie lied.

"The emancipation proclamation freed only the slaves held in the southern states in rebellion against the Union, you see?" Saunders looked at Charlie and watched him nod his head. "The slaves in Delaware, Maryland, Missouri, and even parts of Tennessee and Louisiana, occupied by the Federal forces, were not freed."

Charlie stared at Uncle Sol in disbelief. Saunders continued, "You see, Lincoln didn't free a single slave. He couldn't, actually, without the consent of congress. He was attempting to keep England and France, both of whom were Confederate sympathizers, out of the war. Both countries had made a pile of money, as had the North, with the slave trade. When the slave trade was outlawed, all three had made a lot of money off the Southern states, and all three decided it was an immoral thing."

"I see," Charlie nodded. "Miss Harman never told us all that."

"Of course not," Saunders replied. "I lived during those times, I know the truth. Miss Harman is from up North with the rest of them 'holier than thou' types. She don't want you to know."

Charlie looked like someone who had finally been awakened to the real world. Things were not as he had learned them. Saunders continued, "Miss Harman teaches you that the founding fathers were all perfect and sinless, right?"

Charlie nodded in agreement.

"George Washington never lied and all that other shit," Saunders laughed. "She teaches you the war was over slavery and the South was evil."

"You're right," Charlie agreed.

"She's not the true problem," Saunders leaned forward and gave Charlie a hard look. "The true problem is these fellows like your grandpa who take the Yankees' side because he hasn't the balls to risk his money or property to speak the truth."

Charlie's head dropped to the floor. Again, Uncle Sol was bringing up his grandfather in a way that demeaned the man. He loved hearing the stories about the war, but something about the way Uncle Sol always made his grandfather sound was a bit upsetting to the boy. He wanted to think his grandfather was like the boy in Sol's story, but deep down he understood that it wasn't in his grandfather's nature to be heroic.

"Ah, what's the use discussing it now," Sol waved his hand in the air as if he were trying to push a pesky fly out of his face. "Weren't none of us did enough to win that war. I can't really blame one man."

"I went to the public library this afternoon as soon as school let out," Charlie changed the subject. "I can't find anything about the Civil War in this area, Uncle Sol."

"What you doing that for?" Sol raised his eyebrows. "Either you don't believe my story is true or you trying to get ahead of me to see how it ends. Which is it?"

"I was just curious is all," Charlie gave a sly grin. "I wanted to see what I could find. You said there was a skirmish down in town, but you haven't mentioned if that's part of the story or not."

"There was a skirmish in town," Sol smiled at Charlie's impatience. "We gonna get to that pretty soon. We got more fighting off in Virginia yet."

Charlie nodded and asked, "Uncle Sol, do you mind if I go home each night..."

Sol looked up, noticed Charlie was hesitating, and replied, "Hell no, I don't mind you going home at night. You think I wanted you to stay with me all the time?"

Charlie tried to stifle the laugh. "I'm trying to ask you something. Would it be all right if I write your stories down when I leave from here each day?"

104

"Hmmm," Sol rubbed his forehead. "I don't reckon it would hurt nothing at all. Why'd you ask?"

"I wouldn't feel right without your permission," Charlie held his hands out, palms up. "They are your stories."

"Charlie," Sol reached over and patted the boy on the leg, "they're your stories now. I'm giving 'em to you cause ain't nobody else gives a damn no more. Now where were we?"

"Spring of Sixty-three," Charlie perked up on the seat and waited.

"Right," Sol nodded in agreement as he dug around in his brain looking for the correct place to take up his story. "Now, the 64th Alabama Infantry was sent back to guard the railroad between Fredericksburg and Richmond when the spring campaign began. So them boys missed the Battle of Chancellorsville, and that's when Stonewall Jackson was shot by his own men and died."

Charlie's face betrayed his surprise. "He was killed by his own men? Miss Harman said he was killed in battle and the war might have turned out different had he lived."

"She's right about that," Sol agreed, "on both accounts. He was killed in battle and we might have won the war if he'd lived. It was at night, and he was out scouting the Yankee lines. When he rode back, his own men thought he was the enemy and opened fire. He didn't die right away but after they amputated his arm in a house several miles away."

"I learn so much from you, Uncle Sol," Charlie was shaking his head. "I hope you don't ever get tired of teaching me war stories."

"Don't worry 'bout that," Sol scratched at his scraggly beard. "Now I'm gonna take up the story after the battle. Lee reorganized his army after Chancellorsville, and the 64th was moved to James Scales' brigade. Sammy got his wish. He was assigned to Pender's division at last. Those boys were marching north with their heads held high. They'd whipped the Yankees in ever battle they'd fought in."

****

105

They marched northward through Maryland and into Pennsylvania. The men couldn't have been in higher spirits. They'd whipped Hooker's army with only half of their forces. Sammy prayed they were marching north to fight the battle that would end the war and gain the South the independence they deserved, but deep down he didn't believe it would happen.

The dust rising among the shuffling feet was choking. The dirt stung his eyes. Sammy worried about his men succumbing to sun stroke and continually checked on their welfare. One soldier had called him 'Aunt Polly' earlier because of his worrying over them so. Some of his men were barefoot, but they kept up with the column.

Sammy rode down the road on his horse, staring at the horizon. It was a different road, but the scenery was the same. A line from a poem he'd heard somewhere before leapt into his mind—something about 'down this road followed by his ragged band.' It gave him hope. If something so minute could be brought out of his damaged memory, surely the rest would make an appearance someday.

Sammy noticed his troops' expressions. They were in high spirits, but he couldn't help noticing there was something sinister behind the mask. They'd never be the same again, regardless of the outcome of the war. This bloody war had scarred them. Most had given up the thought of surviving to the end. Dreams of tomorrow had long since been stolen from them. The one thing that wouldn't survive if they managed to outlive this war was innocence. They'd all seen things men should never see, and they'd seen it more than once. And there was still no end in sight.

Basil recognized Sammy's mood and nudged his horse beside his commander. He asked, "Care to ride out in the field away from the men a few moments, Colonel?"

Sammy shrugged and steered his horse away from the plodding men. Out in the field, out of earshot, Sammy asked, "What's bothering you, Captain?"

"Me?" Basil pointed toward himself. "You're the one that's acting strange."

"I'm worried, Basil," Sammy shook his head. "Got things starting to bother me."

"Like what?" Basil looked surprised. "You've got the best troops in the army. You're one of the best commanders I've ever been around, and best of all, you've got the best adjutant in the entire Confederacy."

Sammy smiled and looked at his best friend. "You're right about most of that."

Basil grew serious and asked, "Seriously, what's the problem?"

"This war is the problem," Sammy rubbed his temples. "I'm growing concerned with myself. I'm beginning to…"

"To what?" Basil's interest was peaked.

"I'm almost embarrassed to say it," Sammy looked toward the ground. "It's that I'm beginning to enjoy it."

"War?" Basil asked. He was taken aback by the statement. "I'd have never guessed that with you."

"Do you think something's the matter with me?" Sammy asked.

"You don't strike me as a ghoul," Basil smiled. "What part do you enjoy? It's not the killing is it?"

"Not that," Sammy answered quickly. "No, not that at all. I'm not sure how to explain how I feel."

"Try me," Basil encouraged him.

Sammy stared into the blue sky and asked, "In battle, have you noticed how the sky seems brighter? The water tastes purer and the leaves are greener."

"What the hell are you talking about?" Basil stared into the sky. "It looks the same to me."

"I'm talking about in combat," Sammy wanted Basil to understand what he meant. "All your senses are on full alert. Colors are brighter, and you feel as if you could walk through the Federal lines without being harmed. It's that strange feeling. I don't know the word for it. Maybe I'm the only one that feels the excitement, the feeling of euphoria while I'm knee-deep in hell."

"I understand that part," Basil gave a laugh of relief. "Sure, we all feel that way. Don't mean I want to get shot at to feel it again."

"I see," Sammy said.

Basil patted Sammy on the shoulder and said, "All men become addicted to that feeling. Enough of anything and you grow accustomed to it, not really enjoy it, but it gets like…being at home. It's not an unpleasant feeling at all. I can understand it."

Sammy looked back over his shoulder at the ragged band that followed him. They reminded him of corpses, trudging slowly to their deaths. It was as if they'd already begun to decay, consumed by the poison that is war.

Basil asked, "Does it bother your conscious when men die under your command?"

"My conscious?" Sammy asked more to himself than to Basil. In truth, he hadn't given the idea much thought. He said, "These men are not fighting for me. They're fighting for the rights the United States Constitution guaranteed them. They're fighting against a despot that would make this country subject to laws by a central government. Besides, the ones that die are in a better place now. There's no more marching, dying, exhaustion, or hunger. They'd be fighting now if I weren't their commander."

"Just a curious thought," Basil mumbled. "I've seen you worry over the wounded and dying before."

"They are my men," Sammy replied. "Of course I worry over them. We're in a state of war. Men will die. Just look at them, Basil. Marching up this road as if dragged by an invisible force to their deaths. They know that some of them won't be coming back, but they still march on. They don't have to go. They can slip off into the night and disappear, but they won't. You and I both know they're not marching up this road for me. They're marching up this road because they know it's the right thing to do."

Sammy noticed they were approaching a small town. These towns depressed him. They were untouched by the hands of war and flourished while the Southern towns were decimated.

Basil asked, "Shall I unfurl the colors?"

"Might as well," Sammy replied. He smiled as Basil rode back to the column of troops and gave the order. At each town they passed through, they would unfurl the flags and hold them high for all to see.

Basil had just returned to join Sammy when they both noticed a traffic jam ahead. There seemed to be a commotion in the town square.

"What now?" Sammy asked. He said, "Let's ride forward and see what's the matter."

They got as close as they could to the crowd of soldiers gathered in town. Sammy could see an officer mounted on his horse in the center of the square. It was Joseph Hyman of the 13th North Carolina Infantry. Sammy looked at Basil and said, "General Scale's not gonna like this."

Hyman stood in his stirrups and shouted, "Ladies and gentleman of Pennsylvania, how happy you should be. You've been fighting to have us back in the Union, and now here we are. I've been in favor of us returning to the Union for some time now, and we've finally come back like the prodigal son. As you can see, we are Southern gentlemen, not quite the barbarians you've sent against us. We're not raping your women, stealing your food, or burning your houses. We were even born in the United States, speak the English language. Nothing like the hordes of Dutchmen you've sent against us."

Sammy noticed Brigadier General Scales forcing his horse through the crowd of men. His kepi sat high on his head, looking as if it would fall off at any moment. The man wasn't happy. He finally reached the back of Colonel Hyman and reached out with his hand, stretching for the man's collar. Hyman never saw him approaching.

Scales grabbed his subordinate's collar and jerked him backward, almost unhorsing the man. He screamed, "Colonel Hyman, what in the hell is the meaning of this?"

Hyman spun around and gave Scales a sheepish grin. His face turned red in embarrassment. "Just having a little fun, General."

"You've stopped the entire column," Scales shouted as he jerked his thumb over his shoulder down the line.

"The men needed a little rest and something to keep their spirits up, sir," Hyman reached up, grabbed the neckline of his coat and pulled it back in place. "I meant no harm at all."

"Fine," Scales snapped, "now get your men moving. Enough of this nonsense."

They trudged on up the road through the dust and heat. They were days away from the battle that might decide the war. The men's spirits were high, but the heat did all it could to dampen Sammy's own spirit. The heat made his head pound, and he wondered if it was a result of the wound he'd suffered back at Shiloh over a year ago.

The last day of June ended like any other. Sammy decided to take supper among his men and roll up in a blanket alongside them. Basil had rounded up a couple of camp stools from somewhere, and he and his commander perched near the fire. It was still rather warm, and they didn't sit near the fire for warmth but for light.

The next morning dawned, bringing light to the first day of the month of July. Sammy's regiment was back in line marching toward a small town called Gettysburg. There wasn't a man in his entire regiment that had ever heard of the town. It was the position that General Robert E. Lee had chosen as the rallying point of his entire army against the advancing Federal horde.

There was the sound of firing early that morning from Pettigrew's brigade ahead. Sammy saw Major General Dorsey Pender riding toward the front. His expression told him something was wrong. Sammy felt comfortable enough with his new division commander that he rode into the edge of the road to intercept the brave man. Pender slowed his horse and raised his kepi into the air as he approached Sammy.

Sammy asked, "Everything all right, General Pender?"

"The usual nonsense, I'm afraid, Colonel," Pender returned Sammy's salute as he eased past. "Just have your men ready to move. I'll send back orders as soon as I'm sure of what is happening."

Sammy moved back into the road. There was nothing he could do except keep his men moving toward the front. The last Sammy had heard was that the Federal army was still back in Virginia. There had been no sense of urgency until now. He began to fret about what was happening up ahead. He hoped it was nothing that would foul up General Lee's plans.

He rode along and listened to a conversation between a boy who looked to be no more than sixteen and another man. The man he was speaking with kept hacking on him about not eating breakfast in the morning. The boy's face was pale, and he wore an expression of deep sadness.

"You shore you ain't sick, Bob?" the man asked again. "You don't look so good. You shoulda ate something."

"No," Bob replied, "my time has come—it's over. My body will be lying out here, my spirit having flown to be with my Lord, before this day is over. I just feel it; know it."

The man began to laugh and poked Bob in the ribs with his elbow.

"You may laugh," Bob said, "but my time has come. I've got a twenty dollar gold piece in my pocket that my pa gave me for good luck. Could you make sure that gets back to him?"

"You gone take it back to him your own self," the man replied. "Now I don't want to hear no more of that silly talk."

Sammy made a mental note to check on this boy at bedtime. He was obviously upset. There wasn't even a hint that there might be any action today. He wondered what could have affected the boy to cause such a state of melancholy.

Ahead, Sammy heard rifle fire and then the boom of a cannon, followed by more artillery fire. He noticed his men perk up. They began to glance at their colonel as if to ask what was occurring down the road. Sammy didn't know any more than they did. The roar of battle began to grow as they continued to trudge on toward the sound. Unconsciously, the men began to pick up their pace.

From the sound, they understood they were several miles from the action. Soon Pender came back down the line in a foul mood. Brigadier General Alfred Scales was near Sammy, and thus he was able to overhear their conversation.

Scales asked, "What in hell's happening, General?"

"Heth has gotten us in a fine mess," Pender was shaking his head. "He's run into Federal cavalry and mistook them for militia. Now he's gotten us into a big scrape, and we have two corps jammed on this tiny country lane. When we get to the front, if we do today, be prepared for action."

"Right, sir," Scales nodded as Pender rode on past.

The brigade didn't reach the field until a little after two, and things had quieted down for a little while. Pender rode up and ordered Scales's brigade to deploy to the right of the Chambersburg Pike. He rose in the stirrups and said, "Gentlemen, one more push and we have them. As soon as Perrin's brigade is in line on your right, we will move in and win this war."

The men all erupted in cheers. It was after four before they moved forward and engaged the enemy troops on the ridge ahead. They moved past the McPherson barn on their left and across a branch before starting up the ridge. It was there that Sammy noticed it first. The Federals had practically broken just across the pike, and he saw at once that he could swing his regiment around and catch the Federal line in enfilade.

General Scales saw what Sammy was doing and rode forward cheering his young colonel. He yelled, "That's the way, young man, that's the way!"

Soon the fire began to take effect. Enfilade meant they were firing down the line, which meant if you overshot, you would still hit someone. The fire was devastating, and it was over as quickly as it began. The Federals soon began to melt away, back toward the town ahead.

Artillery fire erupted from the direction of a large seminary to the Confederate right front. The shell burst overhead, spraying Sammy's regiment with case shot and shrapnel. Sammy noticed Lieuteant Colonel Patrick South beginning to reel in the saddle. He rode that way. More artillery fire began to rain down on the regiment. The Federal artillery had the range now. It would only get worse.

"You all right, Pat?" he asked as he rode up to his wounded captain. Instantly, he felt foolish for asking. Shrapnel had torn through Captain South's chest. Smoke was boiling from the wound because of the hot metal. Captain South was eased to the ground by his men. It was an obvious mortal wound. It amazed Sammy that he'd managed to stay in the saddle as long as he did.

A strange thought entered Sammy's mind. From somewhere other than the last year, he remembered something from the book of Revelation. *"Behold a pale horse, and he that sat on him was death, and hell followed with him."*

General Scales soon arrived and ordered Sammy to reform his regiment so they could advance and drive off that troublesome artillery. Sammy began to scream at his men to get back on line with the rest of the brigade. They were soon moving forward again, but they wouldn't get anywhere near that artillery. He could see them already beginning to pull back with the retreating infantry.

As they topped the rise near the seminary, a sharpshooter fired. Sammy could actually feel the wind off the bullet as it went past and struck Lieutenant David Wallace in the neck. Sammy turned to see his eyes grow wide as a stream of blood shot from his carotid artery. The poor boy began to slowly lean to his left and fell out of the saddle, crashing to the ground in a heap, expiring almost immediately.

"He was a noble boy," Sammy said to no one in particular.

They were soon ordered to halt. He glanced around at the terrain for the first time. The trees were mutilated by rifle fire. Some of the bushes and weeds looked as if they'd been mowed. There was a horse standing in the field ahead with its entrails ripped open and piled on the ground beside him. Still he was attempting to walk away, clueless as to what had happened. The smell was of a typical battlefield. The strong odor of sweaty men in hundred-degree heat mixed with black powder smoke. The faint smell of blood could be caught occasionally.

Scales soon had his brigade moved into a tree line off past the seminary to the right. It was growing dark. Sammy remembered the young boy this morning who'd said he would die today and decided to quench his own curiosity as to whether he survived the day or not. He found the man who'd been talking to the boy.

The man saw his colonel approaching, staring at him, and wondered if he was in some kind of trouble. He leapt from the ground and gave a rigid salute.

"As you were," Sammy waved the man back toward the ground. "You've worked hard today; you all have. Now I want you to rest. What's your name, sir?"

"Henry," the man replied in a nervous tone, "Henry McRae."

Sammy asked, "The young boy you were speaking with this morning—I believe Bob was his name. Is he here?"

"No, Sir," Henry replied as he began to shake his head. "He was the first one killed in our company. Bullet hit him square in the forehead. He was dead before he touched the ground, sir."

"I'm sorry to hear that," Sammy began to move away. He began to grow depressed. Deep down, he felt responsible. Perhaps he should have ordered the boy to the rear, and he'd still be here. But how was he to have known the future?

He found him a tree off away from the rest and began to reminisce about Lillian. He remembered the smell of her body, the beautiful soft hands and sweet smile. Those times together were almost like a dream that can never come true. Perhaps, when this war is over, he would go back there and marry that beautiful girl who loved him so.

Maybe he would be dead tomorrow. He tried to have a premonition, but nothing came. He was to the point of not caring anymore, not expecting to survive this war. Perhaps not even this battle. He drew the conclusion that he'd never get home. Never know who his family was or what had become of them. They'd have come to believe that their son or sibling died at Shiloh, never knowing he rose to the rank of colonel, commanding a regiment of almost a thousand men. He pushed the thought out of his mind, deciding then and there he would die like a man if he must die.

He thought back to the young boy named Bob and calculated that he himself deserved to die for not ordering that boy to the rear when he had the chance. Sammy began to see his men as what they were. They were dead men walking. The thought

114

almost seemed surreal. They were nothing but walking corpses. They'd received a death sentence in this war, and they just continue to function until their lives are cashed in.

The stress of the day and the energy-draining heat soon wore his mind down. Sammy was soon asleep. Lying there on a tree root, he slept as if he were in the best bed around.

July the second dawned, revealing signs of another hot summer day. Basil was already complaining about the heat before the sun had cleared the horizon. Sammy didn't have the energy to complain. He hadn't felt this bad since the day he'd drank with Colonel McMillan back in Fredericksburg. He continued to lie on the root and stare through the branches toward the lightening sky.

Soon orders were passed down the line that they were to be prepared to enter action at a moment's notice. General Lee had given orders for today's battle to begin on the right, and each unit would attack en echelon, which meant one brigade at a time. Lee hoped to catch the Federal army shifting troops toward the right. So, theoretically speaking, once Sammy's regiment went in on the left, there would be nothing there to hit.

By noon, it became apparent that the attack was not going to occur as planned. For some reason unknown to Sammy and his men, Longstreet was still not in position on the far right. Sammy wondered if this might be an omen of evil portent for the action today but quickly pushed the thought out of his mind, continuing to hope for the best.

It was late in the afternoon when Sammy heard the fire begin on the right. Just when he had begun to think the attack wouldn't happen today, it had opened with a fury. Sammy watched his men spring up and prepare themselves as they jumped into line of battle. Basil was walking toward Sammy at a quick pace. Sammy met Basil and motioned for him to follow him to the front of the regiment.

Sammy walked to the front of his men, who had formed ranks without being given orders. He shouted down the line, "Gentlemen, we are ordered to enter the battle en echelon. That means we are at least a good hour away from moving out. The attack must work its way down the line from right to here. Now stack your arms where you stand, and sit down in the immediate vicinity, prepared to go at a moment's notice. Don't be up moving around in this heat. Conserve your energy. Save yourselves to whip the damned Yankees all the way to Washington and beyond!"

His men gave a shout at the announcement. They soon stacked arms and spread out on the ground behind the line of rifles. Sammy, Basil, and the other officers stood out in front of the line listening to the attack as it gradually grew nearer.

It was getting almost time to enter, as they could tell the attack was only a division or so away. Suddenly, Sammy's attention was drawn to the front right. He knew something important had happened. He motioned to his staff to stay put and half-jerked Basil as they moved in that direction.

His consternation began to grow as he noticed that most of the men gathered around the man on the ground were members of Major General Dorsey Pender's staff.

Sammy moved his way through the gathering mob and saw Pender lying on the ground. His pants were torn open at the thigh, and his leg was opened up by artillery shrapnel. The man was in obvious pain. Sammy moved away as they loaded him aboard an ambulance and moved him toward the rear.

He waited for the order to move across the field and toward the center of the Federal lines, but he waited in vain. There was a communication breakdown upon Pender's wounding, and there was no one in authority to give the order for the division to move out. Darkness came and went, yet no orders came. Sammy grew frustrated and discouraged.

He and Basil spent most of the night alone, leaning against the tree Pender had been wounded beneath. They discussed whether Lee would order a retreat after one day of successful fighting and then a day of disaster. It was too hot to sleep, so they spent most of the night talking about every subject they could think up.

The next morning it became obvious they wouldn't retreat without another effort to win this battle. Sammy watched Lee ride down the line, pausing occasionally to inspect the Federal lines through his field glasses. Later in the morning, Sammy and Basil watched Confederate artillery being stealthily moved into position facing the ridge across the field.

"Looks like we'll get another shot at this thing," Basil said. His face betrayed his concern about it succeeding across that vast expanse.

Sammy noticed there was no cover between this tree line and the ridge almost a mile away. He said, "If it'll end the war, I'm all for it."

"Sorry I don't share your enthusiasm," Basil shook his head. "We go across that field, and there's a good chance one of us won't make it back. A damned good chance neither of us will."

"You know what Stonewall used to say?" Sammy smiled at Basil.

"Not sure, no," Basil gave Sammy a quizzical look.

"He said that a man is just as safe on the field of battle with bullets flying past his head as he is at home in bed. He understood that God decides the day you will die, not man." Sammy fought off the urge to smile when he'd finished.

Basil wasn't in agreement. He said, "It's just that sort of thinking that got the man killed."

Sammy could contain the smile no longer. Basil shook his head. He just couldn't make light of the situation that appeared to be developing in front of him. He said, "Maybe you are a ghoul, Sammy."

"I've probably been called a lot worse," Sammy laughed. "Drilling these men in Montgomery was probably one of those moments."

About one in the afternoon there was a single cannon shot to their right. Sammy and Basil looked that way in unison as another cannon fired. At that instant, it seemed the entire world was coming to an end. All the Confederate artillery opened fire at Cemetery Ridge, the ridge occupied by the Federals. In a matter of minutes, the Federals began to return fire. Shells exploded overhead and knocked branches out of the trees. Sammy watched his men hug the ground as a baby would its mother in times of fright.

117

The sound was enormous. He'd heard nothing like this during the entire war. The artillery fire became one continuous roar. It seemed to last forever. The sound began to grate on men's nerves. He saw panic flash through the eyes of a few and began to walk among them as if he were on a Sunday afternoon walk. They couldn't hear him above the din, so he just motioned for them to lie flat.

It went on for almost an hour before the Federal guns stopped firing. The Confederate artillery continued to fire another ten minutes and then fell silent. Sammy saw the 34th North Carolina under command of Lieutenant Colonel George Gordon rise from the ground and move out of the tree line into the field beyond.

Sammy spun and almost ran into Basil. Sammy yelled, "This is it! Form the men!"

Basil turned and started shouting for the regiment to form in the field beside the 34th. Men were up, moving forward, happy to be out from under the artillery barrage. Sammy ran out into the field and drew his sword. He started to show them where to form but realized they'd been through this enough times to form on their own.

Basil moved up alongside Sammy. Sammy continued to face his men, watching them form with his back to the enemy. Basil was facing east looking toward the enemy lines. He shook his head and said, "I can't believe we're going across this field into that."

"We've driven their artillery away," Sammy continued watching his men. "It won't be that bad now."

Basil looked at Sammy. "And, just how do you know that?"

"They stopped firing the last ten minutes," Sammy replied.

"Right," Basil nodded and turned to watch the men as they finished coming on line.

Sammy raised his sword in the air and shouted, "Are you men ready to pay them sons-of-bitches back for that hour of hell?"

The entire regiment cheered. Sammy said in a lower voice, "Men of the 64th Alabama, I want you to make me proud here today. We can end this war in the next few minutes if every man does his duty."

The regiment didn't cheer, but Sammy noticed the solemn expressions as what he had just told them began to sink in. Sammy turned to face the enemy. Basil followed suit. Sammy whispered, "I have a bad feeling about this one, Basil. I need you to stay back and take care of yourself."

Basil had begun to believe what Sammy had told him about this being easy. He frowned and looked at his commander and best friend.

"Don't let the men know we have any doubts," Sammy whispered again. "If that hill can be taken, we'll take it. I just have a feeling something is not quite right."

As the order was given for the line to move out, Basil mumbled to himself, "How did I get myself into this shit?"

"You're a good man, Basil," Sammy said in a low tone, "and you're gonna survive this war. Now, do as I said and stay back."

Basil nodded in agreement. He asked, "But, what about you?"

Sammy turned and his eyes met his adjutant's for the first time. "There are times when a colonel's life doesn't count. I'm goin' up there and driving off those barbaric sons-of-bitches or I'm gonna die in the attempt."

"Sir," Basil began to protest, but the expression on Sammy's face told him it would do no good.

As they left the slight protection of the vale and moved toward the top of the hill, Sammy gave the order for the officers and file closers to fall back behind the line to their proper positions. They were a mere hundred yards from the tree line and still had over a half mile to reach the Federal line. For the first time, Sammy could see from one end of the assaulting line to the other. They were stretched almost a mile long with a large gap between the left and right wings.

"At least we're in reserve," Basil told Sammy as he motioned ahead toward Fry's brigade in the front line.

"We can count on those boys there," Sammy replied. "They're Alabama and Tennessee boys."

119

Basil nodded and wondered if it really made any difference where any of these men called home.

They kept moving without a single shot of any kind being fired by either side. It was the most beautiful thing Sammy had seen thus far in the war. He'd never seen a Confederate line that wasn't as crooked as a ram's horn, but today was different. The lines were almost perfectly straight. The men were in no hurry; they were saving their energy for the fight they all knew was coming across the field.

Then, a single shot rang out from the cannon across the way and then another. Soon Federal artillery opened all down the line, even from the round hill on the far right. Shells began to crash and explode around the lines.

"Guess we didn't drive 'em all off," Basil said.

Sammy watched men instinctively duck when a shell would explode overhead. Still, the line remained perfectly straight. They continued advancing without hesitation. Not a man wavered. A shell landed in the midst of the 34th North Carolina to his right. It didn't explode, but struck a private in the chest and tearing him apart. A couple of sergeants standing behind him stopped in shock. They were covered with the poor man's blood. The shell had buried itself in the ground just in front of their feet without exploding.

They swept into another vale that offered limited protection. The enemy lines were not visible down here, although the artillery shells continued to explode overhead. Sammy and Basil ran forward as the entire line of twelve-thousand men halted to dress their ranks for the final push. The pause didn't last but a minute, not near long enough, because being in a protected place under this kind of fire made a man want to remain. Not a man wanted to go back out into the open. Every one of them also realized that the worst was yet to come. They'd have to pass through rifle fire and then canister fire from the artillery. The cannons would act like one huge shotgun spewing thousands of small round balls through their ranks. It was the deadliest ammunition this war had produced.

They left the vale at the same steady tramp as before. The artillery fire began to get more accurate. Luckily, Sammy's men

120

were in the second line and didn't receive as much as Fry's line in front. They marched onward, closing to within three hundred yards. That was when Sammy first noticed what lay ahead. Just thirty yards from the Federal lines was a fence. His men would have to charge and break the fence down to continue. *That shouldn't be a problem, he thought. It won't be the first fence that's become a casualty to my men.*

He was already studying the Federal position beyond the fence. A small rock wall stood about three feet high. The Yankee infantry was lying behind that wall, using it for protection, their rifles resting on top. It was nothing as formidable as what Sammy's men had at Fredericksburg, but it offered some protection to the Federal riflemen.

They had moved to within two hundred yards, and still the Federal line held their fire. Sammy was thankful for that at least. The longer they waited the closer he would be when he ordered them to charge. If they could get up close and Fry's men could take the first volley, Sammy would order his line forward and they'd be among the Federals before they could reload.

When Fry reached a hundred yards from the Federal main line, the Federal artillery opened fire with canister. The infantry opened fire a moment later. Sammy saw Fry's Alabama and Tennesseans taking severe punishment. The men weren't close enough for the canister to take as much effect as the bullets. Fry gave the order and Sammy watched his men surge toward the fence. The line of men struck the fence as one, yet the fence didn't budge at all. Fry was forced to order his men to climb through. They provided excellent targets to the Federal riflemen as they began to climb through and over the fence.

Sammy couldn't believe his eyes. Someone should recommend the fence builder for a medal of honor. Had the fence gone down, Fry would have saved a lot of lives. Sammy realized that it was now or never. He ran forward and shouted, "Charge! Charge!"

The line surged ahead. He watched his men slam the fence a second time, yet still it didn't give. They were forced to climb through. Sammy bowed and crossed through the fence. A boy was climbing over and was hit. He fell on Sammy's back, knocking his colonel to the ground. Sammy shook his head and began to rise, when he felt arms lifting him. It was Basil who thought his commander had been hit.

For the first time, Sammy noticed the sound—officers shouting orders above the din, the screaming of the wounded, and the sound of canister tearing through human flesh and bone. The latter sound made him cringe. It sounded and looked like hell on earth. He began to wonder if this was Armageddon.

"Are you all right?" Basil shouted.

Sammy turned and their eyes met. Basil was taken aback at what he saw. Sammy noticed the look of shock. Sammy's eyes were almost glowing red. Basil had never seen a man change the way Sammy had. He looked as if he had become possessed by demons. A strange thought crossed Basil's mind. The story of the man in the Bible who had a thousand demons called Legion. He blinked, but the sight was still disturbing.

Sammy took his shoulder and knocked Basil to the ground. He screamed, "I told you to stay back!"

Basil lay on the ground and watched Sammy turn and charge the Federal line along with his men. It was a sight that would never leave Basil's memory if he lived a thousand years. Just yards from the rock wall, he watched Sammy crash to the ground. He attempted to rise but fell again.

Basil leapt to his feet and moved forward. The 64th Alabama was fighting valiantly but was simply melting away before his eyes. There weren't enough men to take the hill. He kept his eyes on his fallen friend. There were two men who were moving back toward the rear. They already understood what was about to happen. Basil grabbed both men and spun them around, motioning toward the body of their commander lying on the ground beyond them.

They raced forward again with Basil in tow and grabbed Sammy. Basil grabbed another soldier still fighting and ordered him to help them move their commander to the rear. They carried him rearward as the battle continued to rage behind them. Basil motioned to the south where there was a gap in the fence, and they passed through the fence there.

Basil fully expected to get a bullet in the back at any moment. They continued on with Sammy until they gave out. The body was dead weight. The Confederate charge had been repulsed at this point and men were streaming back across the field. Basil rounded up six more men to carry Sammy. When they reached the protection of the vale, they lowered Sammy to the ground. Basil bowed over his commander.

Sammy opened his eyes and grimaced through the pain. "Basil, did we take that hill?"

"Not quite, no," Basil said, "Where are you wounded?"

"In the arm and leg both," Sammy replied. "I can't walk."

"It's all right," Basil reassured him. "We're almost back to our lines. Let me round up some fresh legs."

Sammy watched him move off. The men who'd been carrying him continued to wait with him as they caught their breath. One of the men offered Sammy his canteen. Sammy took it with his left hand as blood ran out of the sleeve on his right arm.

Basil was back in moments with another set of men willing to carry their commander to the rear. Basil had them place Sammy on one of their blankets to make carrying him much easier. They moved into the open again, but this time there was no hurry. The Federals had ceased firing and were making no attempt to follow up their victory by pursuing their broken foe.

They moved into the trees and on beyond. Basil wasn't gonna stop until he found a surgeon for his commander. Behind Seminary Ridge, they located a temporary hospital and carried Sammy there. A surgeon was working on a man with a broken arm.

Basil walked up to the surgeon and said, "The colonel of the 64th Alabama is wounded and needs attention."

The surgeon gave Basil a disgruntled look and announced, "Place him at the end of the line. I'm busy. He can wait just like all the others."

Basil raised the flap on his holster and eased the Army Colt out as the doctor turned and continued to work on the man's arm. Basil eased the barrel of the pistol against the back of the surgeon's head. He said, "I don't believe you understand me. I'm not asking you, I'm ordering you. And I will say this in advance—if he dies, I will kill you."

The surgeon shrugged indifferently and slowly turned around. He said, "Show me the way. You've convinced me."

They moved over beneath the tree where the litter-bearers still waited. These were men who would follow Sammy to the gates of hell, had actually done that here today, and they wanted to see that he was gonna be well taken care of.

The surgeon squatted beside the wounded officer and asked, "Where are you wounded, Colonel?"

"Arm and leg," Sammy mumbled.

The surgeon ordered the soldiers to remove his coat. The men grabbed their commander up and began to wrestle the coat off of him. Sammy let out a groan against the pain. Basil told them to take the coat off easily. The men looked at Sammy apologetically. The coat was soon removed, and the surgeon rolled up Sammy's sleeve past the elbow. He dabbed at the wound on the outside of his arm at the elbow with a handkerchief. He announced, "It's superficial. The bullet just skimmed the skin. This wound will be fine. Now let's look at the leg."

The soldiers looked at the doctor. He shook his head. "Remove the damn boot. Do I have to tell you every move?"

The men removed Sammy's right boot. The surgeon rolled his pant leg up above the knee. He dabbed at the wound with the handkerchief and pried the skin apart. Sammy clenched his teeth. The surgeon said, "This wound is a bit more severe. Bullet went through but missed the bone. It would probably be safer if we just amputated."

Sammy reached down to his side and slid his Army Colt from the holster. He pointed it at the surgeon's forehead and announced, "You're not taking my leg."

The surgeon looked from Sammy to Basil and back. He shook his head and said, "You two must be twins. Hell, you want to shoot someone over every little perceived slight. It's clear you don't want me doing my job, so if you'll excuse me, I'm going to help men who want my help."

124

The doctor stood and moved away in disgust. Basil looked at Sammy and asked, "What do you want me to do?"

"Wrap the wounds," Sammy squinted into the afternoon sun. "I'll be fine. See if you can locate me something for the pain."

"That we can do," Basil motioned to the soldiers.

When they had finished dressing his wounds, they placed him beneath a nearby tree with the other wounded that'd already been treated. The laudanum Basil had found did the trick as long as Sammy didn't attempt to move. Basil left to retrieve Sammy's frock coat. Sammy lay with his back against the tree watching the surgeons working. There was already a pile of amputated arms and legs four feet high beside each surgeon's table.

Basil soon returned with the coat. He said, "Sammy, do you know how lucky you are?"

"I don't feel very lucky at the moment," Sammy replied.

Basil paused and smiled at his best friend. "There's seven bullet holes in this coat. They was trying to kill you all right, but them Yankee's can't shoot for shit."

Sammy laughed and then grimaced against the pain. "Don't make me laugh; it hurts."

Basil asked, "What can I get you, sir?"

"Go back and check on my men," Sammy wasn't worried about himself. "I need a casualty report, and I need to know which officers are still with us."

"Sir," Basil objected, "the regiment will be fine. I'm not leaving your side."

"I'm fine, Basil," Sammy ordered, "just go get me that report and then you can come stay here tonight."

"Right," Basil patted Sammy on his left shoulder and moved away.

Within an hour, Basil was back. His face betrayed the fact that he was bringing bad news. He collapsed on the ground beside Sammy and leaned back using his right arm as a prop.

After a long moment, Sammy said, "Well, spit it out. It can't be that bad."

Basil shook his head and exhaled loudly. "It's damned bad, Sammy. They're all gone."

"All?" Sammy's eyes widened. "We couldn't have lost every man."

"Not the men, sir," Basil corrected himself. "We've lost all the high-ranking officers. Lieutenant Colonel South was killed the first day. Major Burnett was killed soon after crossing the fence. A lieutenant commands each company. Captain Smallwood is the only surviving captain, and he commands the regiment in your absence. He has a handkerchief wrapped around his head where a bullet creased his forehead. We only got a hundred and forty-seven men answering roll call."

Sammy was wrong. It was that bad. He stared down at his feet and said, "We'll have a few stragglers come back in once they find us. We always do."

"Right," Basil agreed as he tried to sound cheerful.

"In the meantime, we're gonna need to promote some officers," Sammy reached up and rubbed his forehead with his left hand. "Captain Smallwood will be my new major."

"I'll inform him," Basil said. He waited, but Sammy said nothing. After a long pause, he asked, "And who do you want me to inform you're promoting to lieutenant colonel?"

"Inform yourself," Sammy said and looked at his best friend. He wanted to congratulate Basil, but under the circumstances of his promotion it didn't seem proper.

"Right," Basil agreed. His face betrayed the responsibility Sammy had just placed on him.

The next morning, Basil had Sammy placed in a wagon with other wounded officers. Sammy was lying on the outside against the side board. His wounded right arm and right leg forced him to rest on his left side facing the side board. He attempted to focus on the wood just inches from his face but found it impossible because of its close proximity. As the wagon lurched into motion, the wounded men all gasped. Sammy wondered if any of them would survive the trip back to Virginia in an army wagon. It jolted them to their very bones and made his wounds ache. Luckily, the sky had grown cloudy and there'd be no sun today.

They rode west back toward the gap they had passed through three days earlier to begin this fight. As they passed over

126

the first day's battlefield, Sammy forced himself up onto his left elbow to stare at the scene. Bodies lay in heaps out on the fields they were passing. Most had turned as black as Africans. Their heads and faces were swollen to a grotesque appearance. They were filthy, and their expressions were wild and horrifying. No matter how far he looked, there were bodies strewn across the fields. He lowered himself back down into the wagon and fought back the tears. Some of those men out there were his men. They'd come here only to die. *What a waste, he thought.*

It soon began to rain. The other officers in the wagon complained, but Sammy found it a welcome relief from the heat. The long trip back was one of constant misery. Some of the officers' wounds were covered with maggots. He listened to men praying for the good Lord to take them from this world of suffering. Blood was actually dripping through the cracks in the bed of the wagon. Despite the ordeal, Sammy made it back to Virginia. He understood, however, that he would never be able to erase the scars of this campaign from his memory.

CHAPTER SEVEN

Charlie trudged up the hill carrying a long object under his right arm. Sol studied him curiously as he drew nearer. He soon recognized the object as Charlie approached the porch.

"Where you get that stereoscope?" Sol asked.

"My parents gave it to me for my birthday," Charlie smiled. "You didn't know that yesterday was my birthday, did you?"

"Well, I should a knowed something was up when you didn't stop by to see your Uncle Sol." Sol leaned forward and shot a stream of tobacco juice off the porch.

"Sorry about that," Charlie plopped into his chair beside Sol. "Had relatives in from Jackson and couldn't get away."

"There you go being sorry again," Sol shook his head. "What you got a picture of in that thang?"

"Jesse James," Charlie perked up. He handed the stereoscope to Sol. "It's a photograph of him dead in his casket. My dad was up in Jackson a few weeks ago and bought this. I just got it yesterday afternoon."

Sol took the stereoscope and peered inside. Each eye focused on one of two pictures that looked almost identical, but were just different enough to make the scene appear three dimensional. He asked, "How old are you now?"

"Twelve," Charlie replied. "You ever seen Jesse James's picture before now?"

"Not that I recollect," Sol continued staring into the stereoscope. "He fought for the South, you know."

"I heard he was an outlaw too," Charlie reached up and patted at a cowlick that was bothering him. "Miss Harmon said he was a blood-thirsty guerilla. She says he was fighting only for himself."

"Miss Harmon is something else," Sol mumbled as he handed the stereoscope back to Charlie. "She thanks she knows it all. Jesse weren't no outlaw 'til the war was over. He fought in the partisan forces all right, but he was no outlaw. He was a fightin' for what he believed in same as the rest of us."

128

Charlie smiled. He figured Uncle Sol would contradict what Miss Harmon had been teaching him. Charlie said, "Uncle Sol, I'd like to ask you for a favor."

Sol eyed Charlie a long moment. He asked, "What favor?"

Charlie wasn't ready to reveal what he had planned just yet. He said, "I'd really like you to consider it awhile before you answer."

"Hell, boy," Sol spat another stream of tobacco off the porch, "I got to know what it is before I can stew on it."

Charlie smiled. "I want something from you for my birthday."

"What would that be?" Sol asked. He began to suspect it was gonna be something unpleasant by the way Charlie kept avoiding the actual question.

Charlie cleared his throat, betraying his nervousness. "Sir, I want you to come to my house and have dinner with my family this Saturday night."

"Dinner?" Sol asked louder than he meant. "You mean to tell me you want me to eat your family's food for your birthday?"

"That's all I want," Charlie replied. "My mother wants to meet you since I talk about you so much. And my father has been impressed with how much you've taught me about the war."

"Hmmm," Sol paused in deep thought. "I suppose it's the least I could do for you."

"Thanks," Charlie smiled. "Now, let's get back to the story. We just retreated from Gettysburg and Sammy is wounded."

"He was wounded," Sol grimaced in thought. "He was taken to Winchester and nursed in a nice home there by an old widow woman. She was genuinely happy to have some company and worried over that boy 'til he was well."

Charlie nodded, waiting for Sol to continue. Sol said, "Basil came by to visit with him as much as he could. You know he was a running the regiment with Sammy absent and couldn't come by ever day. One day Basil came by and told Sammy that he couldn't put his entire life on hold hoping to regain his memory, cause it might never come back. He told Sammy he wanted him to write Lillian back in Fredericksburg and ask her to marry him. Sides, it would do his mental health good having a wife. It would help him

129

fight off the depression that had seemed to take over his life at the time."

"Did he?" Charlie asked eagerly.

"Did he what?" Sol raised an eyebrow.

"Did he write her?" Charlie was on the edge of his seat again.

"Yep," Sol replied, "as a matter of fact he did. But don't get too excited on me. She wrote back. It had been almost six months since they'd spoken. She told him that she would always love him cause he'd been her first and all, but she had met a lieutenant from some Virginia regiment and they'd become engaged. Basically, she was telling Sammy he had passed up his chance, and just like everything else in his life, things had gone all wrong."

"I wish he would just go back to Mississippi and marry that Mary girl," Charlie shook his head in despair.

Sol couldn't contain the smile. He knew the story was driving Charlie crazy. He felt as if he were torturing the boy by dragging it out, but the story had to be told the way he was telling it, even if the boy had to wait.

"Now, the rest of the summer was spent reorganizing Lee's army. Sammy was out of bed by the end of August and back in charge." Sol leaned back in his rocker and looked toward the roof of the porch. He continued, "News from the west was real bad. Vicksburg had surrendered on the day Sammy left Gettysburg in that wagon, and Chattanooga had fallen to Rosecrans without a shot. He'd flanked Bragg out of town. Longstreet wanted to take his corps and go there to help Bragg destroy Rosecrans before it was too late. Lee finally granted the movement, but forced Longstreet to leave Pickett's division of Virginians behind. Sammy had requested to take his regiment west with Longstreet, and his men were placed in Law's all-Alabama brigade. They were placed on trains and sent south, racing against the clock to arrive in time to save Bragg and turn the tide of the war."

****

130

The train ride was exhausting. They left Virginia and traveled down through the Carolina's and into Georgia. Sammy's regiment was bringing up the rear of Longstreet's entire corps, and he began to wonder if his men would arrive in time to join the fight.

The leg wound had yet to completely heal, and Sammy still moved about with an obvious limp. Most of the men were riding in boxcars, on open flat cars, or riding on the tops of cars. Sammy and the officers of his regiment were lucky enough to obtain a seat in a passenger car.

They rode all day and through the night to reach Georgia. They were halfway across the peach tree state late one night when Basil decided to bring up something that had been bothering him. He had waited until all the other officers were sleeping. Sammy was sitting next to him watching the night pass by the window.

Basil nudged his best friend and said, "Sammy, I got something been bothering me that I would like to ask you about, but I'm not sure how you'll take it."

"Basil, you're my best friend," Sammy couldn't understand why he'd act so nervous about speaking with him about anything. "You know good and well that you may speak freely with me."

Basil was nodding in agreement before Sammy finished. "I realize that, but this has really bothered me. Back at Gettysburg, do you remember any of what happened once we crossed that fence?"

"Pretty much," Sammy was bewildered. He couldn't understand where Basil was going with this. "Why?"

"Do you remember driving your shoulder into my chest and knocking me on my ass?" Basil was speaking almost at a whisper in case some of the other officers were not quite asleep.

"Vaguely," Sammy smiled. "I didn't hurt you did I?"

"No," Basil shook his head. "I saw your face, Sammy. I'll never forget that look."

"What look?" Sammy asked. He truly had no idea what Basil was talking about.

"Your eyes were red as if filled with blood," Basil whispered even lower. "I thought you were possessed or something. Hell, I

131

thought you were a demon. When you knocked me on my ass, I thought for a moment you meant to kill me on that hill."

"Basil," Sammy shrugged, "I would never harm you. I was trying to save your life. I'd told you to stay back, and there you were, up front with me."

"I know, I know," Basil replied. "I thought you were hit. I came back up there again after you went down."

"I appreciate that too," Sammy smiled. "I'd be off in Elmira Prison Camp, or worse, if I didn't have the most stubborn and insubordinate adjutant in the army."

Basil felt better just talking to Sammy about what had happened there. The man seemed to be back to his old self. Still, he would never erase that image from his memory.

They arrived on the field during the late morning of September 20, 1863. There had been heavy fighting the day before. The carnage was tremendous. They continued marching to the front, all the while listening to the roar of battle. It was obvious they were in time for some serious fighting. As they neared the front, passing over the ground won by the Confederate forces the day before, Sammy noticed a ditch full of Confederate soldiers piled on top of each other in heaps. The fighting here had been fearful.

Basil pointed at the scene and said, "They weren't killed in battle, Sammy. Someone brought them up here to be murdered."

They moved on through rolling hills and thick forest with the occasional field cut out in the wilderness. The place looked wild and uncivilized. He heard cheers ahead and a lull in the fighting. Some men were still fighting; he could still hear the sounds. But something monumental had just occurred.

They came out into an opening and found Major General John Bell Hood, their division commander, along with his staff. Hood was speaking with a courier. He said, "Tell General Longstreet that we have taken the enemy by surprise. They left a gap in their line, and my troops just exploited it. Tell him I'm pressing on with my men."

The man saluted and rode away. Sammy saluted Hood and said, "I'm Colonel Sam Rodes commanding the 64th Alabama

Infantry of Law's brigade. We've just arrived on the field, sir. We're the last of your division. Any idea where I can find General Law?"

"Advance straight ahead," Hood motioned with his head. His left arm was paralyzed from artillery shrapnel that had ripped off his bicep at Gettysburg. "He's up there advancing after the retreating enemy. If you want to get in this fight, you'd better hurry forward. Them Yankees will be back in Ohio as fast as their legs can carry them."

"Right, sir," Sammy turned and motioned for his men to follow him. They moved forward at a trot. There was no time to align them just yet. He would find Law and then organize his men for the push against the enemy.

They hadn't gone but a few hundred yards before they reached a large field. On the other side was a steep hill teaming with men in blue uniforms. The enemy had stopped running and regrouped there. Confederate units were adjusting their lines in the tree line and preparing to attack the hill. Sammy asked for directions and found General Law sitting on his horse studying the hill almost three hundred yards away through his binoculars.

Sammy cleared his throat. "General Law, I'm Sam Rodes of the 64th Alabama. We've just reached the field, sir."

Law lowered the glasses and looked at the newest member of his brigade that he had yet to meet. His eyebrows elevated noticeably when he saw how young the man before him appeared. After an awkward pause, Law said, "Align your men here and prepare to advance with the rest of the brigade."

"Right," Sammy saluted and spun to move back to his men. He almost ran into a rider on horseback. It was General Hood. He stopped at the edge of the tree line and pulled out his binoculars and peered across the field. Sammy stepped back and was in the process of walking around Hood's horse, when a bullet struck the general in the upper thigh. Hood reeled in the saddle. Sammy moved forward and prevented his commander from collapsing to the ground. Hood was a large man, much too heavy for Sammy, but Sammy managed to keep him aloft long enough for help to arrive.

Several staff officers helped him lower the general to the ground. Hood's leg lay splayed out from his body. It was obvious the man's femur was broken about four inches from the hip socket. *He'll lose the leg, Sammy thought, and possibly his life as well.*

He moved back toward his men. Basil already had them formed in line of battle when he got there. Sammy walked up and said, "We're going in momentarily."

Basil eyed Sammy's frock coat with obvious concern. He asked, "Are you wounded, sir?"

Sammy peered down and noticed there was fresh blood on the lower left skirt of his coat. "It's not mine. It's General Hood's."

"General Hood's dead?" Basil's eyes grew wide.

"Not yet he ain't, but he's gonna lose a leg regardless." Sammy turned to face his regiment. His troop strength had climbed back up to almost five hundred men since the terrible losses at Gettysburg. He yelled, "Men, we're about to enter battle here, and I would like you all to bow your heads and pray with me."

The men bowed their heads, most took a knee before bowing. Sammy began his prayer by quoting from the book of Psalms and made the prayer short and sweet. It was to instill spirit into his men more than to ask for protection. He said, "Yea, though I walk through the valley of the shadow of death, I will fear no evil, cause I'm the baddest son-of-a bitch in the valley."

When he'd finished and his men realized he was through, they all burst into cheers. Basil turned to Sammy and shook his head. "First time I've heard a prayer like that one. You sure you're not possessed?"

"Trying to instill a little courage is all," Sammy grinned at how well his prayer had gone over.

The order soon arrived to advance. Colonel James Sheffield of the 48th Alabama now commanded the brigade. With Hood wounded and out of action, General Law now commanded the division. The regiment moved across the field toward the steep hill beyond. There was no doubt this was gonna be as bad, if not worse, than Gettysburg. But strangely, Sammy didn't have any bad feelings about this fight.

Bullets began to whistle overhead before they were halfway across the field. That was one good thing about attacking an enemy so high up; they tended to overshoot. They moved onward toward the tree-lined hill. Sammy wondered why the Confederate high command hadn't noticed the obvious. It would be much better to flank this position, surround the hill, and force these Federals to surrender. Most of the Federal army had evacuated to Chattanooga. Now, Longstreet and Bragg chose to hit their last remaining stronghold from in front.

They reached the opposing tree line suffering only minimal casualties. But that was about to change. Sammy marched along behind his men as they began to scramble up the steep slope. It was fall, and leaves were falling off the trees. He watched his men in their slick brogans slipping and grasping at bushes and roots to pull their way up the steep hill. At the same time, they were forced to endure the severe rifle fire being poured down on them from above.

They managed to climb halfway up the slope before they were forced back by the severe fire. Sammy and Basil fell to the bottom of the hill with their men and immediately set about reforming them. Staff officers were there shouting at Sammy to move his men back up the slope. Sammy felt like explaining to them the necessity of flanking this hill but decided they were just the messengers from the man in charge. It would do no good to make suggestions to them. He soon had his regiment started back up the slope.

They moved back up the hill, going a little farther than before, only to be pressed back again. They fell back, reformed, and moved up again. Three times they were repulsed, yet still Sammy led them forward for another try. They may lose this battle, but it wasn't gonna be from a lack of effort.

It was growing dark the fourth time they made their way up the bloody hill. His men made a stand just thirty yards from the Federal main line and kept up a constant fire. They received a severe fire in return. All the Confederate commands on each side of the 64th Alabama were suffering heavily. Still, they stood their ground, fought, and died.

135

The fighting had almost died down. The sun was setting, and the forest was growing dark. The Federals had fallen back almost fifty yards and stopped firing for the most part.

Basil nudged Sammy on the shoulder. "Sir, follow me; I think you need to see this."

Sammy followed his second in command toward the left of the regiment. Basil stopped and pointed toward a strange shadowy figure. Between the lines was what appeared to be a man. He wore high riding boots, a black cape, and had long, flowing, white hair. He had his back to Sammy as he walked among the dead. He appeared to be studying the faces of each body. After he had walked about twenty yards, he turned and started back toward the 64th. That was when Sammy noticed it. The man's eyes were glowing out here in the darkness. They were bright green. Sammy wasn't sure, but he thought he saw fangs hanging from the man's mouth.

Basil nudged Sammy again and said, "Let's get the hell out of here."

Sammy didn't argue. He followed Basil back toward the center of the regiment. They both plopped on the ground behind a large oak tree. Sammy was exhausted. Neither spoke of what they had just seen.

Sammy heard a private nearby talking with another soldier. He said, "I saw it too. It's a witch. That's what ran the Chickamauga Cherokees out of this land. They moved on west to get away from the witches."

Basil looked at Sammy, but it had grown too dark to see his reaction. Sammy didn't want to think about what they had seen out here. He wanted to think it was just a man, but what man would be walking among the dead bodies between two enemy lines? It would be suicide out there.

After dark, he noticed lights in the valley below the hill. He wondered if it was safe to move about now. Soon a rumor spread down the line that the Federals had retreated toward Chattanooga. Sammy moved down the hill with Basil and stumbled out into the field. There they encountered women searching for loved ones. One of the women asked Sammy which unit he belonged to.

Sammy told her an Alabama unit. She seemed to be looking for Georgia boys.

The wounded were so pitiful that Sammy couldn't fight back the tears that ran down his face. It was the first time he'd shed tears on a battlefield. He looked into each face he passed, holding his lantern close to see if he recognized anyone. He and Basil came up on a man lying on the ground with his lower jaw shot away. The man couldn't talk at all, what was left of his tongue seemed to loll from the back of his throat.

Sammy handed the man a piece of paper and a pencil and asked, "Is there anything I can do for you?"

The man scribbled on the paper. Sammy stood up and held the pencil close to his lantern. There was a single word on the paper that read "Victory."

The next morning, Sammy learned that the Federals had retreated into Chattanooga during the night and were reforming there. He wondered why the high command had allowed it to happen. He thought about General Robert E. Lee and how he would have surrounded this hill and then pressed on against the enemy before they had a chance to reform.

That afternoon, as they began to trudge slowly toward Chattanooga, the rains came. He heard a report that the Battle of Chickamauga had caused 35,000 casualties. Sammy had no way of knowing it at the time, but he'd survived the two bloodiest battles of the war.

As Bragg's army began to envelope the city of Chattanooga, where he hoped to lay siege to the Federal army and force their surrender, Sammy received orders to take the 64th Alabama Infantry back to Montgomery, Alabama, and refill his ranks with fresh recruits. The trip back to Montgomery proved to be a sad one. Sammy couldn't help but think about leaving Montgomery almost a year and a half ago with seven hundred men. Now he was returning, his regiment a mere shadow of its once former self. The 64th Alabama Infantry reached Montgomery with just a hundred and ninety-one men.

CHAPTER EIGHT

Charlie answered the door and was genuinely shocked at the sight that stood before him. Uncle Sol stood there in an old gray suit. His normally long, scraggly hair was plastered down flat, and he held a bouquet of daisies.

Charlie smiled, "Are those for me?"

"Damn, boy," Sol shook his head. "They for ya mama. Now, ain't you gonna ask me in?"

Charlie laughed and stepped to the side to make way for his best friend. He motioned toward the parlor and led Sol inside. His father was sitting in a Victorian chair reading a journal. Charlie announced, "Dad, Uncle Sol has arrived."

Thomas Rich lowered the paper and stood. He extended his hand. "Mister Saunders, how's the arthritis?"

"About the usual, Doc," Sol took his hand. He was obviously nervous. It was the first time Charlie had ever seen the man anywhere but on his front porch. Sol said, "Just call me Sol, like I told the boy."

"Sol it is then," Thomas smiled, "and I'm just plain Tom."

"Tom," Sol released his hand and nodded.

"Have a seat," Tom insisted.

"Not yet," Charlie objected. "I want to take him to meet mom."

Charlie grabbed the old man by the elbow and herded him toward the kitchen. They arrived to find Misses Rich pulling a turkey from the oven. There was a black lady helping with the cooking. Doctor Rich earned enough money that he had hired his wife a maid and cook.

Charlie announced, "Mom, this is Uncle Sol. He brought you flowers."

Misses Rich turned and wiped her hands on her apron. "I better put those in water; they're beautiful."

"Nice to meet ya, ma'am," Sol bowed formally. "I want you to know that boy of yours sure is polite. I can tell you did a good job raising him."

"Thank you," Charlie's mom blushed. She placed the flowers in a glass of water and turned, extending her hand. "Just call me Helen."

"All right, ma'am," Sol nodded and then shook his head. "I meant Helen."

Charlie took Sol back to the parlor, where they made small talk until dinner was prepared. At the table, Sol was truly concerned about the impression he would make and made every move precise. He wiped his mouth after each bite.

Helen paused between bites and said, "Charlie tells me you know a lot about the Civil War."

"I know a good bit, ma'am," Sol continued to stare at his plate with his head lowered. "I seen a little fightin' myself."

"Really?" she asked louder than she meant. "Did you fight at Vicksburg?"

"No, ma'am," Sol replied. "I missed that one. I was at Shiloh though."

"They say it was awful there," Tom spoke up. "My father was a surgeon at Vicksburg they say, although he's never mentioned it."

"He was at Jackson," Sol corrected Tom. "I don't mean to sound like a know-it-all, but he was at Jackson while Grant laid siege to Vicksburg. He done some doctoring up that way for a time."

Tom waved Sol off. "You're not being a know-it-all. I actually don't know any of his history. He's spoken very little of the war. I know Charlie has picked his brain as much as he possibly can, but he can get no more out of him than I could."

"He might not want to remember it," Sol raised an eyebrow. "It was awful times. I hope I ain't upset you folks by telling Charlie them stories about the war."

"Not at all," Helen said quickly. "It's educational. They teach that stuff in school, you know."

"I hear'd about the teaching that Yankee Miss Harmon been a doing," Sol locked eyes with Helen for the first time. "She weren't even born 'til twenty years after it was over, and then she gonna talk to them kids like she knows ever thang."

139

"Don't encourage him," Helen laughed and nodded toward Charlie. "He comes home upset almost every day about her history classes."

"Charlie's a good boy," Sol looked over at his young friend. "He's smarter than most boys his age. He can thank for himself."

Charlie was grinning. Tom Rich asked, "So you've been here since you were born?"

"That's right," Sol replied. "I'm about the last of my folks what's left."

Helen leaned forward over her plate. "You have relatives here in town? Charlie said you were the last of your family."

"None to speak of, ma'am," Sol took a bite of turkey. "Least not yet anyhow."

Charlie interrupted the direction of the conversation by asking, "Uncle Sol, could you tell my folks a story when we get through eating?"

"They don't want to hear no old man talking about that war," Sol replied.

Tom and Helen both answered at the same time. "We'd love to hear one."

Sol stopped chewing and looked toward the ceiling. "Suppose I got time to tell a short story before bedtime."

"Splendid," Tom said.

They finished eating and moved back into the parlor while the black lady cleared the table. Sol bragged on how delicious the meal had been. Helen gave all the credit to her help in the kitchen. Sol then bragged about what a nice place Tom had purchased. He then asked, "Now Charlie, where was we?"

"We just finished the Battle of Chickamauga, and the regiment had gone to Montgomery to recruit more men," Charlie replied.

"That's right," Sol agreed and began to study where he would begin his story. "Sammy and his men spent the winter in Montgomery. Nothing much of note occurred during those cold winter months. Mostly men a tryin' to stay warm was all. Winter weren't near as bad in Montgomery as in Virginia. I don't even thank they got no snow that winter. Sammy had dreamed of independence for the South, but after eighteen hunnerd and sixty four was introduced, his hopes began to fall. In the spring, he'd got his strength back up to a little over four hunnerd men. He was soon ordered back to Longstreet's Corps, which had spent a bloody winter in East Tennessee. Longstreet was ordered back to Virginia and had fought in the Battle of the Wilderness. Sammy's regiment didn't arrive in time to participate, but he was in time for a very bloody battle just a few days afterward. They marched to a small hamlet called Spotsylvania."

****

They arrived on a Wednesday to be placed in the center of the Confederate lines. There had already been serious fighting, and many of Sammy's men hoped they'd missed the worst of it. Most of them fully expected Grant to retire to regroup and reorganize his battered army.

A chaplain they'd picked up in Montgomery arrived at Sammy's tent and asked if he could deliver a worship service that night since most of the men were anticipating a battle on the morrow. Sammy agreed and even said he'd come.

It was almost dark when the man began his sermon. He began, "Today I'll be preaching to you about death and what it means to die for one's country."

Sammy heard several of his men begin to mumble. Before the chaplain could begin, Sammy stood and stared hard at the preacher. He said, "You'll not preach on that subject tonight. These men have seen plenty of death and dying for two years now. You can preach on something upbeat or not preach at all."

Sammy's men began to cheer him. The preacher looked bewildered. He started to protest but noticed the expression on the young colonel's face. He simply nodded his head and began to talk about Jesus feeding the five thousand with five loaves of bread and two fish.

A man in the crowd shouted, "Don't be talking about no food neither; we about to starve as it is!"

The large group of men burst into laughter. The preacher was without words. He looked helplessly toward Sammy. Sammy rose and said, "That's enough. We'll hear the sermon about the fish."

Once he'd finished his sermon, his soul had been stirred. He said, "Men, I've never been in a battle before, but I've decided that if you go into battle on the morrow, I will be right there alongside you."

Some of the men shouted their approval. Sammy rose from his seat and said, "All right, men, go try and get some sleep. We could have a long day tomorrow from the sounds of things."

About midnight, Sammy woke Basil from his sleep and motioned for him to keep quiet. Basil nodded. Sammy motioned for Basil to follow him. They crouched low and moved off through the trees toward the main Confederate line ahead. Sammy would pause occasionally and listen. Basil thought he heard movement— bayonets and canteens clanking off in the distance beyond the main line. Horses were neighing.

Sammy leaned over and whispered, "Something big is coming down out there. You hear that?"

"Yeah," Basil whispered. "What you think's going on?"

"Lee's pulled all our artillery back expecting Grant to withdraw and attempt to flank us again, but I think they plan on hitting us right in the center in the morning," Sammy pointed toward the sound of troop movement out in the darkness. "Our lines make a huge salient around the high ground here, which means it forms an angle. I don't like the idea of them hitting us here in such a weak spot."

"We need to tell someone," Basil whispered.

"Let's go," Sammy elbowed Basil and crouched low as they moved through the forest. They avoided branches and vines until they came up on a small group of men crouched in the darkness whispering. Sammy moved over and squatted beside them. He whispered, "Who are ya'll with?"

"I'm Brigadier General George Steaurt of Johnson's division," one of the figures replied. "Who are you?"

"Colonel Samuel Rodes of the 64th Alabama Infantry of Law's brigade," Sammy whispered back. "I've been loaned out as a reserve for the center. Sir, there's a lot of movement out beyond our lines, and I don't like the looks of this."

"Same thing I was just saying, Colonel," Steaurt whispered back. "I've sent men back to Johnson with reports, and he's told me Lee is sending the artillery back here."

"That's good, sir," Sammy said. "Any idea when they'll arrive?"

"Before daylight I'm hoping," Steuart tried to sound cheerful.

"Basil and I will go back toward the left and see what we can hear," Sammy told Steuart. "Will you be in this vicinity?"

"Yeah," Steuart replied. "Forward anything you learn to me here, and I'll send it on to division headquarters."

"Right," Sammy whispered. He grabbed Basil, and they both eased back through the brush.

Sammy was up all night listening to the troubling sounds moving out in the darkness. He was surrounded by the men of Lee's army, practically thousands of men, and he felt so alone. He wondered how that could be. Basil reclined against a tree and kept nodding off. Sammy wanted to send him back with the regiment, but he needed the man just now. He nudged Basil and said, "Go find General Steuart and ask him if he's heard from the artillery yet."

"Yes, sir," Basil mumbled as he came out of his slumber. "You gonna wear my boots out, Sammy."

"I'll buy you another pair," Sammy spoke at the back of the figure moving away in the darkness.

He thought about what would happen at dawn if the artillery wasn't back in place. This was shaping up to be a recipe for disaster. He heard rustling in the brush behind him and turned. A figure in the darkness spoke. He recognized the voice of Major Smallwood.

"Over here, Major," Sammy whispered. "You sounded like an entire regiment crashing through that brush."

"Sorry," Major Smallwood whispered back as he knelt beside Sammy. "I tried being quiet."

143

"It's all right," Sammy spoke in a hushed voice. "We're far enough away to not be heard. Hell, Ewell's main line is about a hundred yards ahead of us."

Major Smallwood listened into the darkness. He asked, "What's happening?"

"I don't know," Sammy replied, "The artillery was removed late yesterday afternoon. Something big is about to happen. I can just feel it. Me and Basil been listening to troops moving out beyond our lines all night."

"Perhaps they're just moving to the east again," Major Smallwood tried to sound cheerful.

"Perhaps," Sammy whispered. "Or perhaps they're planning on hitting this salient."

Every soldier in the army understood how weak a salient was in a defensive alignment. This particular salient was large, containing about five thousand men. The men had nicknamed it the "Mule Shoe" because of the shape. If the enemy broke through a portion of the salient, the troops on the other side would be caught between a crossfire.

"What time is it?" Sammy asked.

"It's early," Major Smallwood replied. "It'll be daylight in half an hour."

Basil came sliding back through the brush and squatted. He was almost out of breath. He gasped, "General Steuart says the artillery is nowhere to be found. He says to arouse your regiment and have them prepared in case they do hit us."

"All right, gentlemen," Sammy rose to his feet. "Let's go back and get the boys up. This could turn out to be a long day."

The three men moved back to where the men were sleeping in line of battle. They quietly began to arouse the men, but a shot from the front, followed by several more, finished the job for them. Men rose up and peered into the darkness in front of them. Suddenly the darkness erupted with rifle fire. Men could be heard screaming toward the front.

Sammy turned to Basil and said, "There it is."

He debated ordering the men forward without orders, but decided to wait and see how bad things were first. The chaplain from the evening before was racing down the line screaming for the men to aim low and do their duty. A bullet whistled by overhead. The chaplain stopped and turned his head. A ricocheting bullet screamed past overhead, and the chaplain dove onto the ground. Several men began to laugh.

Sammy looked to his right and noticed the sun beginning to brighten the sky. The chaplain rose to his feet about the time an artillery round passed high overhead, trailing sparks from the fuse. He quickly turned and knocked a young private down as he raced toward the rear. Someone spoke up and said, "So much for going into battle with us. I thank he done seen all he wants."

"Just a little dab of fightin' will do for a preacher," another soldier replied.

It amazed Sammy how battle-hardened his men had become. Standing there waiting to go into hell again and they were telling jokes and poking fun at each other. When the war had begun, men would stand and pray aloud before entering the fray. It was as if they had resigned themselves to death and were going to enjoy every moment they had left on this earth. They'd seen too many comrades killed to expect that they'd survive this war.

Soon stragglers began to move back from the front. Men who'd lost their nerve and others that had lost their units because they'd been overrun. Sammy collared one of them and asked how bad it was up there.

"It's damned bad, sir," the bedraggled private mumbled. "They sent ever thang they got agin us. We overrun, and it's just gonna get worser. They broke us right in the middle as you can hear."

"Attention," Sammy yelled. He'd heard enough. It may not do any good, but he decided he would lead his regiment against the massed Federal infantry. It may be a suicide mission, but someone would have to slow the enemy advance and give Lee time bring up reinforcements before his army was destroyed. Turning toward the front, Sammy yelled, "Forward, march!"

The regiment numbered just under five hundred men. He would be charging into a mass of Federals that numbered around twenty thousand. There was no time to think about the odds. They put that many men in that small of an area and it would be a slaughter every time his men opened fire.

They moved ahead, reaching the open area at the main line. Fog hung heavy across the ground, and though the sun was finally up, it was impossible to see more than twenty yards. That too had helped the Confederates because the Federals had yet to realize the havoc they had created. Sammy noticed that things weren't near as bad as he had thought. There were still a lot of men fighting here. The Confederates were on their side of the breastworks, and the Federals were in the ditch on the other. They were massed there about twenty ranks deep, and still men were coming up. Sammy could hear the ones already in the ditch screaming for them to go back. There was no room for all those men here.

Sammy waved his sword and yelled for his men to go to the breastworks. They charged headlong into the heat of the moment. It was an imperiled position. If the Federals gained a foothold along any part of the salient, they would be in danger of being surrounded.

The Federals were frustrated because they couldn't return the Confederate fire. There was no room to move. They were packed in the ditch like sardines. Sammy noticed them throwing their rifles across the works like spears, hoping their bayonets would do the killing for them. Sammy's men began to pick them up and hurl them back over the dirt wall into the massed ranks. He could hear men screaming when they were struck.

Both sides fought back and forth over the works for nearly an hour. Neither side was willing to yield an inch. All the Confederate officers in this area were either killed, wounded, or captured. Sammy learned that he was the senior officer on this part of the field. Subordinate officers he'd never met before came to him for orders. Each time Sammy would simply reply, "Hold your ground. We'll have reinforcements up soon."

There wasn't much for the officers to do otherwise. This was a soldier's battle. The only command decision for the officers to make was whether to stay or retreat. There were no fancy maneuvers, just bloody, close-range fighting.

The sky had grown cloudy, and it soon began to rain. The mud in the trench was almost ankle deep. Lightning flashed across the sky, and thunder roared along with the guns. The trench on both sides of the breastworks began to fill with water. The rain turned into a torrential downpour. The dead and wounded lay in the water, which soon turned a bright red. The entire scene beggared description. It was pure bedlam. Sammy wondered how long men could endure the strain. The fighting seemed to go on forever. He took out his watch. It was approaching ten. Sammy looked toward the rear, but there were no reinforcements to be seen.

He collared a private and said, "Go to the rear and find out what the hell's happening."

"Who do I ask for?" the rain-soaked soldier asked.

"I don't give a damn," Sammy pushed him away. He turned and saw Basil loading a rifle for the soldiers in front of him. Sammy remained bent low as he eased over to Basil's side.

"I'm amazed the rifles work at all in this weather," Basil said.

"This is sheer madness," Sammy yelled. "Send someone over to General Steaurt and find out what he knows."

"Want me to go?" Basil asked.

"Yeah," Sammy replied. He grabbed Basil as he began to leave. He added, "Just be careful."

Sammy watched Basil leave. He looked over the horrid scene. Haversacks and canteens were floating on the water. There were broken rifles everywhere. Men on both sides of the breastworks would hold their rifles up to fire, exposing nothing but their hands. Most of the wounded were wounded in the hands or arms.

Someone tapped Sammy on the shoulder. He turned to find the ragged private. Sammy had half-expected the man to stay in the rear and was genuinely surprised to see him come back at all. The private saluted and said, "I found some chicken-shit staff officer back there. He says the orders are to hold our ground to the last man. General Lee is building a new line of breastworks across the base of the Mule Shoe."

"Thanks, young man; you've earned yourself extra rations tonight," Sammy patted the boy on the shoulder.

"If I live," the boy added and inched his way back up to the works, where he started loading a rifle.

Basil was back soon thereafter. He said, "General Steuart and most of his brigade are captured, Sammy. We got men holding over there, but it's ugly. Major General Johnson is captured also."

"Damn," Sammy said. "I just got orders from the rear to hold our ground to the last man so Lee can build a new line of works across the base of this damned salient."

"How long will that take?" Basil asked.

"Who knows," Sammy shrugged. "We're stuck here until then."

The fighting raged on over into the afternoon. The strain was almost unbearable. Sammy noticed men growing exhausted and falling asleep sitting straight up in the mud, oblivious to the fighting raging around them.

About three, the Federals determined to come over the works in a rush. The move caught the Confederates unaware. It happened so suddenly, the Southerners had no choice but to fall back to the tree line fifty yards in their rear. Sammy raced ahead and stopped them. He soon had them in line and firing on the Federals. The enemy troops were out in the open and growing confused about what to do next. Sammy saw his chance. He quickly ordered a counterattack. He commanded all the men in this sector now. He had about two thousand men under his command. They lunged forward, and the sudden thrust now caught the Federals by surprise. His men raced ahead through the mud, and the few Federals that weren't able to get back over the works in time were bayoneted or clubbed to death. Sammy had never seen men so resolute in holding their lines.

The rain was still falling, and the burning black powder made Sammy's eyes burn. He tried to rub his sleeve across his eyes, but there was powder all over his coat and it just made matters worse. He forced his eyes open and looked skyward, letting the rain rinse his eyes out.

Sammy began to wonder if any of his men would survive this battle. He'd never seen anything like it. Basil yelled, "Gentlemen, there is no better place to die than right here!"

A private yelled back, "I can think of a lot better places to die than in this shit hole!"

Everyone who heard the remark burst into laughter. Sammy had one of those jarring thoughts that seemed to work its way through his damaged memory. He remembered someone saying that life was made perfect by death. It troubled him that he didn't know who'd said that. Whoever it was obviously wasn't here in this mess alongside him or they'd probably reword that statement.

Sammy heard a commotion to his right. The Federals there had decided to come over the works again. They managed to capture the men who were fighting them there. They turned toward their right and began aiming their rifles down the line. Sammy could hear them yelling for he and his men to surrender. Basil jumped to his feet and yelled, "Kill them!"

The men in the immediate vicinity turned and charged the men in blue. Their facial expressions told Sammy they hadn't expected this. He charged along with his men as he drew his sword. Everything was a blur now. The fighting was hand to hand. He saw a big Confederate swing his musket like a club and bash in the skull of a Federal soldier. Another Federal fired from about ten feet away. The bullet struck the Confederate just below the right eye and passed through his head.

Sammy noticed a Federal soldier about to run his bayonet through a man to his left. Sammy drove his sword through the man's abdomen almost to the hilt. The man's eyes seemed to bulge from their sockets as shock set in. Sammy saved one of his men, but still he almost felt sorry for what he'd just done. War had never seemed this personal before. It was the first man he'd actually killed with his own hand, although he always understood that ordering men to kill was the same as if he were doing the killing.

He was about to pull the sword from the man, when another enemy soldier brought his musket high overhead and brought it down with a crash into Sammy's wrist. At the same time, Basil shot

149

the man in the chest with his colt revolver. Pain shot up Sammy's arm. There was no doubt that bones had been broken. He crashed into the mud in pain.

As quickly as this assault had begun, it ended. There weren't enough Federals to hold this part of the line. They were soon all killed or captured. A very few were able to get back over the works and into the ditch on the other side.

Sammy lay in pain, holding his right wrist with his left hand. Basil was at his side. He asked, "How bad is it?"

"Damned bad!" Sammy screamed. Some of the water from the ditch got in his mouth, and it tasted of blood. "Broken arm!"

"I'll get you to the rear," Basil began to help Sammy up.

"Never mind me," Sammy said. "You're in command now. Hold this line. I'm not gonna die from a broken arm."

"Right," Basil turned back to the works. He quickly got two soldiers to attend to Sammy.

The men came over and one of them said, "We'll get you to the rear, sir."

"You'll do no such thing," Sammy objected. "Just get me over against the breastworks so I can keep my head out of the water. I'm not leaving my men."

The men shrugged, and together they helped drag Sammy through the mud, blood, and water to the pile of dirt. Sammy lay back against the embankment, cradling his arm against his belly. The wrist throbbed with each beat of his heart. Basil let everyone know he was in command and quickly returned to the side of his best friend.

"I've taken command," Basil was shaking his head. "You can get out of here now. Go to the rear and get that wrist seen to."

"I'm fine," Sammy mumbled. "Listen—check on the ammunition. We've been fighting a long time. I've already brought some up this morning, but I'm willing to bet we're about out again."

"Will do," Basil said.

"Get me a report on casualties also," Sammy wiped at the water pouring down his face. "And find my hat," he added. "I can't see a damned thing in this deluge."

"There's nothing worth seeing here," Basil laughed and patted Sammy on the shoulder before moving off.

A brave Federal lieutenant stood on top of the works firing his pistol into the mass of Confederates. Sammy turned his head and saw him. A young boy near Sammy yelled, "Sir, look at that man shooting at us."

"Well, shoot back, damn you," Sammy yelled.

The boy raised his rifle and sent a bullet into the lieutenant's chest. The day had been a long one, but the evening was passing even slower. Sammy wondered if they would be notified when the works were completed in the rear. He wondered if night would ever come. He figured darkness would surely end this unmerciful fight.

Basil came back. He saluted and said, "Sir, we're down to less than half strength. The color bearer was bayoneted fourteen times. Should we fall back?"

"Keep fighting," Sammy said.

"I got more ammunition coming up," Basil patted Sammy on the shoulder and moved away again.

Sammy thought he may have found the answer to life down here in the mud and blood. With the battle swirling all around him, he began to think he was born for warfare. This was actually feeling like home to him, as if it were a place he belonged—had belonged all his life but didn't know it until now. He made up his mind not to worry anymore about where he'd come from or who he was. He was Samuel Rodes, the god of war and death.

Darkness arrived and yet the fighting continued. There was no letup in the weather either. Sammy slept off and on as the battle raged around him. It was almost three in the morning when orders finally arrived for the men in the salient to fall back. Lee had kept his word. Once his engineers had completed the line, he'd sent for them. Basil held Sammy by his left arm as they made their way toward the rear. Sammy had been so exhausted that when he tried to rise, his legs didn't seem to want to work.

Before they left the scene, Sammy looked at all the bodies piled in heaps around him. The enemy and his men were all mixed together. It was the worst he'd seen thus far in this war.

As they crossed the breastworks in the rear, fresh troops were there to relieve these exhausted soldiers. Sammy saw General Lee sitting on his horse riding among the men. He kept telling them how proud he was of them. He rode up next to Basil and Sammy and said, "I hope you're not wounded too badly, Colonel."

"Thank you, sir," Sammy replied. Lee rode on past. Sammy looked at Basil and noticed his mouth gaped open. "What?" he asked.

"That was old Marse Robert himself," Basil said.

"I know," Sammy laughed. "Now let's find me a surgeon."

"They just gonna want to cut that hand off," Basil replied.

"I may need to borrow your colt," Sammy smiled, "I lost mine early yesterday morning in that mud back there."

"We'll get you another if you keep that hand," Basil laughed. "Unless you can shoot left-handed."

They located a field hospital. Wagons loaded with men arrived continuously. Some of the wounded were screaming, and several were begging to just be shot. One man kept repeating over and over again, "I want to die."

CHAPTER NINE

"Did he lose the hand, Uncle Sol?" Charlie asked as he climbed onto the front porch and took his seat.

"I had a good day today," Sol said seriously. "Thanks for asking, and how was your day?"

Charlie smiled and shook his head. "Sorry, you feeling all right today?"

"Tolerable," Sol mumbled. "That Miss Harmon teach you anymore nonsense today?"

"Not much history today," Charlie replied. "Mostly math and literature. She likes Mark Twain."

"She know he fought for the Confederacy?" Sol asked.

"He did?" Charlie answered with a question.

"For a short time," Sol reached into his pouch and took out a plug of tobacco. "He deserted. He wasn't a warrior type."

"I see," Charlie replied. He waited for Sol to begin chewing the tobacco. He'd learned that if he acted interested, Sol would just drag things out longer in an attempt to torment him. He said, "My folks loved that story you told about Spotsa…whatever it was. They didn't have no idea things got that bad."

"Spotsylvania," Sol corrected him. "And yeah, it was damned bad, but it weren't the worst battle. Not it nor Gettysburg, like most folks want to thank."

"Really?" Charlie asked.

"Yep," Sol spat a stream of tobacco juice off the porch. "You be shore and tell ya ma what a fine meal that was."

"I will," Charlie replied. Sol had told her that very thing about ten times that afternoon. There was really no point in repeating it. He was ready for some war stories. Charlie fought the urge, could contain it no longer, and asked, "Did he lose the hand, Uncle Sol?"

Sol eyeballed Charlie a long moment. He loved torturing the boy with anticipation, but he immediately realized that Charlie was in a bad state of curiosity. He decided to let the boy off easily. He replied, "No, he didn't lose the arm. Now listen without being so damned nosy."

"Yes, sir," Charlie lowered his head.

Sol pinched the smile from his face. He asked, "Now, where was I?"

"He got wounded in the right wrist, Uncle Sol," Charlie looked at him incredulously. "Are you getting dementia?"

"Yeah," Sol smiled, "damned dementia causes my joints to ache, but we called it rheumatism back during the war."

Charlie shook his head. He couldn't wait for the story, and Sol was dragging this thing out to the extreme. He said, "I think I'll go home if you're not gonna tell me the story."

"All right, boy," Sol laughed. "He was carried back to Richmond and put up in a private residence like all high-ranking officers were back then. He refused to let them amputate, although they was a wanting to cut his hand off halfway between the wrist and elbow. They did what they could and placed a crude splint on his wrist to hold it in place if it were to heal."

"Uncle Sol," Charlie interrupted. "I saw scars on your wrist before—lots of times when your sleeve slipped up your arm. You were telling the story, and when you extended your arm, your right wrist was all scarred up."

Sol peered at the boy a long moment. He said, "It's a long story about my wrist there, Charlie. I was out a hunting and reached in a hole on the side of a hill. I was a thinking about some gold might be hid in there, but it was a raccoon. He liked to ate my arm off. What this got to do with my arm, boy?"

"I just noticed it, Uncle Sol," Charlie replied. "I didn't know where you got those scars."

"Damn, boy," Sol shook his head. "Would ya just let me tell the damned story?"

"Sorry, Uncle Sol," Charlie replied. "I'm listening."

"Sammy was a staying with an old maid in Richmond, Virginia. She was called 'Crazy Bet,' but her real name was Elizabeth Van Lew." Sol leaned forward and let another stream of tobacco fly into the yard. "She was a Union sympathizer and helped all the Yankee prisoners that was being held in Richmond. She willingly took Sammy in to keep the authorities off her ass. See, she acted crazy to keep the authorities from catching her and her antics. She wore her oldest clothes and shredded bonnets.

154

The woman was nothing to look at. She'd make your eyes hurt. Anyway, she took good care of Sammy so's the authorities wouldn't question what she was up to. That's when Sammy started having them bad dreams."

"Bad dreams?" Charlie asked.

"Yeah, bad dreams," Sol scratched at his scraggly beard. "He dreamed of a woman in her late forties. She was introducing him to a beautiful young girl. That gal was a couple years younger than Sammy. He'd never seen a more beautiful gal than her. Sammy didn't know what the nightmares meant, but they definitely meant something."

"What did they mean?" Charlie asked.

Sol stared at Charlie a long moment. He began to shake his head. The boy would never learn. The story would be completed when it was time and not a moment before, yet still he had to ask. Sol said, "Now, Sammy received a letter from a girl he'd long given up on. Her name was Lillian, and she'd moved with her family from Fredericksburg to Richmond to escape the path of the Yankees. She was just living about five blocks away and wanted to come see Sammy when he felt like company."

"What did he say?" Charlie almost leapt from the chair.

"What you want him to say?" Sol asked. "He's a southern gentleman; I mean, what *can* he say?"

"So he got to see Lillian again?" Charlie was almost standing now.

"Yeah, she come over to see him," Sol smiled at the success his story was accomplishing. "Made Crazy Bet almost feel sorry for a wounded Rebel."

"That is really great," Charlie eased back into the chair in an obvious state of ecstasy. "I had always hoped they would end up married before the war was over."

"Hold your taters there, boy," Sol held up a hand. "I didn't say they went and got married. She was engaged to a lieutenant last time they had spoken."

"Did the lieutenant get killed?" Charlie was holding out hope for the story to end the way he had dreamed it would.

155

"Boy, what am I going to do with you?" Sol shook his head. "Now, she come and seen her old love, but the lieutenant was still alive and she was still gonna marry him."

"Damn," Charlie said before he realized it.

"You ought not talk that way," Sol raised an eyebrow at Charlie. "Your momma wouldn't approve."

"Sorry," Charlie lowered his head. "I just want to know what happens to Sammy soon. It's driving me insane. Can I be honest with you, Uncle Sol?"

"Sure," Sol nodded at the boy. "What you got up your sleeve?"

Charlie looked at the floor of the porch and finally worked up the courage. He said, "I think I know where this story is going."

"You do, do you?" Sol asked. He stared at Charlie through his piercing eyes. "Where's it going?"

"Would you tell me if I guessed ahead of you?" Charlie asked. He watched Sol nod his head as if he were agreeing with him. Charlie asked, "Are you Sammy?"

"Sammy?" Sol asked. "Where in the hell did you get that idea?"

"Sorry, Uncle Sol," Charlie lowered his head again. Another thought dawned on Charlie. "Didn't you say Basil was from Mississippi?"

"Yeah," Sol squinted his eyes at Charlie.

Charlie asked, "What part?"

"Hell, I don't know; don't make a damned no way!" Sol's voice boomed out louder than he meant.

"Sorry," Charlie lowered his head. "Go on with your story."

"Well," Sol rubbed his forehead, "Lillian came and seen Sammy at Crazy Bet's house. She told him she had a future husband in Lee's army, a fightin' Grant at North Anna. See, Grant was still trying to get around Lee's right flank and take Richmond, but Lee was too sharp for him."

"So," Charlie paused for a long second, "she didn't marry him?"

"Marry him hell," Sol shook his head again. "Damn, boy, don't you understand plain English? She married some lieutenant

156

that weren't amounting to nothing in Lee's ordnance department. Now pay close attention to this part."

****

Sammy arose every morning and shaved as was his custom. He would spend a long half hour just staring in the mirror and wondering who this boy was that looked back at him with the same questioning eyes he was producing. He'd changed over the years, as short as those years were. But his appearance was still the same—thin mustache over his upper lip, clean shaven everywhere else, and the red hair. He'd given up hope of someone ever recognizing him and telling him who he was or where he was from. Each morning, he would ask himself who this stranger was that stared back at him in the mirror. It wasn't long after that when the nightmares started.

His wrist was always in torment. There were times when he began to wonder if he should have had it amputated. He focused on the pain. It was the only thing left in his life that made him feel like he was still living. Sammy had trouble believing his life was truly real. There were quite a few moments that made him feel as if it was all a dream.

He walked around Elizabeth Van Lew's home and looked at the flowers and beautiful trees. Sammy would force his hand to move and attempted to kill the pain with his mind, but he could never accomplish what he wanted. He remembered what Basil had said about him being a ghoul. Maybe he was a ghoul. He had no way of knowing. He was bitter; there was no doubt about that. Everyone he'd become close to had gone away in the end, everyone except Basil. He tried to cheer his poor mood with the understanding that he still had his best friend. Yet, Sammy was still bitter with what life had dealt him.

Sammy walked down town into the heart of Richmond and visited an apothecary. He bought more laudanum. It ridded him of the pain and actually ridded him of the feeling of loneliness. He watched the citizens who'd missed the entire war while he'd fought so hard, and he thought about his legacy. He would leave

157

everything he'd seen with these thankless people. They could have his everything, his empire of dirt even. He would let them deal with what he'd become. He'd become what he was for them.

He stepped from the apothecary and took a large sip of laudanum. He waited and felt the medicine begin to take effect and walked across the empty street. Sammy thought about the fact that there was nothing half as lonesome as being totally alone. He worried about the effect the laudanum was having on his young body and quickly deduced that he had not yet begun to defile himself.

He made his way back up the street toward Elizabeth Van Lew's house. The daily fare was provided by the Confederate commissary department. It consisted of a thin slice of bread and a small plate of soup. He'd eaten enough of it already to understand that it would only make him hungry for more. Sammy worried about his men back in the lines, attempting to survive on less than what he was eating here in his nation's capital.

The last night he spent at Crazy Bet's had given him a nightmare he would not soon forget. There was a girl in his dream, a girl that should have meant something to him. It was as if this girl had lived forty years before him and barely broke through his disabled memory. Sammy began to wonder if he was losing what was left of his damaged mind. The dream had seemed so real. An older lady in her late forties was introducing him to a beautiful girl, a girl of his dreams. The scene was surreal. The girl was actually interested in him. He couldn't imagine anyone that beautiful being interested in someone as childish-looking as him. It made him wonder if he was dreaming about a woman that may not exist.

As troubling as the dream had been, he'd awoken ready to return to his men. Sammy wondered about what state of affairs his regiment was in with Basil in command. He didn't worry about the job that Basil would do in command, but still he worried. He bid a final adieu and mounted a horse for Gaines' Mill, a small community just east of Richmond. He found his men there, just south of Gaines' Mill at a small hamlet called Cold Harbor.

Basil was genuinely glad to see his best friend. The poor Mississippian had been worried about his commander and best friend since his wounding at Spotsylvania three weeks before. Sammy arrived to share a tent behind the breastworks at Cold Harbor with him. Basil had not expected to see him arrive so soon, and he had actually expected him to arrive without his right hand. He hugged Sammy and gave the splinted wrist a good inspection. Basil said, "Sammy, I didn't expect you back so soon. I thought shore you was gonna lose a limb this time, but I prayed every night you'd return and here you are."

"Yep," Sammy held Basil as close as he could with his left hand, "here I am."

"Sammy, we dug in as fast as possible," Basil jerked a thumb back over his shoulder. "You know they given us hell ever time we see battle. Our men done killed three times more men than we got in our entire regiment. I told our boys to do you proud, and they did."

"You think they'll hit us here?" Sammy asked.

"They can try," Basil smiled, "but, they'll be messing up if they do. We're entrenched like a fat tick on a dog's back and ain't a damned thing they can do but to come and die."

"Good news," Sammy replied. "I couldn't sleep for worrying about you and the boys. I ain't got no family now but ya'll, and I worry over you boys like a momma hen over her brood."

"That hurts," Basil lowered his head. "I thought you trusted me was the reason you promoted me to your second in command."

"I trust you," Sammy smiled and patted Basil on the shoulder with his left hand again. "I don't have no more family to speak of. I can't afford to lose you. How's Major Smallwood?"

"Dead, sir," Basil lowered his head. "He was hit in the head by a sharpshooter at Bethesda Church two days ago. Was out overseeing the men digging entrenchments and was shot in the head. Dead before he hit the ground. He never knew what hit him."

"Damn," Sammy shook his head.

"That's not the big problem," Basil jerked a thumb over his shoulder. "We dug in here before Richmond. If Grant overruns our position here, well, the war is over. He'll have Richmond and there's no use fightin' no more."

159

"They won't overrun us," Sammy replied as he stepped past Basil to inspect his lines.

Basil followed along behind. He'd enjoyed independent command over the regiment, but he'd also missed Sammy. They walked from one end of the regiment to the other before returning to the center. Sammy's men were extremely happy to see their commander back in charge. He'd made them wonder if he was the man for the job when he was first given command back in Montgomery in 1862. Now, over two years later, they would follow this man to the gates of hell and burst through those gates if he ordered them to.

Sammy turned to Basil and announced, "They may overrun another portion of this line, but you can place the entire Yankee nation in front of the 64th Alabama Infantry here and we'll kill them all. You've done an outstanding job in my absence, Lieutenant Colonel Basil."

"Thank you, sir," Basil replied. He'd done all he could, but he didn't feel near as confident as his commander.

The next morning dawned warm, and the day would grow much warmer as it wore on. Something out beyond the early mist bothered Sammy. He'd had this feeling before at Antietam and it had proved that his sixth sense was actually alive and well. He mentioned to Basil that something big was about to happen, but Basil thought it was only because it was his first day back in command.

Sammy had experienced this feeling back at Spotsylvania that long night just over a month ago. There were certain things that just didn't feel right. He knew deep down that the morrow would bring something big. There'd been feelings like this before.

As the morning wore on, Sammy began to wonder if Basil hadn't been right. Maybe he'd just seen too much in the last year and expected the worst every day. It saddened him to know that he may not see a battle here today. That was the true shock of what was occurring in Sammy's life at this moment. He longed for the Federals to hit him in these massive entrenchments. He wanted to punish the Northern horde. Perhaps Basil had been right all along. Perhaps Sammy was a ghoul.

It had grown into the afternoon when the sound shook him to his core. The earth seemed to tremble beneath his feet. The tread of thousands of men brought Sammy to his senses. He'd heard the sound once before—it was the sound of his men marching across the wide field at Gettysburg against the enemy. He recognized instantly that the sound wasn't coming from his men who were waiting behind their entrenchments. It was the sound of Grant's army being sent against an entrenched foe attempting to hold their capital.

Sammy realized that Grant was gambling everything he had on one massed assault. If he could overrun the Confederate army here, he'd win the war. If it failed, he'd just lose another large group of his men. He'd lost them before at Shiloh, Vicksburg, the Wilderness, and Spotsylvania. It didn't bother him. Men died in war, and he didn't worry about the losses. It would be worth losing ten thousand men to win this war. It would be worth losing ten thousand just to cause the Confederates to lose more men that he understood they couldn't afford to lose. It was a war of attrition that he alone understood. Sure, he was referred to as a butcher, but he would win the war in the end.

Sammy rushed forward to the breastworks. He had to be proud of Basil. He'd dug the trenches into the shape of a V. The Federal troops moving into the position would be caught in crossfire. Troops entrenched on each side of the line would catch the Union troops in enfilade. Sammy loved it. Two years ago, he'd been just as upset to see the enemy lose their lives as his own men. Now, he loved to see those enemy troops being killed. Perhaps they were getting just what they deserved. Sammy raced down the line encouraging his men to kill without impunity. He wanted them to slaughter the enemy. Those men had either decided to punish people who wanted their freedom or they were foreign-born and didn't even know what they were fighting for.

Sammy rushed forward and peered over the breastworks that his men had built in his absence under the direction of Basil Manly. The works were perfect. They had works built over chest-high and had placed head logs on top to fire beneath. The Federals wouldn't have a chance against such a line.

161

He watched them moving against his works through an open field. The scene was horrifying—not because he thought they would break his line, but because he knew that the long line of gleaming enemy bayonets were about to be one large mass of writhing humanity. The ground would turn red with blood, and it wouldn't be that of his men.

A boy tugged at Sammy's cloak. It was a young private, who didn't seem a day over sixteen. He shouted at Sammy, "Sir, they're coming. Some are shooting at us."

"Let them get a little closer," Sammy said to the boy. He heard Basil at his side.

Basil yelled, "Get ready, my boys; hell is coming for breakfast!"

When the enemy was within a hundred yards, Sammy gave the command for them to open fire. There were over three men per yard behind the Confederate breastworks. While two men loaded and passed their weapons forward, the best shot in the group would fire the rifle. Those men fired until their shoulders were black and blue. Cold Harbor wasn't a simple battle, but it turned into simple murder. Sammy wondered what kind of man would send his troops to be slaughtered in such a way.

The sun rose, and the heat became unbearable. Still, Sammy encouraged his men to continue the killing. The heat became heavy and dry. The roar of rifle and cannon fire became so loud that Sammy noticed his men's mouths moving but couldn't hear any sound. There was nothing. He quickly deduced that what was occurring here was not war but murder. He almost felt ashamed of what he was allowing to happen.

Another solid line of blue coats emerged from the tree line over a hundred yards away. The scene within the next twenty minutes astonished Sammy. He was unable to ever write what he'd seen occur at Cold Harbor just east of Richmond that day. Column after column of Union troops moved forward against his line. It seemed the entire Union army was hurled against his part of the southern line, and still his men held. They continuously mowed the enemy ranks down. Yet still the Yankee troops came on. Sammy thought about all the battles he'd seen before, and they all paled in comparison to this. He heard men shouting, cheering, and screaming, but it was far worse than anything he'd ever witnessed before. The best part for him was the fact that it was the enemy's troops instead of his own. It was almost joyous for him as he watched his enemy die before his very eyes, caught between a crossfire.

The day was extremely hot, and the sun beat down on the wounded out before his lines. A staff officer told him that it was over a hundred and ten degrees in the shade. Sammy could believe that piece of information. The smoke was blinding and the atmosphere so stifling that it seemed to fill their mouths. Yet, the firing continued, and the enemy continued to die. The entire scene became incessant.

Sammy was soon satisfied that on this hot June day, his men had killed a thousand other men. Each one of his men had killed at least twenty others, perhaps as much as a hundred men apiece. All they had to do was load and shoot. The only reason they'd failed to overrun his line was because they were forced to pass over their own dead and wounded to reach the abatis. The ground in front of his line was covered with the dead and the wounded. There was no possible way they could miss the blue ranks. Men were piled up in front of his works like cord wood. Sammy could have walked all over the field without touching the ground, just stepping on the bodies.

Basil approached Sammy when the firing died down. He had a private in tow. Sammy returned his best friend's salute. He asked, "Who you got there, Basil?"

"Private Duncan," Basil replied. "I got to show you something."

Sammy nodded and waited.

Basil pulled Duncan's shirt down so Sammy could inspect his shoulder. Sammy looked at the boy's shoulder and waited. Basil said, "All our men look like this."

"Bruised?" Sammy asked.

"Bruised, "Basil replied. "They've all fired like hell today. We've killed a hell of a bunch of Yanks today."

163

Sammy looked at Private Duncan. He asked, "How many times you fired today, young man?"

"At least a hundred and twenty, sir," Duncan replied. "My gun got so hot that I had to swap it with a fallen comrade's a couple of times. The powder would flash before I rammed the ball home. It was damned nerve-wracking at times, but we whooped them Yankees asses today, sir."

"Very good, Corporal," Sammy replied.

"I'm no corporal," Private Duncan objected. "I ain't nothing but a private."

"You weren't," Sammy patted the young man on the back, "but you're a corporal now."

"Thank you, sir," Private Duncan saluted and stepped away from the two high-ranking officers.

That night the dreams returned to Sammy once again. The dark-haired girl with the beautiful face was staring at him, almost begging him to come home to her. He awoke in the dead of night wondering where this girl was. She had to be someone from his past. He awoke depressed over the fact that he couldn't solve this mystery.

Sammy dressed and walked with Basil to the main line. The Federals were bad about sending over 'feelers' in the form of a cannonball toward the Confederates. It actually bothered Sammy a bit that they would fire over their own wounded to attempt to frustrate their enemy. He wished he had artillery worthy of returning their fire. The Confederacy had never produced field artillery good enough to compete with the Federals.

It was rare for these random shots to do any damage. They almost seemed lazy-looking out here in the light. You would hear the artillery fire and see the cannonball slowly rise in the air. It felt as if you could actually avoid its trajectory. The projectile seemed to rise so slowly, and the men had become so accustomed to them, that they paid them no attention anymore.

On this particular morning it mattered. If they had been paying attention this time, one of the regiment's captains would have lived another day. Captain Osborn was eating a biscuit when the shell struck him in the head. Most of his head disappeared instantly, the skull disintegrating and vanishing in a mist. The face remained as it peeled inside-out onto his chest. A fine mist of blood sprayed on everyone sitting nearby. Osborn's brains fell onto the ground before his body. He never knew what hit him.

"His spirit is at rest now," Basil mumbled.

Sammy pointed at several men sitting nearby and said, "Wrap his body in a blanket and bury him with full military honors."

"Sir," Basil turned to Sammy, "another five feet and that would have had your name on it."

Not long after the incident, there was a white flag raised by the Federal troops across the way. A message was sent over from the enemy asking for a truce to bury the dead. The stench was already unbearable. Sammy had been listening to the Federal wounded trapped between the lines. They were begging piteously for help, yet there had been no one from the other side seeking their relief until this moment.

The message was passed up through the chain of command to him. The message was strange. The enemy soldiers in blue across the way weren't worried about their own wounded, and why should they be? They were worried about the stench created by the smell of the dead bodies that were blowing into their very faces. Sammy grew frustrated against his enemy. They'd enlisted men from across the Atlantic Ocean to fight for what they themselves were unwilling to risk their own lives for.

Sammy watched the long and deep trenches dug for his enemy soldiers when the armistice was finally worked out. The memory of watching the Federals being buried with very little respect in the Virginia ground was sickening to him. He watched the Federal soldiers make hooks out of their bayonets to bury all the dead. They didn't even have the courage to lay their hands on their own dead and drag them to a burial ditch. Sammy began to wonder why he would care so much for those poor Europeans who were giving their lives for nothing. He watched them throw their European relatives into the long, dark trenches without ceremony of any kind and without respect. It troubled him, but not as much as when he'd first witnessed the beginning of the war.

He lay on his cot that night, attempting to sleep, when he'd seen the dark-haired girl again. Her hair was the color of wheat on a sunny day, not light, but not quite dark either. She had dainty hands with arms wrapped around his as they strolled through a rose garden. He had no idea where they were, but they were together, and that's all that really mattered.

The girl in his dream was graceful and gave him a reason to live again. The cute smile, the dark, admiring eyes. He awoke thinking of her, admiring her. He'd been alone as long as the war had been going on, but he'd always felt as if he had someone. And now he finally knew who that someone was. She didn't have a name just yet, but she had a face. That meant something to Sammy. He'd always felt her by his side. She'd been beside him all along. Now he would find her. He knew he would all along. He'd spend the rest of his life with the girl he'd loved before this gore had begun.

CHAPTER TEN

"How you likin' yourself now that school has let out for the summer?" Sol raised an eyebrow as Charlie stepped onto the porch and took his seat.

"I love it," Charlie replied. "No more Miss Harmon and all her gas for three whole months."

"Maybe she'll go back up north and spread her nonsense about," Sol leaned forward and shot a stream of tobacco juice into the dirt beyond the porch. "I need to have a serious conversation with ya, boy."

"Sure," Charlie smiled, "you're my best friend. You can talk to me about anything."

"I'm getting old, Charlie," Sol leaned back in his chair. "Hell, I'll be sixty-eight next month. Your pa seems to think I got consumption. It'll probably be the death of me one day. Now, my story is very important to tell, but I don't want you worrying none about my health. You don't have to sit on this porch with me all summer. You need to go rip and romp with other boys your age."

"Uncle Sol," Charlie was shaking his head. "You're gonna be fine. I haven't even heard you cough very much."

"It ain't bad yet," Sol corrected him. "Your pa seems to thank I could live another two, maybe three years with it. Hell, I'm an old man. I done lived my life. I ain't scared of dying, and we're about to complete the story anyhow. But I was serious 'bout you spending time with boys your age."

"I got friends, Uncle Sol," Charlie continued to shake his head in disagreement. "John Woodard spent the night with me last week. I have plenty of time to play. I come here and talk with you 'cause I enjoy it. I'll still come here when the story is finished."

"I just wanted to make sure." Sol seemed to relax.

They sat there in silence a long moment. Sol glanced at Charlie and noticed the boy in deep thought, staring at a spot near his feet.

"What you calculating there, boy?"

"Nothing," Charlie lied. He didn't have the nerve to tell him that he was ciphering how old Sol would have been when the Civil

War had begun. He knew Sol said that Sammy was very young. If Sol was about to be sixty-eight, that meant he was born about 1845, which would make him about seventeen at Shiloh.

Charlie looked up and lied again. "I was just waiting for you to tell me some of the story."

"Hmmph," Sol grunted. His facial expression told Charlie that he hadn't bought that lie. "What's the word on Cuba?"

"Cuba?" Charlie's eyes lit up. He was surprised Sol even kept up with the news. "I heard dad talking to mom about it last night. He said we're preparing to send the marines in to quell the uprising of the blacks."

Sol raised his eyebrows. "Don't you find that entire situation a bit strange?"

"How so?" Charlie asked.

Sol shot another stream of tobacco off the porch and wiped his mouth with the back of his hand. "Well, according to that Miss Harmon, the Civil War occurred because the North wanted to help the blacks."

Charlie was nodding his head, not quite following the old man just yet.

"Now they gonna go invade Cuba because the blacks there are protesting for fair treatment by the non-blacks." Sol watched Charlie's reaction with interest.

"I suppose that doesn't make much sense," Charlie rubbed his head in thought.

"Why sure it does, Charlie." Sol laughed to himself. "United States business owns sixty percent of Cuba's sugar industry. With them damned Yankees, it's all about the money. Don't you see now? They took up for the blacks back during the Civil War because it was profitable for them. They against the blacks now because it is profitable. Charlie, every war ever been fought been fought over one thing, and that thing is money."

Charlie's face lit up as he finally understood what Sol was saying. He thought about having Miss Harmon come up here with him and try to explain her way around what Uncle Sol was telling him here today. After a long moment, Charlie said, "That's why I like to come up here so much. You teach me how to think for myself. A person doesn't get that in school."

"Nope," Sol shook his head. "All you get in school is government propaganda. How the founding fathers never sinned and all that shit."

Charlie was nodding his head in agreement. Sol decided it was time to get off the soap box. He asked, "Now, where we at in the story?"

"We just finished the Battle of Cold Harbor," Charlie replied.

"Did I tell you what that great general named Grant did there following the battle?" Sol asked.

"No, sir," Charlie eased forward in the seat, eager to learn something new.

Sol cleared his throat. "Well, first off, he had about nine thousand men killed or wounded in a little over twenty minutes, and his giant ego wouldn't let him admit he'd made a mistake. He'd messed up and didn't want to admit he'd been beat by old Bobby Lee again. Back in them days, if'n you asked for a flag of truce to gather your wounded, it was considered the same as admitting you'd been defeated. I'll never forget that June as long as I live. It was hotter than hell, probably a hundred and ten in the shade. Well, them Yankees was suffering between the lines all the next day. They was a begging for water and such. Grant's own generals came to him all day, begging for him to ask Lee for a truce so they could tend to those poor men. Grant's pride wouldn't allow him to do that, so he just went to bed. The next day they begged him again, so he tried to pull a trick on Bobby Lee. He asked Lee if he wanted a truce to tend to his wounded. Lee didn't take the bait. He told Grant that he didn't have any wounded between the lines. Grant was so flustered that he went to bed that night, again leaving those men untended in that heat. The next day, after his generals was a begging him to do something, he decided to try and trick Lee another way. He had a captain to write Lee asking for a truce. He had the captain sign the message as commander of the Union army. Lee weren't a buying it. He replied that if Grant wanted a truce, he would allow it, but Grant would have to ask. Grant went to bed that night all stirred up and wounded in his pride. The next

169

day he finally decided to request a truce of Lee, but by then there were only two wounded men left. The rest had died."

"That's truly sad," Charlie was shaking his head in disbelief. "Why would men love a commander like that?"

"They didn't love Grant," Sol was shaking his head. "They loved McClellan because he cared for his men. Grant didn't care about nobody but Grant. You see, Charlie, most of the Union army was made up of foreigners who come over for a better way of life. They would make them citizens as soon as they got off the boats and then put them in a uniform to fight for their new country. Most of them poor bastards didn't have no clue what they was even a fighting for. There were several divisions in the Army of the Potomac that didn't even speak English."

"How'd you learn all this stuff?" Charlie asked.

"I lived during them hard times." Sol thought back to his younger years. "I read all the journals and kept up with things better back then."

Charlie shook his head and waited.

Sol said, "Now, Sammy kept having them strange dreams, and one night things began to come back to him. He knew where his home was and who his family was. So, he went to General Lee himself and asked permission to take his regiment home to recruit."

"Sammy got to meet General Lee?" Charlie's eyes bulged from their sockets.

"Just the one time," Sol said. "Lee heard of Sammy's plight and took one more step to help the young officer. He told Sammy he wanted him to go to Montgomery first, where there were several more small regiments unattached to anyone. Lee wanted him to organize himself a brigade and then go to his home and raise a regiment there if possible. He then sent Sammy into Richmond to see President Davis with a letter."

"He saw President Jefferson Davis also?" Sammy looked as though he were about to pass out.

"Just the once," Sol said again. "He went to the White House of the Confederacy and met Mister and Misses Davis both. He carried the letter, but he didn't have a clue what was inside.

Davis was most polite to the young officer. He insisted that Sammy take supper with his family and asked all sorts of details about what Sammy had seen during the war. I thank he was most impressed because of Sammy being a war hero and where he was from. It was at that dinner that Sammy learned what Lee had placed in that letter. He'd recommended Sammy be promoted to brigadier general in the Confederate army. Davis agreed, and during the meal, he surprised Sammy by referring to him as General Rodes."

"Wow," Charlie's senses were overloaded with the twist this story had taken. "Let me stew on this a second. First he met Lee," he watched Sol nod in agreement, "then he met Davis," again Sol nodded in agreement, "and then he was a general."

"Yep," Sol smiled at Charlie. "He was Brigadier General Samuel Rodes of the Confederate States of America—but not really."

Sol watched Charlie's face go from elation to disappointment. Sol said, "Well, technically he was; it's kind of complicated. You see, the president could make you a general, but congress had to approve it to be official. And that slow-acting body would fool around until the war was over before they voted on it."

"Oh, I see," Charlie nodded. "So he led a brigade and acted like a brigadier?"

"Yep," Sol laughed. "He was a general, just not voted on by congress. It's the same thing. He arrived in Montgomery and spent a week recruiting and organizing the other five regiments before they set out for home."

****

He came home with an incompletely healed bullet wound in his leg, yet the limp was gone. The damaged wrist still gave him trouble when he attempted to grasp things.

Brick, Mississippi, at the time, consisted of two-story brick buildings. The buildings formed a square with an opening on the upper northern side and an opening on the eastern southern side.

From the air, it looked like an L, and an inverted L, placed in close proximity to one another.

Sammy had finally remembered everything from his past. Although, he'd left for Shiloh almost two and a half years earlier, it seemed a lifetime ago. He could still remember the promises he'd left behind when Company I, Sixth Mississippi marched out of town. He couldn't wait to see his parents and, most especially, the girl he'd left behind. There would be a great deal of shock after all these years. He could see them asking him questions already. They'd want to know where he'd been, why he hadn't bothered to write, and how eagerly they had been waiting for his return.

Sammy sent Basil ahead to town with specific instructions. He was to tell them a brigade of Confederate infantry was en route to their town. Every townsperson was to be waiting in parade formation along the streets for the men to arrive. Basil had ridden ahead and left Sammy at the head of his brigade in a state of anxiety. He couldn't wait for Basil to return and tell him his home town was prepared for his coming.

Sammy understood what the Bible had meant now. He'd read in Matthew that you should keep watch, because you do not know the day, nor the hour. He couldn't wait to see what his folks would say when their boy had left a lowly second lieutenant and returned a brigadier general. His mother would be happy to see him, but his father would be so proud that he'd attained such rank in defense of his country.

Ahead, Sammy saw a rider approaching. The dust rose behind the man's horse until he got near enough for Sammy to recognize his best friend, Basil.

Basil galloped up and saluted. His horse was panting from the hard ride he'd just endured. Basil said, "Begging the General's pardon, but I'm out of breath."

"Take your time, Colonel," Sammy smiled. Basil was now the colonel of the 64th Alabama Infantry. Sammy had staff officers to take care of the task that Basil had just done for him, but Sammy trusted no one better than Basil, and he wanted this task to be done right. Sammy asked, "Did you inform the town as I told you?"

172

"I did," Basil replied. "I wasn't able to complete my mission, sir."

Sammy stopped smiling and asked, "Why not, Colonel Manly?"

"Per your orders from two weeks ago," Basil stopped and panted for a moment as he collected his thoughts along with his breath, "my folks are there. Imagine me, a colonel. They didn't believe it, but they're still there as I asked. But, I digress…"

Sammy had prepared this moment to be so perfect, and now Basil was telling him it hadn't gone as planned. Sammy interrupted, "Why is your mission not complete?"

"I had to get the hell out of there before the Tories came." Basil shifted uncomfortably in the saddle.

"Tories?" Sammy asked.

"There's a group of Tories been tormenting the town for the past year or so." Basil cleared his throat and scratched at his thin, bearded chin. "They kill anyone at any time. They're not Confederate or Federal, but they're out for themselves. They're a band of thieving and murdering bastards."

"I see," Sammy said aloud to himself. "We'll take care of the Tories when we get there."

"Sammy," Basil interjected, "I don't want to worry you none, but these people are frightened. They're scared. They've been tormented by this band for over a year."

Sammy smiled. Nothing was going to ruin his mood at the moment of his homecoming. He asked, "Basil, are they gonna be waiting or not?"

"They're gonna be waiting, sir," Basil didn't want to get his commander's hopes too high. "Not sure how proud they're gonna be, though, to see more troops enter their town, Confederate or Federal."

Sammy ignored the last sentence. His mind was made up. He was headed home, and the only thing he could remember was the way he'd left that small Mississippi town. Neither Basil nor anyone else would dampen this moment for the young war hero.

They camped just north of town before entering to a procession the following morning. Basil tried to ease Sammy into

173

what awaited him but had no luck whatsoever. Basil had told his friend that things were not the same as they'd been almost three years ago. Things had changed and so Brick, Mississippi, had changed. The people there were worn out with the war. They wanted it over and were in no mood for heroes, regardless of where they were from. Sammy either didn't listen or refused to believe it.

He was beside himself the next morning. Basil was riding by his side. They were entering the town like conquering heroes. Sammy and Basil in the lead, followed by the 64th Alabama and the other regiments he'd organized at Montgomery, Alabama. Basil was abnormally quiet. As they neared the town, Basil began to show signs of dread. He squirmed in his saddle.

Sammy turned to Basil and asked, "What the hell's wrong with you?"

"Sleepless night, sir," Basil replied without making eye contact. He'd been to Brick, Mississippi. He'd seen the fear in the common citizens' eyes. Basil wasn't sure what those people had been through, but they had a look of distress. He wasn't even able to locate Sammy's parents, nor his girl, and he wasn't even sure they'd be there waiting. That was what was bothering Basil the most. It was the thought that after all this time and all these miles, Sammy would arrive to find he was still alone. It worried him to no end. He wondered what would become of his dear friend if he learned he was still alone after all the tribulations he'd been through.

Sammy looked ahead and saw his hometown appear at the end of a long, dusty road. It was just a mile in the distance. He said, "You better wake up; we're here at last."

"Yep, here we are," Basil agreed.

"And to think we both were from the same state all along," Sammy smiled a broad grin.

"Yes, we were," Basil agreed again.

Sammy looked at Basil and asked, "Your folks are gonna be waiting for us also?"

"That's right," Basil smiled. "Course they already knew I was a colonel, and that's thanks to you."

"You earned it, Basil." Sammy reached out and patted Basil on the back. "You truly earned it. You deserve to be in my position or better."

"I'd have to disagree with you there." Basil held up a hand.

They'd reached the northern entrance to town. Ahead, both men could see the townsfolk gathered along the sides of the street and under the awnings of the buildings. They entered the opening of the two buildings and headed straight ahead along the street. The road carried them to the bottom of the L and turned to the left. A small area called "the commons" was located in the middle of the square. There were a few trees there, and people thronged in the open area.

Sammy led his men down the road past the opening at the south side of town and turned back up the road heading back north. Across the way, to the west, he could see his men still filing southward following his lead.

Along the sides of the street, he saw familiar faces that were expressionless and dour. Worn-out people attempting to survive in a time of strain. Four years of ugly war had enervated these people. It was nothing as Sammy had expected. He'd prepared himself for the cheers of seeing a hero return. Deep down, he understood this wasn't going to happen.

He completed the circle of the town commons and returned to the west side of town. He'd missed her presence the first time but now he saw her. She was standing beneath the porch of old man McGraw's barber shop amidst a group of the town's more prominent citizens. Sammy could tell by her expression that she didn't recognize him. *Hell, he thought, no one here recognizes me.*

He climbed from his horse and passed the reins to an aide. Basil stepped beside his commander and faced the same direction. Sammy walked toward the barbershop with his best friend. Sammy neared the steps with Basil alongside. They approached like two conquering heroes. Sammy stepped onto the board sidewalk, careful to keep his hat pulled low over his eyes. The people began to step back, wondering who he was coming to address. The mayor was on the southern part of town waiting, yet this Confederate officer, wearing the uniform of a brigadier general, seemed to show little interest in the town's leader.

Sammy stood before her and gradually raised his head. His face appeared before her like some old ghost from her distant past, risen from the grave. She stared hard into his eyes. It wasn't the same boy who left her. He'd changed a lot, although he had attempted not to change. He reminded her of an older man. He hadn't aged much, but his expression told her he was mentally older than anyone she'd ever met. The wrinkles around his eyes from the strain told her that she was looking into a totally different person's face. War had changed this boy. It had scarred him physically as well as mentally.

Sammy could hardly believe that he was married to such a beautiful girl. He would spend the rest of his life waking up to that beautiful face every morning until he died. It was almost more than he could bear.

Sammy said, "You look like someone just stepped on your grave."

That was when she fainted at the sight of him. He could have never guessed this morning's sun would change his life forever yet again. Simon Rich, the town physician, was standing behind her and caught her fall. Basil watched the proceedings closely. He watched Sammy and wondered if he now understood the way things had appeared to him.

She regained herself quickly. Several ladies close to her began to cool her face with fans. Something was awfully wrong. Sammy could sense that, but still he waited patiently for her to recover.

When she spoke, it wasn't at all cordial like he'd imagined it would be. The girl appeared elusive. Sammy thought about the words she'd spoken to him when he'd left this place almost three years ago. She'd said, "I will wait for you, however long it takes. I'll wait for you forever. And if you don't return, I'll never marry again."

It looks like forever turned out a little too long, he thought. The girl he'd married before going off to war seemed distressed. Sammy wanted to ask her to come and talk to him, to tell him what they'd done to her.

The night before he'd left with the company, they'd sat under a moonless sky and stared at the stars. She'd told him that she would always love him no matter where he went or what he saw. Sammy's world began to spin. He felt disoriented, and his stomach began to churn. Pain was something he'd learned to deal with. He fought the feeling of despondency, the dejection that all he'd promised to do had actually happened. Yet here he was, cashing in a long-held bond, only to learn it had been revoked.

He watched as Phoebe Cameron attempted to explain, but soon, lost in bewilderment, turned to Simon Rich for help. It was at that moment that Sammy began to truly understand the situation as it was. Simon had no answers but stood speechless, looking from Phoebe to Sammy and back again.

Sammy turned and noticed his first cousin approaching at a run. The boy yelled, "Is that you, Taylor?"

Sammy opened his arms just in time to be swallowed up in the arms of his cousin. They held each other tight for a long minute. His cousin began to sob in his arms and railed against the way the town had been treated since the war had begun. Sammy listened to him as he sobbed about the way the Tories had treated everyone here, how they had become the punishment of Lincoln and ripped their world apart.

Sammy said nothing. He continued to stare at Phoebe, held close in Simon Rich's arms. He wasn't really listening to his cousin, not until he heard him say something that cut him to his very soul. His cousin said, "Your parents would have been proud of you."

Sammy pushed his cousin away and asked, "What did you just say?"

"I said," his cousin began to repeat and then stopped in mid-sentence. "I'm sorry, Taylor."

"Sorry, Taylor?" Sammy asked. Sorry wasn't going to cut it.

He wanted to know what his cousin was saying just now.

****

177

Once people began to recognize Sammy, he began to get mobbed by old acquaintances. Friends and relatives saw the commotion across the square and moved that way to see their long-lost son. It was a time for great celebration for the townspeople but a bitter home coming for the boy born Taylor Cameron. Between hugs and hearty handshakes, Taylor's cousin Silas began to recount the horrid details of what had happened since he'd been gone.

Several people would interrupt to ask why Taylor had not even bothered to write home. Taylor patiently explained what he'd been through to each inquiry. Silas would pause and continue the story. When they'd gone across that field at Shiloh, Company I had thirty men. When the fighting was over, there were only five left unwounded.

"We thought you was dead," Silas was shaking his head. "Do you remember why I wasn't wounded or killed in that battle?"

"The events of that day are still a little vague to me," Taylor replied.

Silas was nodding and smiling. "Cause you forced me to stay back holding Captain Campbell's horse. You wouldn't let me go with ya'll."

"He's good at that sort of thing," Basil added from behind Taylor.

Taylor stepped back and motioned Basil forward. "This is Colonel Basil Manly, commander of the 64th Alabama Infantry Regiment—and my best friend," he added. "We've been through hell together."

"Yep, we have," Basil smiled. "Especially in Colonel Robert McMillan's tent at Fredericksburg in January of sixty-three."

Taylor looked hard at Basil. The man definitely knew how to cheer him up. Taylor, or Sammy as Basil knew him, would only feign being in a good mood. He refused to let all these people see him so despondent when they were so proud to see him come home at last.

Taylor nodded toward McGraw's barbershop and pushed Basil and Silas toward the door. He excused himself from the crowd for a few moments. As he began to close the door, he realized his entire brigade was standing at attention. He shouted for the men to stack arms and find some shade.

"Just look at you," Silas said with all the pride he could muster. "You left here a junior lieutenant and returned a general officer just like you promised."

Taylor ignored the comment. He asked sternly. "What happened to Momma?"

Silas lowered his head and stared at the floor. "Taylor, she mourned herself to death. She just couldn't live with the fact that her only son marched off to die at the age of seventeen. She cried ever day for what remained of her life. She died six months to the day after we marched away."

Taylor fought the urge to cry. He looked at the floor momentarily and then asked, "And Dad?"

"He was shot by the Tories for a five dollar gold piece he had in his pocket."

Taylor said nothing for a long moment. He turned and looked out the window at the crowd beyond peering inside at him. Phoebe was sitting on a bench resting her head on Simon Rich's shoulder. Everyone else was smiling and slapping each other on the back at his return. They were especially proud of the rank he had attained fighting in Robert E. Lee's army in Virginia.

Taylor turned back to Silas and asked, "Who are these Tories?"

"They not really Tories," Silas replied. "They're just a bunch of renegades that have taken over because of all the lawlessness this war has created."

Taylor realized Silas was stalling. He asked, "Who are they?"

"Reuben Morton is the leader," Silas finally blurted out. "He's the one that shot your pa. There are about twenty of them."

"Reuben Morton?" Taylor asked out loud. He saw Silas nodding in agreement. "He was in the company at Shiloh. What is he doing out of the army?"

"There were just five of us survived that battle without injury—Reuben, Israel Thomas, Clark Johnson, Jasper Williams, and myself." Silas took a deep breath. "We all just came home after Shiloh. Captain Campbell was killed, and we thought you was killed. We didn't have no officers, so when we reached Corinth, we just kept walking right on home."

"I see," Taylor thought back to all those days he was out searching for someone in Corinth that would recognize him. It all made sense now. "Do you have any way of getting in contact with Reuben and his gang?"

"Sure do," Silas smiled. "Reuben's father, Caleb, is over in Jackson on business with the Yanks. He's supposed to be home around dark this afternoon. He keeps his boy informed of everything happening around here. Reuben hides in the mountains until he thinks there is something worth raiding in town. There's a couple different towns he raids."

Taylor smiled. "That's perfect. Follow me."

The three men walked out the door and back into the crowd. Taylor stepped out into the sun so everyone could see him. He said, "I have an announcement to make."

Everyone quieted down to listen.

"Are you people tired of these Tories tormenting you?" He shouted. He listened to the people yell in acknowledgement. Taylor waved his hands signaling everyone to quiet down. "I have a brigade of eight hundred infantry here to protect you, but we can't be expected to stay here away from the army. Here is all I ask of you. Stay indoors off the streets until tomorrow afternoon, and I will rid you of this pestilence."

The crowd was roaring in approval. They'd been putting up with Reuben Morton for too long now. The man had returned, and finding there was no one in town who could govern him, he turned to robbery, pillage, and murder. His gang had even raped several girls.

Taylor then asked the townspeople to put up his infantrymen for the night to keep them out of sight when Caleb Morton returned from his trip. Taylor turned back to Silas and Basil. He said to Silas, "Now, here's what I want to do. When Morton gets back tonight, I want you to tell him there are two Confederate officers in town looking for a place to hide a large sum of Confederate gold. If he pries, tell him they are Samuel Rodes and Basil Manly. Tell him

180

they are alone with a wagon full of gold that they plan to bring into town at noon tomorrow."

"Oh, that'll bring Reuben and his gang in here like flies after shit," Silas said as he reached over and patted Basil on the shoulder. "You're good cousin, very good."

"Basil, let's you and I get our men hid for the night," Taylor said. "We got a big day tomorrow. Silas, we'll stay with you tonight. I need to know if he took the bait or not."

"You're both welcome," Silas said, smiling from ear to ear, "and I can guarantee the bait will be swallowed hook, line, and sinker. What about Phoebe?"

"I don't know," Taylor rubbed his forehead and stared toward the floor. "Looks like she's moved on. I'm gonna have to take a couple days to figure things out."

"I'm Sorry, Taylor," Silas said. "Hell, she married him after your mother died. No one would have guessed in a million years you were still alive. Try not to feel hard toward her."

"I don't feel hard toward her at all." Taylor turned and peered through the window at the dark-haired wife that was technically still married to him, and another man at the same time. "I feel betrayed."

"But Taylor—" Silas's face grew stern. He hated to be the one to deliver this information, but it appeared he was the only one who had the heart. He took a deep breath and swallowed. "Taylor, she needed someone to help her care for your son."

Taylor looked up with a start. His face drained to white. He felt it coming before it actually happened. His knees buckled and he crashed to the floor. Basil and Silas both grabbed for him, catching him just before his head struck the hardwood flooring.

****

Basil recognized Sammy's mood and gave him plenty of room. The shocking experience of learning his family had either died, been murdered, or just up and remarried was a lot for his best friend to have to deal with in one day. Most shocking of all was to learn he had a son that he'd never seen. Basil began to cipher in his mind the boy's age.

181

Sammy had left for Shiloh in late March two years and five months ago. That meant his son was almost two now. Almost two and Sammy had never laid eyes on him, hadn't even known he existed. Basil couldn't imagine the turmoil his best friend was going through at the moment. He refused to put himself in Sammy's place because he didn't know that he could deal with the misery of it.

It was almost ten when Silas finally returned from his mission. He burst through the door and announced, "The bait has been taken, cousin. Ole man Morton was late getting back."

"You sure he bought it?" Taylor asked.

"Oh yeah," Silas smiled. "We had it all worked out before he arrived. He always stops at Lucas Henry's Tavern when he gets back into town for a shot of whiskey. We had everyone in the place worked up over the two Confederate officers in town with a wagon load of Jeff Davis's gold. We all played off like we weren't paying him any attention, but you should have seen his eyes light up. He killed that glass of whiskey and was gone before his seat got warm."

"Very well," Taylor replied. "Now I want you to sit down here, and let's go over the plan. I want to get this right."

Basil and Silas sat down at the kitchen table with Taylor. Taylor said, "The layout of this town makes a perfect trap. Silas, do you have any idea which entrance he'll come through?"

"South side every time." Silas said firmly. "His damned bunch have a hideout in Whippoorwill Hollow. Ole man Morton was headed that way when he left. They'll come roaring in here about noon tomorrow looking for two Confederate officers with a wagon load of gold."

"They're gonna find two officers here," Basil said, "me and Sammy—I mean Taylor. Damn, it's gonna take a while to get to know you by that name."

"This is gonna be beautiful," Taylor began to sketch what he intended to accomplish with his two best friends.

Taylor tried to get some rest, but sleep refused him. He exited Silas's house and paced on the front porch. He felt as if his life was over now before it had really even begun. During the entire war, his life would see moments of great elation and then moments of deep despair. Just when he thought everything was coming together for him, he was forced to deal with the reality of home.

Thoughts raced through his mind. What would he do from here on out? At his weakest moment, he could only think of returning to Corinth or Richmond to see if he could get Mary or Lillian to reconsider him. Yet he had a son, and that complicated everything. He had a wife also, but he wasn't sure if she loved him anymore. *She is in bed with another man at this very moment, he thought. That doesn't sound like love.* Taylor figured he had two options here. After dealing with the Tories, he would force her to make a decision. She was legally still his wife. They had a son together. Why would she not want him back? Failing at that, he would return to the war. War felt like his home now anyhow. He was still in the army and only here on recruiting leave.

War was something he'd shamelessly come to love. He'd learned to live by the feud. Without war, he was nothing. Maybe he'd become a ghoul after all, but war had given him a sense of being. In war he felt indispensable. It was true he'd endured agonizing wounds and been to the lowest depths of hell, but that pain could never compare to the pain he was dealing with today.

The three had risen early the next morning to be sure everything was in place for the trap. By eleven, the ambuscade had been set. Now the only thing needed was the Tories. Basil and Taylor waited inside Lucas Henry's Tavern. Basil decided a shot would do them both good and demanded his best friend and his cousin join him.

Taylor was intent, all absorbed in everything going correctly with the Tories. He didn't want a single one of them to escape. The entire afternoon had been planned out to the minutest detail. He stared at the large oak tree in the center of town. That large, grassy, shaded area had served as the town picnic site for years. He had other plans for it this afternoon.

It was a quarter till noon when twenty-one hard-riding armed guerrillas came charging through the south entrance. Several fired their pistols into the air. Leading the group was Reuben Morton. Taylor continued sitting at the table watching as the trap was closed. He'd had barrels and wagons placed across the north entrance. There was no way out of there. He sat where he could see his men run wagons across the south entrance. Those twenty-one treacherous fiends were going nowhere now.

Reuben and his men were so intent on getting that wagon of gold that they didn't notice the wagons rolling across their only exit. They continued to the northern buildings and made the turn, stopping in front of the tavern.

Reuben, still sitting on his horse, began to yell. "Where are those damned Confederate officers?"

As instructed, no one replied. Reuben looked around and noticed the streets were eerily deserted. He yelled again, "I'll give ya'll just thirty seconds to deliver those two assholes to me or I'm gonna turn my men loose on your town. We'll burn this place to the ground!"

Taylor stood and motioned his head toward the door. "He wants us, Basil. Let's give him what he wants."

Taylor stepped through the door first, followed closely by Basil. Taylor kept his hat low over his eyes to prevent Reuben from recognizing him. Taylor asked, "What ya'll want with us?"

"Where's the gold?" Reuben demanded.

"What gold?" Taylor asked.

Reuben was losing patience with this obviously elitist bastard. He raised his arm and leveled the pistol at Taylor's chest. "Mister, you got just ten seconds to give me that wagon full of gold before I make it where we can see daylight all the way through you."

"Gentlemen!" Taylor shouted. "He wants the gold! Let's show it to him!"

At that, every window in town flew open, and the barrels of seven hundred infantry rifles were extended. There was no way twenty-one men could survive once they all opened fire.

The look on Reuben's face was priceless. He turned in the saddle and looked around town. That was when he noticed the exits were blocked. Sammy removed his hat and walked closer toward Reuben's horse.

184

Reuben's eyes seemed to bulge from their sockets. He looked as if he'd seen a ghost from his distant past. He smiled and said, "Oh, it's you, Taylor. I'm glad to see you're well."

Taylor's voice was low, almost a growl. He said, "Now throw them weapons on the ground before I make ya'll look like sifters."

Reuben tossed his pistol and motioned for his gang to do the same. Taylor turned to Basil and ordered, "Take these prisoners under arms. We're gonna have us a court martial trial."

"Yes, sir," Basil replied and ordered several soldiers to secure the prisoners.

Taylor walked back toward the door to the tavern and met Silas walking out. He said, "Silas, I want you to go organize the witnesses either for or against these men. I'm gonna rule as the judge in this trial. If these men have someone they want to represent them, they better find them within the next hour. I want you to see to it."

"Right," Silas replied and turned up the street.

"One more thing, Cuz," Taylor added. Silas stopped and turned. "You're no longer a civilian. You're a captain on my staff. Now salute before you go."

Silas noticed Taylor smiling and did his best to give a crisp salute before going on about his assignment.

It was almost incomprehensible for the townspeople. Taylor had disarmed all twenty-one of the outlaws and within thirty minutes was in the process of trying them in a military court. Reuben Morton had asked the town's leading citizen to defend the men in this case. That man was a man who could not refuse men whose lives were on the line. He was the town doctor, Simon Rich.

Taylor thought about how ironic it was for Reuben to ask the man who'd stolen the judge's wife to represent him. It seemed as if he was daring the judge to sentence him to death. He never realized that it was his father, Caleb Morton, who'd hired the good doctor. It was the only hope the old man had for his wayward son.

Taylor didn't take the time to ask each man how he pled, but simply looked at Doctor Rich and asked, "How do your clients plead?"

185

Simon Rich paused a long moment. He'd been instructed to say *not guilty*, yet he didn't know what to add in addressing the judge. He refused to call his wife's "husband" by any honorable name. *Your honor* was definitely out of the question, and *General* would place his social status above the good doctor's. After a long, awkward pause, he said, "Not guilty, and furthermore, I'd like to object to a military court trying these men. It's an illegal act. These men aren't in the military."

"I beg to differ, sir," Taylor held up his index finger. "Reuben Morton signed up for three years in the Confederate service in March of 1862. Is he acting under any orders or is he a present member of the Confederate Army?"

Simon Rich lowered his head. The judge of this court was asking for an answer, yet he knew he would lose his case as soon as he replied. He decided to try a different tact. "Sir, I understand. But things have become even more complicated with your return."

"What in the hell does my return have to do with his lawlessness?" Taylor sat at a desk that Silas had placed in the town commons.

All the local citizens gasped at Taylor's use of his language. A true Southern gentleman would never curse in public, especially in front of the ladies.

Yet, Taylor was angry. He'd been risking his life for the innocent civilians of the Confederacy. He was at the front, fighting bravely, while these cowardice people had been murdering and pillaging because they were too scared or lazy to fight. He no longer cared what people thought of him.

Simon Rich said, "Not guilty."

"Very well," Taylor nodded at Basil. "Prosecutor, you may call your first witness."

Basil stood and called his first witness. The list was long, but there wasn't a soul in the crowd who would testify for the defendants when the prosecution rested. Men had testified to the thievery. Women had testified to the depredations they'd been subjected to. There were even two witnesses to the murder of Taylor's father.

186

When Basil rested his case an hour and a half after the trial had begun, Taylor turned to Doctor Rich and said, "Call your first witness."

Simon stood and shifted nervously from one foot to another. He and Reuben had been whispering throughout the trial. Simon said, "I have no witnesses to call."

Taylor asked, "So you're telling me that the defense rests."

"No, sir," Simon lowered his head. "My client wishes to take the stand himself against my wishes. But I fear he must because we haven't had time to find witnesses for the defense due to the speed of this trial. I must object and ask for an extension for me to locate potential witnesses."

"Denied," Taylor responded quickly. "You mean to tell me the prosecution found forty-three witnesses in one hour, and the defense can't locate a single witness in the same amount of time? Do you know what that tells me?"

"No," Simon replied. "I have no idea."

Taylor didn't like Simon's tone of voice but decided to let it pass. "It tells me you're attempting to buy these murderous outlaws some time, and it's not going to happen. Now, call your witness or rest."

Simon turned and motioned for Reuben to take the stand. Reuben attempted to look remorseful. He took the stand and placed his hand on the Bible as Basil took his oath.

Simon asked, "Reuben Morton, is there something you'd like to say to this court?"

"Yes," Reuben raised his head. "I consider myself a friend of the judge of this court. I know I'm not a perfect man. I'm innocent of killing his father out of cold blood. It was an accident. I didn't mean for it to happen the way it did. I grew up with most of you, ate dinner as a kid at your homes. I beg you to not allow this travesty to happen. I have members of my gang who are no more than fifteen years old. I do sincerely regret my actions. I throw myself at the mercy of this court and especially my young friends who are too young to be tried in a court of law."

Simon cleared his throat. "Is that all, Reuben?"

"That's all," Reuben lowered his head.

Taylor didn't hesitate. He turned to Basil and asked, "Do you have any questions for this witness?"

"No, sir," Basil replied.

"You may return to your seat," Taylor said to Reuben. Reuben, with head lowered, slowly returned to his seat beside Simon.

"I've heard enough to make a ruling," Taylor said to everyone present. "I find these men guilty of numerous crimes against the Confederacy, their homes, and even their own people. I sentence each of them to death."

There was a gasp that went up from most of the citizens. It was the moment they'd all been waiting two long years for, but they hadn't realized how it would make them feel when this moment came. It was true that most of these men deserved to die, but it was a total different thing when they'd testified against these men and felt somewhat responsible. It was just the beginning of their sorrows. Taylor Cameron was about to announce another shocking sentence.

Taylor ordered Reuben Morton to stand before his desk for sentence to be passed. He noticed the man was standing there on trembling knees. He said, "These men preying on the innocent and loyal citizens of this nation deserve swift and just punishment. I hereby order that they be hanged in not less than one hour from this very minute. Reuben Morton, you should order your men to prepare to meet their maker immediately."

Taylor stood and left his desk. Basil and Silas followed close behind. Other members of the brigade moved forward to take the prisoners to the city jail until time for the hanging.

Taylor walked back inside the tavern and ordered three rounds of whiskey for him and his friends. Basil killed his immediately. Silas looked at his cousin in wonder. He asked, "Are you really hanging all them boys?"

"Damned right I am," Taylor replied. "If it had been you with five dollars' worth of gold in your pocket, they would have shot you down like a mangy dog."

"True," Silas lowered his head. Both men had grown up with some of these boys. They'd gone to school and fished in the same streams together. True, some of those men deserved to die, but some were just too young. He asked, "Even the kids?"

"Kids my ass, Silas," Taylor replied. "You telling me they're brave enough to terrorize innocent people but too young to fight for their country or hang for their crimes?"

"I suppose not," Silas agreed. He hadn't thought of it that way.

There was a knock at the door. Taylor wondered what kind of idiot would knock on a tavern door without just entering. He turned to see a young, beautiful girl peering in at him. It was Phoebe Cameron. She asked, "Taylor, can I speak to you alone?"

Taylor paused. His eyes betrayed the love he still had for her. He said, "Please come in."

Basil, Silas, and Lucas Henry exited behind her. Taylor waited.

She walked near and said, "We need to talk."

"We do?" Taylor asked a little more sarcastic than he'd meant.

"Yes," her eyes appeared beseeching. "What happened to that innocent boy that left me almost three years ago?"

"He's dead," Taylor replied. "Killed not from warfare but from broken promises."

"What was I to do?" she asked.

Taylor shook his head. "At least wait until the war was over to see if I'd come back."

"That's not fair," she objected. "I didn't receive a single letter from you for six months. Silas even told me he saw you shot in the head. How'd you live through that?"

"I was cared for by a girl that didn't even love me." He turned and poured himself another shot of whiskey.

Phoebe decided to change the subject. "You never drank before you left."

"I never drank until I returned," Taylor lied. He didn't feel like explaining the one time he'd drank in Fredericksburg or he would have to add that he was drinking while she was fooling around with someone besides her husband.

"I'm sorry," Phoebe lowered her head. "We have a son together."

"I know," Taylor replied.

Phoebe looked shocked. "How'd you know?"

"Silas had to tell me," Taylor uncorked the bottle and poured himself another stiff shot. "Hell, no one else in this town had the courage to do it."

She turned and stared out the window. "Are you really going to hang those men?"

"I am," Taylor replied.

She began to slowly shake her head. "How can you do that?"

Taylor fought to control his temper. "Do you remember my father?"

"Of course." She slowly turned to look into his eyes. What she saw frightened her. This wasn't the innocent boy that had left her for a glorious war. Before her stood a completely different person. War had aged him mentally. She felt as if she were the same girl that had watched him leave, but he wasn't the same boy. That boy had died at Shiloh, and some demon had possessed his body there. Phoebe tried to understand this thing he'd become; she tried to understand his dispassion. How callus he'd become toward human life.

In Taylor's mind, he was about to rid the world of an ugly blight. Those men didn't deserve to share the same world, same life, with men like the faithful soldiers he'd been leading these bitter years. He couldn't understand why she would beg for the lives of these despicable individuals.

Deep down, Phoebe understood that those days of innocence—when they'd first met and married—were gone. They'd been erased by a long and bitter war that wasn't quite over with.

She decided to try another tactic. "Taylor, you can't do this thing. You don't have any idea what's gone on here while you've been gone. It would be hypocrisy."

"Don't speak to me like I haven't seen war. I've seen the ugliest things men could ever do to one another, and I'm not through yet." Taylor killed the shot and began to refill the glass. He appeared pompous and arrogant. He was nothing like the person she'd been in love with, and that hurt her.

"Taylor," she lowered her head and began to speak in a low voice. "I've heard all I want to hear about war. It's been one ugly stain on our nation's history, and it's over nothing but money."

Taylor corked the bottle and thought about taking another shot. The room was already beginning to feel stuffy. One more shot and he might not be conscious for the hanging he planned to enjoy.

Phoebe walked over and forced herself into his arms. "Can you imagine how I felt when they told me you were dead? A month afterward I learn I'm pregnant with your child. Half of my heart's been torn away, never to return. I have so much doubtfulness over what I've done, whether wrong or right. I didn't know which way to turn. You know me; you married me because of my piousness. Can you ever forgive me?"

Taylor lifted the glass and stared into the whiskey that was swirling in the glass before his face. There was no sense in continuing the conversation. The girl would never understand the pain she'd caused him. He'd done an outstanding job of hiding his tears. He'd never been referred to as haughty, but it was a trait he was obtaining from the past few years of experience. He killed the shot and placed the glass on the bar.

There was no possible way for him to express how he truly felt about her remarrying in his absence. No matter how one looked at it, he had been betrayed. He'd been betrayed by the woman he'd been off fighting for. He may have appeared ostentatious, but the truth was that he was hiding his tears. He felt betrayed just like Jesus, when a man denies that He died for his sins. He could never understand why she refused to see this. She only seemed to worry about a group of criminals that deserved to die.

To Phoebe, he emerged as a callous man. He didn't seem to regret what he was about to do here, and he didn't appear to lament the many men he'd led to their deaths in this heinous war.

Taylor turned and stared at the once-innocent girl he'd married, and demanded, "I want to see my son."

191

Phoebe simply nodded in agreement. She said, "Tonight, after this nonsense is over. Is there anything I can say or do that will spare these men's lives?"

"No," Taylor replied

"I'll come back to you," she sobbed into her hands, "if you will spare the lives of these boys. Murder is wrong either way you look at it."

"Let me get this straight," Taylor's eyes grew narrow. "You'll come back to your husband that you're still married to if I spare evil men's lives?"

"Yes," Phoebe replied. She didn't know what else to say.

Taylor looked hard at the girl with her face buried in her hands. As she lifted her face and peered at him, he said, "Get out of my sight."

She peered at the husband that she'd watched leave this town in such a glee. She looked into his eyes, but they were far different than the boy's eyes that had left her. His eyes were empty now, nothing like what she'd known before. This boy had died a thousand times, and there was no bringing him back to the world of innocence.

She turned to leave but paused at the door. Her head was lowered in sadness. She said, "I made Simon leave the house as soon as I learned you were alive. I'm not sure where we go from here. He's staying at his parents' house for the time being."

With that announcement, she opened the door and departed in tears. Taylor had thought Simon had sent her here to beg for the condemned men's lives. He turned and slammed the shot glass against the wall. Deep down, he felt he should be enjoying this execution, but she'd managed to ruin the moment for him.

Back in front of the tall oak tree, Taylor gave Reuben the opportunity to express any last words he may have. Reuben dropped to his knees and begged for mercy. Phoebe watched Taylor's every expression for signs of compassion, but all she saw was the same blank look as before.

Once Reuben had finished, Taylor said, "Reuben, you're a villain, and I'm the punishment of God. If you hadn't committed all these sins, God would not have sent a punishment like me upon you. Now, sentence will be carried out on you and each of your men."

Phoebe buried her face in a handkerchief. War had changed her innocent boy. She finally understood that he didn't consider war to be a bad place like most people did. War was his home now. It was morality to him. It was his sanity, and it seemed to rule him.

Taylor looked at Basil and said, "Hang the miscreant."

She couldn't believe that he hadn't seen enough death and suffering in this war already. It was as if the world had completely revised itself. War had begun to feed on itself and would never stop until every human was deceased. Phoebe understood that a man like Taylor would never change. He'd been through too much, seen more than a man should see in a lifetime in two short years, and he was too far gone to fix. There must be a settling of accounts, and Taylor was just beginning to settle his here today. One man had killed his father, and now twenty-one men must die for that one misdeed. She began to wonder who the villain was here. It appeared from here on out, Taylor could never kill enough to ever be happy again. The only place to make Taylor happy would be a cold, dank grave.

She realized there were a lot of malicious men in this world that didn't deserve to live, but Taylor made it appear that the true heroes may not deserve to live either. He'd fought for his people, and life had abused him for that. The boy had taken umbrage to the way she'd defended the felon before him. He would take no pity on his soul, and he'd probably pray that God not take any pity on him either.

In Taylor's mind, he was standing by his convictions. The man must hang and so must all his gang. She could never change his mind because he understood he was right.

Phoebe began to believe this was all her fault. She was shocked at the state in which he had returned to her world compared to his innocence when he had left. He would take out his hatred for what she'd done on these poor men. She began to

193

wonder how she could ever sleep another night with a clear conscience.

Reuben would be the first to hang. He was placed on the horse with a noose tied around his neck. The condemned man suddenly wanted Taylor to grant him some last words, but he soon realized he would never speak again. He asked Doctor Rich, "Have I no last words?"

Doctor Rich protested to Taylor. Taylor said, "There is nothing this man has to say that anyone here would want to hear."

Reuben began to grow hostile. He became belligerent at the denial of his last request. He screamed vituperations at Taylor as they began to tie the noose about his neck. He stopped in mid-sentence as he noticed a small sneer appear at the corners of Taylor's lips. He understood that his old friend was actually relishing this moment. There was nothing left he could do to pain the man, nothing left to do but die.

After the hanging was complete, Taylor arose from behind the desk near the tree and announced, "He has paid his debts to man. It is God's will to decide if he is even with the world for his many sins. Now, bury these wicked bastards in an unmarked grave and let's forget about them."

After the hanging, several people thanked him for the way he'd handled these evil men, but most returned home in exasperation at the way the war had ruined their little town.

****

Taylor decided to camp in the field with his men. A messenger arrived from Silas telling him the people were over their shock of the day's events and were throwing him a welcome home feast. He should be in town at six.

He wasn't in the mood for any celebration feast but felt he should go there for the sake of appearance. Besides, the people had made it a point of feeding his brigade, and he appreciated that more than anything they could do for him.

He thought back to his days in school. He'd always been nervous, always the runt and overlooked by everyone else. Taylor

194

had been a shy boy. He could never speak in front of a group of people. Now he was returning home a hero, and nothing was as he'd imagined.

At his angriest, he felt he deserved better than the cards had dealt him, but he understood that deserving had nothing to do with it. He'd seen many a good men go under the dirt back in Virginia, Pennsylvania, Maryland, and Georgia. Those men deserved better than they got. Life owes a man nothing. Taylor realized that he was wise beyond his years because of this long, bitter war.

He'd just turned twenty a month ago but felt as if he'd lived a lifetime. He stepped from his tent and walked to Basil's tent not far away. Basil was visiting with his family but immediately jumped from his camp stool to see what his best friend needed.

"We got a dinner invitation tonight," Taylor mumbled. "I want your family to come along also."

"Yes, sir," Basil gave a sloppy salute and a toothy grin.

By the time dinner was over, the sun had slipped below the horizon. Family and friends had built a large fire. Silas stood in front of everyone and said, "Now, everyone quiet down, and let's see if we can get Taylor to regale us with some war stories."

The entire crowd hushed, and all eyes fell on Taylor. He thought a long moment and supposed it was only expected they'd want to know where he'd gone and what he'd seen.

Taylor said, "We died those bitter years. We died without pause—killed and died—and for what?"

He looked out at the dejected faces and wished there was something more he could add. He had the realization that these people couldn't understand what he was talking about because they'd never witnessed the horrible things he'd lived through.

Silas wasn't going to be dejected this easily. He asked, "Did you see some battles?"

"I've been in the eye of the storm," Taylor replied.

Basil decided to save his best friend and commander. "He's just being modest. Taylor is a renowned hero in the Army of Northern Virginia. He's met Robert E. Lee and President Davis himself. He led his men with the utmost dexterity. In the battle

195

report for the Battle of Spotsylvania, Robert E. Lee even called him gallant because of how unflinching he was in the face of danger."

People began to smile, and Taylor noticed them hanging on Basil's every word. He lowered his head, and although Basil wasn't lying, the words made him feel disgraced. Why should he be praised any more than his men that were camped on the edge of town?

Basil was saying, "To be a great leader, a man must first believe in himself. This man has proven he's a great leader on many battlefields."

That was when Taylor noticed Phoebe sitting just beyond the bonfire. She was listening to Basil intently. It was obvious she found it hard to believe that the timid young boy who'd left her for war had returned a hero, praised by none other than Robert E. Lee. She sat in awe at the thought.

She noticed a soldier approaching Taylor with stripes on his coat sleeves. The man gave a crisp salute and said, "General, the men are all bedded down for the night. Pickets are posted around the camp."

"Very well, Sergeant Major," Taylor said.

The Sergeant Major asked, "Will you be needing anything else from me tonight, sir?"

"Yes," Taylor replied. "You've been working too hard, Robert. I need you to fix yourself a plate of this fine home cooking, get yourself a drink, and sit with us a spell."

"Thank you, sir," the sergeant major nodded and moved toward the large table covered with food.

It impressed Phoebe the way Taylor worried over each of his men. War may have hardened him, but he definitely had a soft spot for those men he was responsible for. She turned her attention back to Basil, who was busy telling the story of the first time he'd met Taylor on the battlefield of Sharpsburg, or Antietam as it was known to the Yankees.

Taylor sat quietly as Basil told everyone there everything they'd been through together. After two hours of Basil turning war into a glorious adventure with a brave commander, Taylor watched his best friend finally exhaust himself.

196

Basil sat down beside the man he'd just spent two hours building into the town's greatest hero. He was proud of what he'd accomplished, although he'd left out the worst parts, the parts men tend to try and forget.

Silas stood before the crowd, turned to Taylor, and asked, "Tell us about your wounds, Cousin."

Taylor decided that he may as well play along. Whether he was in the mood or not, these people were genuinely interested in what he'd been through. "I was shot in the head at Shiloh and forgot everything until a couple of months ago. I didn't even know my own name or where I was from. I healed up pretty well from that wound except for the ever-plaguing headaches. I got a flesh wound in the arm at Gettysburg and had a bullet pass all the way through my right leg. I still limp some from that one."

"Where were you at Gettysburg?" Silas asked.

"Fought on the first day and got both wounds in Pickett's Charge," Taylor replied. He listened to the people whispering to each other over the fact that he'd been in that famous charge. Taylor continued, "I didn't so much as receive a scratch at Chickamauga, but Spotsylvania was bad. I had just run a Federal soldier through with my sword, when another Yankee swung his musket overhead and down on my wrist. Broke the thing in several places. It still gives me trouble because I wouldn't let the doctors amputate."

"He has a thing about amputation," Basil broke into laughter. "He pulled his army Colt on the surgeon at Gettysburg when he said he was gonna take off the leg."

Everyone found that part amusing. An older man sitting near Phoebe said, "Can't say as I blame him."

Basil burst into the story about Colonel McMillan at Fredericksburg and the snowball fight. Taylor stood and said, "I'm sure not gonna sit and listen to this story. I need some rest, but don't let me spoil the party."

Basil continued his story as Taylor moved away from the fire. A voice behind him stopped him cold. He turned, and Phoebe was just a foot from his face. She said, "I'll bring Tom to your tent in a little while. Make sure your guards don't shoot me."

Taylor almost asked who Tom was, but he suddenly realized that was the name she'd given their son. He bowed slightly and said, "I'll let them know you're coming."

She arrived a quarter after nine with a sleeping little boy in her arms. Taylor had her lay the young child on his cot. He could see himself in the face of the little boy. He stared at the face a long time without saying a word. Phoebe noticed tears streaming down his cheeks. He continued to watch the small chest rising and falling with each breath. Before him lay something that was actually a part of him, made from him.

"I can't look at him without thinking of you," Phoebe said.

They both sat on camp stools and talked as Taylor stared at his son. He said, "It was all a lie."

"A lie?" she asked.

"All that glorious war-talk." Taylor turned and looked into Phoebe's eyes for the first time. "Let me tell you the truth of a battlefield. Dead men scattered about. The wounded swearing, crying, and begging for their mothers. I've had men who knew they were dying beg me to care for their children. The truth is those were my men. I led them to their deaths. They belonged to me, and I to them. Death can't separate us. I'll live with their memories forever."

"It's sad, Taylor," Phoebe reached out and held his hand. "You don't think time can erase all that?"

"No," he replied. "I can smell the smoke and hear the roar now. I can feel the mud of Spotsylvania and taste the blood of Gettysburg. It is easy to dream of glorious war while in a comfortable home, but seeing war is far different. Men who have seen war never stop seeing it. Late at night, while I'm attempting to sleep, I can actually hear the dreadful screams of the wounded."

"You've got a lot on your conscience, and you'll die if you don't rid yourself of that guilt." Phoebe began to rub the back of his hand.

"I was dead the moment I left you." Taylor tried to control the tears, but there was no denying them. "Ordering men to kill is no different than doing the killing yourself. Now I've become so accustomed to killing, I may have become Death itself. I've had

198

nightmares since I've been in battle, and the saddest part is that the dreams in which I'm dying are the best ones of all."

"Taylor," she was tiring of him sounding so defeated, so melancholy, "what will you do when this war is over?"

He simply shook his head. To be truthful, he had no idea what he would do.

She said, "You can go back to the university you quit. There will be no jobs because we're gonna lose this war, and you know that."

He shook his head again. "I can't lose this war."

"You can't?" she fought the urge to laugh. The way he made it sound, this war was to be decided by him and him alone.

"I refuse to lose," Taylor turned toward the doorway of the tent and noticed it gently moving in the night air. He refused to admit that the war could be lost. "After all those harsh battles I've been through and all those men I've watched die, I'd rather die than see us lose this war."

He turned to see her with tears coursing down her cheeks. She said, "Why do you defend such an unholy war. It's been nothing but a blight on our nation's history. I hate warfare, and don't care if we lose."

"How can you say that after all the men who have given their lives for your freedom?" Taylor gave her a malevolent stare. He paused, regretting his tone of voice. He asked, "What would you have me to do?"

"Quit this war." She moved close to him, staring into his eyes just inches from his face. "Just walk away. You have a son now."

Taylor wiped at the tears coursing down his cheeks. He asked, "Do I have a wife also?"

Phoebe turned and returned to the camp stool beside Taylor's cot. "I don't know what to say, Taylor. A part of me still wants you. You're the father of my child. Another part of me thinks you're something totally different from the innocent boy who left me at the beginning of the war."

"I am something else," Taylor moved toward the tent flap and eased it open, peering into the night. "Maybe we don't need anything or anyone. Have you thought about that?"

"What are you saying?" Phoebe asked.

"Maybe we can just leave this place and forget the war, forget it all." Taylor turned to his wife and looked at her beseechingly. This was something he was sure couldn't happen, not with the responsibility of commanding a Confederate brigade of infantry. But he still wanted to know what she would say. "You've always been my heart, where no one else can ever be. I can't put the way I feel toward you into words, regardless of the fact you've been sleeping with another man for two years now."

He'd done what he wanted to do from the beginning. He'd opened up his heart and laid it all on the line. He continued, "You're still my wife, regardless of what has transpired in my absence. You married me first, and your marriage to Simon is illegal. All that I am or ever will be is sitting right here in front of me."

"I have nothing to do with what you've become, Taylor." She loved him. She may not still be *in love* with him, but she loved him. However, she would never allow him to say he'd become this monster because of her. "You've become what you are from that war you couldn't wait to get involved with."

"I understand that," Taylor replied, "but there has to be some way that we can make everything return to the way things were before."

He noticed she was shaking her head at this remark and realized she was right. Things would never return to what they were before. He tried a different angle. "You know, I've stared at the face in the looking glass since I've been home and wondered what's gone so wrong with the boy I once knew."

"You left me to fight a war, and that's all that's wrong with you." Phoebe saw their son begin to squirm in the sheets and reached over to gently rub his head.

"I was wrong," Taylor said. He'd finally admitted it. He'd been wrong to leave her and fight an ugly war. He'd done his duty, but deep down he still felt he'd done the wrong thing. He looked back on his life and felt a sense of shame. The entire time that he was fighting, thinking he was doing the noblest thing for his people, was a big mistake. His entire life until this point came across as a lie. It wasn't fair, but it was life. That was the moment he realized that the innocent young boy who'd left so long ago had grown into a bitter old man. He asked, "Where do we go from here?"

Phoebe shook her head. The answer eluded her. She loved him, but she had grown to love Simon. The man was the extreme opposite of Taylor. Where Taylor had become a being who specialized in taking lives, Simon was a being who'd worked hard to save those lives.

Taylor realized he was in a conundrum with no escape. He truly didn't know whether she still wanted him or not. He wasn't even sure he wanted to know the answer to that question.

Phoebe said, "I long for the end of war."

"Only the dead have seen the end of war," Taylor replied. "If it's not this war, it'll simply be another somewhere else. Don't worry about where we go from here. I can't come home until it's over anyway."

"I will not have Simon in our home again until we figure this thing out."

Taylor opened the tent flap and stared into the cold, dark night, across the sea of tents that housed the men he commanded. He said in a quiet voice, "Do you still pray before bed every night?"

"I do," she replied.

"Say a prayer for peace." Taylor turned back to her with tear-filled eyes. "Say a prayer for all the fallen boys. Say a prayer for yourself and our son. Say a prayer for me, because I can't come home until it's all over with."

"Taylor, your mother made sure you got the best education available." Phoebe rose from the stool and walked into his arms. "She taught you to be so pure and sinless. She made sure you attended the finest schools so you would succeed in this life. She would roll over in her grave if she realized what you've become—callous killer."

"I've killed with impunity, it's true." Taylor thought about the irony of it all. "I don't understand what's occurred in my life. There's

201

been so much death. I remember leaving this town to all the cheers of the citizens. I remember how proud you were to see me going off in that lieutenant's uniform. All the girls encouraged us, told us we were fighting for them. Now I return to learn my girl has turned against me. Everything I've ever done seems to be a sin now."

"I'm not against you." Phoebe interjected. "I've learned how ignorant we were to encourage our boys to go die in war. I'm against war."

"I left my parents for you." Taylor began to shake his head. He was determined he'd shed his last tear. There was nothing left but the feeling of bitterness. "My poor mother mourned herself to death. I lost her because of you. I lost both parents basically because I thought I was going away to make you happy."

"That's a lie." Phoebe's eyes grew wide with anger. "You couldn't wait to get in this war. You were a cadet at the university, and that professor had you sold on how glorious war would be. Now don't blame me. There is enough blame to go around without placing it all on my shoulders. I only told you what I thought you wanted to hear."

"I'm sorry," Taylor replied. "Are you mine or not?"

"I have no idea at this point." She lowered her face into her hands and began to weep again. "I don't know what I want at this point. I feel I should wait and see what the future brings, but I don't see how I can possibly hurt Simon now. He's given me and Tom so much. When this war is over and you return, we'll sit down and work something out. I just wish…"

Taylor noticed her hesitation. He asked, "Wish what…that I hadn't returned?"

"You know better than that." Phoebe looked into his eyes. "Your mother tutored me. She made me the lady I am today. It was as if I'd been to finishing school."

"And I fought a war," Taylor mumbled. "I fought a war for my family and my country. I came home to learn I'd done that for another man to take my wife—a man who was too much of a coward to fight for his family or his country."

"I'm so sorry," Phoebe lowered her head.

"I have to thank you for one thing." Taylor watched her look up, her eyes questioning him. "At least I know I can feel again, even if that feeling is nothing but pain."

She cast her eyes back toward the ground. He saw tears streaming down her cheeks again. Taylor regretted that he'd said that last part, regretted that he'd hurt her, although she'd destroyed him.

Taylor realized for the first time that it was over. She had evaded his question. The bitterness began to build. Somewhere in the last two years of his life he'd lost his one true love and now understood he would never get that back. He would never let her know how deeply she had grieved him. It was time to let her have reason to forget him. That was what it appeared she was asking for here tonight.

He turned back to the tent flap and stared into the dark night. "After the things I've done and seen, I've concluded that I was born to be a warrior. War is my wife now. I was born to wade through the darkest storms, and it's what invigorates me. Without battles, my soul would probably die anyway."

"Don't talk that way, Taylor," Phoebe was shaking her head. "I don't believe a word of that."

He wished he could say she was right, but deep down he truly believed every word he'd just spoken. After she'd taken their son and gone, he began to think about the path his life had taken. It was as if he was on a runaway train, not in control of his own destiny at all. It was a runaway train that would never get him back home.

Taylor sat just inside the tent flap. He'd tied the flap back around to the outside of the tent wall. The night had become deathly quiet; not even a whippoorwill protested for lack of sleep. Memories of his parents flooded back to him in waves. He thought about how hard his mother had worked to make him so unadulterated in every task he performed. At some point, he was forced to admit that she hadn't succeeded. As long as Taylor lived, there would always be that sensation of disgrace.

He could see Phoebe standing on the veranda promising him that she'd wait for him forever, and he remembered feeling her warm tears when he held her to his cheek. All of that was folly now.

There was nothing left for him to accomplish in this place. He would give an order in the morning and march northward to attach his brigade to Hood's army in North Alabama. He wondered if it would be a cowardly act to run away from his problems. It really didn't matter. There was a war that needed to be fought, and he'd cleaned up the lawlessness in his hometown.

He waited patiently for the dawn. It was still an hour away. There had to be a better place, a place of happiness somewhere in his mind, but it was elusive at this point. He needed to change the way he felt but was unsure how that could possibly be accomplished. It was the first time in his life when he felt that loving someone was the wrong thing to do. Taylor was attempting to give her his entire world, but she seemed unwilling to accept it. This war had turned the entire world upside down.

As soon as the sun began to light the eastern sky, Taylor went to Basil's tent and instructed him to have his adjutant wake the men. It was time to leave.

Basil rubbed at sleepy eyes and asked, "Leave? Hell, we just got here?"

"There's a war to fight, Basil," Taylor turned to exit the tent.

"I know. But hell, we deserve a few weeks of rest." Basil sat up and attempted to argue with Taylor. "Would you just wait a minute?"

"Basil, if you want a furlough," Taylor paused in the doorway of the tent without turning around, "I'll happily give you a couple of months, but I have to go."

Basil swung his legs over the side of his cot, propped his elbow on his knee, and placed his forehead in his hand. "All right, all right, I'll get on it."

Taylor was frustrated at how quickly word had spread through town that he was departing. It seemed everyone had come by his tent to try and persuade him to stay longer. He could hardly wait for his men to finish breakfast so he could make his escape.

As his men formed for the march out of town, Taylor noticed all the townsfolk gathered on both sides of the road to see them off. Phoebe stood just under a shade tree. He pretended he didn't see her as he climbed into the saddle and nudged the horse forward. Basil was waiting astride his stallion. He wanted to argue with Taylor about leaving so soon but realized his commander had made up his mind. Taylor could be strong in his convictions at times, and Basil realized the futility of further argument.

They eased the horses out onto the road ahead of the line of infantry. Someone yelled, "We love you, Taylor!"

Taylor nodded his head in reply. An old lady yelled, "You be careful and come home in one piece now!"

Basil sat erect beside his commander. He was proud of his best friend and felt an honor riding out of town at his side. It made him feel like some kind of conquering hero.

An old man yelled, "We'll never forget what you did for us by killing them Tories! May God go with you, son!"

Phoebe watched him slowly pass by. She thought he was lost. He had no place left to call home, nowhere to go. She felt like he blamed her for the path his life had taken, but deep down she knew who he really blamed. Taylor could never forgive himself for what he'd become. He'd spent the last few years doing what he thought was goodness, but he could never understand why his heart hurt so bad.

Silas spurred his horse up alongside Taylor's and smiled. "Didn't think I'd be back in the army so soon."

"Now, here you are," Taylor replied. He fought the urge to turn and take one last look at Phoebe. His heart had grown bitter. A funny thought passed through his mind. Since he'd grown to love bitterness, perhaps he should take his heart out and eat it. It would be a black heart, covered with scars. *More foolishness, he thought. I must clear my mind for the battle that is awaiting me down this long, dusty road.*

Phoebe had seen right through him the moment she saw him. There was no goodness left inside. The war had destroyed all of that by showing him things a man isn't supposed to see. She wanted to shout for him to turn back, to stay with her. At the

205

moment, she felt like racing down the road, grabbing the bridle, and demanding that he come home. Suddenly, she realized it was all her fault for not demanding him to stay with her and forget this war. She glanced around and thought about what people would say if she did beg him to stay. She hesitated, and in that moment of hesitation, she realized she might regret this moment for the rest of her life.

Taylor fought the urge to cry and swallowed hard as he fought the tears back. A lump rose in this throat. He couldn't let his men see him in such distress. He thought about how he couldn't wait to get back here and hold her in his arms. He'd made up his mind that he would never let her go. To the left of the road was a rose vine in full bloom. All he had left was memories of a better place and time. He glanced back over his shoulder for one last look at the girl he'd left behind, staring at her through watery eyes, and then spurred the horse forward as if to say goodbye.

Silas noticed the mood and said, "When we get back home, cousin, she will still be here waiting."

"I couldn't change her mind," Taylor replied, "or her heart. It's over, Silas."

"She'll be here waiting; I assure you of that," Silas began to argue. "You're a hero now."

"I don't feel like no hero," Taylor mumbled. He wanted to change the subject, so he turned to Basil, and said, "We ought to catch up to Hood around Decatur or thereabouts."

"Right," Basil agreed.

"He's heading into Tennessee, and we still have a chance to win this war." Taylor turned as he was talking to include Silas in the conversation. "We take Nashville and enter Kentucky, it's gonna cause the biggest stink in the Northern press."

"Taylor," Silas began to sound disconcerted, "well, both of you really. I need to let ya'll in on something. I have never been in combat. Hell, Taylor, you wouldn't allow me to go in at Shiloh."

"I probably saved your life, Silas," Taylor continued staring at the long road ahead.

"I understand," Silas wasn't through yet. "I still need you fellars to take good care of me. I don't want to be a volunteer aide that looks like some kind of dummy when we get in the thick of it."

"Now, Silas, you know I have always taken good care of you." Taylor shook his head.

"I want to fight the same as the rest," Silas understood what Taylor was insinuating. "I don't want to stand in the back and hold no more horses."

"Your point is duly noted." Taylor smiled at Basil and then turned back to Silas. "In the next battle, you have my word that you will not be in the rear holding horses."

"Thank you." Silas looked past Taylor at Basil. "Please don't tell the men about this conversation."

"Your secret is safe with us." Basil smiled and nodded. "Taylor, you deserve to be home longer. You've earned that. It's almost like you've only come home to say goodbye."

Taylor shook his head. He would hear no more talk about staying home. The town only gave him a feeling of betrayal now. His wife had lied to him, betrayed him. The town had betrayed him by not protecting or caring for his parents.

They camped that night just south of Richland, Mississippi. The next morning they would reach Jackson, the state capital, and take a train north to Corinth.

That night, after Taylor had gone to bed, Basil asked Silas for a moment alone. Silas wasn't sure what Basil could possibly want. They walked off into the darkness away from the camp.

Basil paused and said, "I'm worried about Taylor."

"How so?" Silas asked, his voice betraying his concern.

"He seems so psychologically fatigued. It's difficult to put my finger on." Basil rubbed his head. "I mean, it's not the deal with his family, it's been this way for some time. It's like the war has worn him down mentally. He appears to be a young man on the outside, but it's like he's aged a hundred years on the inside."

"I've just been so happy to see him alive that I haven't really noticed." Silas thought a moment and then asked, "What would you have me to do?"

"Just be there for him." Basil looked back toward the tents to make sure no one was eavesdropping. "Try and keep his spirits up. Just like the thing with his wife. It's just not like him to simply give up like that."

"I'll do my best." Silas patted Basil on the shoulder. "And thanks to you, he made it home. You're a great friend, Basil."

They boarded the train the next morning and roared off northward toward Corinth. They would change trains there and travel eastward on the Memphis and Charleston Railroad, the "Backbone of the Confederacy." From Barton, Alabama, eastward, they would be forced to walk, the track having been destroyed by two opposing armies. Four days later they arrived in Tuscumbia, Alabama, only to learn that Hood's army had left for Tennessee the day before. After being ferried across the Tennessee River to Florence, Taylor had his brigade marching hard in the wake of Hood's forces.

He hadn't known how he would get Phoebe off his mind, but staying busy definitely helped. His cousin Silas was a big help. He kept Taylor distracted and even began to raise his cousin's spirits again. Together they'd decided that when this war ended they would go into business together. They would build carriages like his father had done. Until then, there was a war to fight, and Taylor was itching to get at the enemy one more time.

As the column moved northward, Taylor, Silas, and Basil happened upon a man sitting on a fence watching the brigade make its way up the road. The man sat there smoking a pipe and watching the advancing line of men with passing interest.

Taylor reined up and asked, "What's your name, sir?"

"Spencer Lyman," the man replied. "You boys part of Hood's bunch?"

"That's right," Taylor replied. "How old are you?"

"Twenty-seven," Spencer replied. "You boys are about a day's march behind Hood. You probably catch him up around Columbia somewhere's."

Taylor ignored the comment. "Why are you not in the army?"

"I'm an overseer," Spencer replied.

"A what?" Silas asked.

"An overseer," Spencer replied. "You see, the Confederate congress passed a law that says anybody what oversees twenty slaves is exempt from the war. I oversee twenty-one of old man Fox's servants."

"I see," Taylor eyed Spencer a long moment. "Well, if there was any such law, it's been long since forgotten about because we need every man in the ranks. We're losing this war."

Spencer sat back on the fence. He wasn't sure what Taylor was saying.

"Silas, get this man a rifle and put him in a company back there." Taylor turned to Spencer and said, "Welcome to the army, Spencer Lyman."

Spencer's eyes grew wide. He began to argue his case. "Now hold on there, Colonel, I know..."

"It's General, and there'll be no more argument about it." Taylor nudged his horse forward.

"General," Spencer was pleading now, "at least let me go home and tell my family."

"There's no time for that." Taylor stopped the horse and turned to Silas. "Have one of his servants go to his house and tell his family that he's joined the army."

CHAPTER ELEVEN

"You lose your best friend?" Sol asked.

Charlie plopped into his chair. "No, sir. Your story has gotten me in the dumps. I hope it gets better."

"Well now," Sol sucked at his front teeth with his tongue. "Used to be you just couldn't wait for me to finish. Now you don't want to hear no more."

"I do want to hear more." Charlie looked up, his eyes wide in protest. "It's just sad—real sad, Uncle Sol."

"Hell, it ain't no fairy tale," Sol shook his head. "It's the damned truth. Life don't always treat a man right."

"Sorry," Charlie lowered his head.

"There you go being sorry again," Sol shook his head. "What am I gonna do with ya, boy? Sides, the story ain't done. It has a happy ending anyhow."

"It does?" Charlie perked up. "By the way, my mother wants you back over for dinner this Saturday."

"I can't turn down that woman's vittles." Sol's mouth began to water at the thought. "Your ma is just too good to me."

Charlie tried to constrain the smile. "Don't get too excited. Parson Peters is gonna be there too. He'll be trying to get you in church."

"Damn," Sol shook his head. "Them vittles is awful good. Guess I will have to put up with his sermon to get 'em."

Charlie was ready to get back to the story now that he understood it had a happy ending. He asked, "So, that hanging down there in town was the skirmish you were referring to?"

"That's right," Sol nodded. "Only shooting done was by them damned Tories, and they was a shooting up in the air. The hanging was nice."

Charlie looked at Sol in disbelief. He could never tell if the man was serious or just playing with him. He asked, "Is that why everyone calls that large oak 'the hanging tree'?"

"Yep, that's the one," Sol replied.

"All the boys dare each other to sit under it every Halloween," Charlie said. "I never knew it was because of a real hanging."

"It is," Sol said. "Them boys got buried out in the cemetery in an unmarked grave."

"Our town cemetery?" Charlie asked.

"That's the one," Sol said. "Now, where were we?"

"Marching into Tennessee, "Charlie said.

Sol asked, "Did I ever tell you about crossing the Tennessee River?"

"You mentioned that ya'll were ferried across."

"The pontoon bridge was taken up by the time we arrived," Sol spat a stream of tobacco juice off the porch. "Most of it, least ways. We had to be ferried across the river in small boats. Took most all day just to get one brigade over."

"Wow," Charlie's eyes widened. He loved the little things he learned about the war from Sol.

"We marched northward," Sol was back telling the story, "eyes on the horizon, down another long, dusty road. Men slowly marching to their own deaths. That's the way it works in warfare. Makes you wonder about the strange creature God created called *man*."

"I have to agree with you there," Charlie nodded.

"We didn't catch Hood until Spring Hill, on the 30th day of November," Sol was in deep thought. "I'll never forget that day. We marched past S.D. Lee's sleeping corps and found General Hood at a house called Rippa da Villa or something like that. Had to have been a Frenchman lived there I bet. He was in a fitful mood. He'd trapped the Federal army, and his subordinates had allowed them to escape. Twenty-three thousand men had marched past his entire army during the night within a hundred yards. Ole Hood was fit to be tied I tell ya."

"That many men? That close?" Charlie asked in disbelief.

"That many men, that close," Sol replied. "It was a damned shame. We may have changed the course of the war, but who knows."

****

211

He woke every night because she haunted his every dream. She would continue to haunt him for the rest of his life; he had no doubt. There was no way he would ever belong to anyone else. He could picture himself already, living alone in an old cabin—the life of a hermit until he grew old and died.

Taylor had come to realize that he had a giant hole through the middle of his soul. There would never be enough happiness left in life to fill that void. Death would be the only thing that could kill the bitterness. He was vehement about that. He felt weary with this load that seemed more than he could ever bear. He was tired, bone tired, of this war and what it had done to him. This war had created him, made him the monster he was today.

His brigade trudged on up the road, away from Spring Hill and in pursuit of the Federal army that had escaped Hood's trap last night. Taylor couldn't believe what had happened. He'd found Hood in a foul mood at the plantation home called Rippa Villa. The man was frustrated and ranting about the failings of Frank Cheatham and John Calvin Brown. When Taylor had reported to Hood, the man had simply told him to find Cleburne and fall in with his division.

It made Taylor proud that Hood would assign his men to Cleburne's division. That division was known as the crack troops of the Confederacy. The Federal army feared Cleburne's men, and that suited Taylor just fine. He wanted to hit them now; he needed to hit them.

Somewhere down this dusty road might be the end of this war and a new life for him. Besides, it was obvious that the war would end if this campaign wasn't a success. It truly felt like the darkest days he'd seen so far in this bitter struggle.

They'd marched all day before he caught up with Major General Patrick Cleburne and his division. They were drawn up south of Franklin, Tennessee, on a ridge called Winstead Hill. It was obvious the army was about to advance. Cleburne was polite but told Taylor to get his brigade in line to the right of Brigadier General Mark Lowrey. Lowrey was the reserve brigade for Granbury, and Taylor's men would serve as Govan's reserve.

They were still filing on line when Basil rode up to Taylor and said, "My regiment's on line, Taylor."

"Very well," Taylor replied. He continued to stare across two miles of open fields toward the entrenched Federal force.

Basil cleared his throat. "This ain't gonna be very pretty."

"Hood's campaign has been one damned blunder from beginning to end," Taylor replied. "This would never have occurred in Lee's army. It's like we're going to war with our brother's kids or something."

Taylor could hear his men complaining about the absurdity of making such a charge. Earlier in the war he would have agreed with them, but now he was empty inside. It didn't matter if Hood had ordered him to charge the gates of hell itself, he would have gone willingly. He would go here today without a complaint whatsoever. A private near Taylor shouted, "Sir, if we go down there, we're all gonna die!"

"We all gotta die," Taylor replied. Life was cruel, there was no refining it. He regretted what he'd become, his dispassion. He wasn't the same boy who'd left his home, his mother and father, and his wife.

Silas stepped next to Basil and asked, "What does Taylor want?"

"Revenge," Basil replied, "and he's about to get it."

"Revenge for what?" Silas looked shocked.

"His life." Basil replied. "Everything—hell I'm not sure, but I can see it as clear as day. He wants revenge for ever being born I guess."

The order was given, and the brigade moved off down Winstead Hill toward the waiting Federal lines across the way. When the first artillery rounds began to pass overhead, Taylor turned to Silas, passed him an envelope, and said, "Take this message back to General Hood."

Silas just looked at the envelope in disbelief. He asked, "Now? We're just going in; I won't know where to find you."

"Never mind that," Taylor thrust the envelope at his cousin, "I'll send someone back for you. This must be delivered."

Silas began to shake his head. He refused to take the message. "You're not doing this to me again, cousin. I'm going in with ya'll."

Taylor's eyes flashed. His countenance didn't even resemble that of a human. The man was becoming transformed for the battle ahead. He was animal-like. His voice was more forceful now, demanding, "That is an order, Captain. I'll have you arrested immediately!"

"Yes, sir." Silas reluctantly took the message and spun the horse. He rode to the rear, stealing glances of his cousin and Basil marching into battle with their brigade.

Taylor hadn't lied to Silas. He'd promised he wouldn't order him to go to the rear to hold any horses. He hadn't promised he wouldn't send him on a message-delivering mission.

They marched onward as the first line of infantry opened fire. Cleburne's front two brigades quickly overran this weak line placed out in the open without protection of breastworks. Cleburne came roaring down the line on his horse once the line had broken. He was screaming at the top of his voice. "Go into the works with them!"

Instantly, Taylor realized what his new commander was saying. The enemy had broken and were racing rearward to the protection of the breastworks at the main line. If the Confederates would race along with them, the main line wouldn't be able to fire for fear of hitting their own men. He quickly gave the order to advance at the double quick. There was no time to worry about maintaining the line. It was of great importance for them to reach that line with the rest of the division.

Closing on the main line, Taylor could see a cotton gin to the right of the road. The enemy behind the entrenchments held their fire as long as possible. When they opened up at last, they were forced to kill many of their own men as well. It was as if they'd charged into a hail storm. They struck the main line and it broke. The Confederate soldiers were caught up in the moment. The rebel yell was being screamed all up and down the line. Taylor felt fantastic again. He was in the chaos of battle. He was home.

214

To his left he saw General Granbury shot in the head. He crashed to his knees in the middle of the Columbia Pike. His hands were covering his face, with his elbows resting on his knees. He was dead, yet his body didn't appear to realize it just yet. It was a macabre scene.

Taylor and his men naturally funneled through the gap in the road. They were no longer headed straight for the cotton gin, but that didn't matter anymore. There was a breach in the line and he realized it needed to be exploited. He didn't try to correct the alignment. It was as if his brigade was a living animal, had taken a mind of its own, and understood what he expected them to accomplish.

They raced on down the Columbia Pike toward a retrenched line about fifty yards beyond. They stumbled over the dead and trod across the poor wounded lying in the road. They no longer cared about their fallen comrades. If they were forced to make this fight, they wanted it done quickly.

The scene appeared as hell on earth. Pandemonium was everywhere he looked. It would be a scene Taylor would never be able to erase from his memory. The slaughter was horrific. He felt glorious again for the first time in ages.

They broke through the retrenched line and into the yard and road in front of a modest brick home. It was almost dark now. The scenes appearing here couldn't be described.

Taylor turned to Basil and shouted, "This is it! It's over if we can keep pushing!"

"Right!" Basil replied. His eyes betrayed the shock of what he was witnessing. The fighting here was hand to hand. Clubbed muskets were being swung overhead; men's skulls were cracking like one would break an egg.

Taylor saw a Federal officer run a Confederate major through with his sword. He saw the major fire his pistol into the enemy soldier, and both collapsed in the road ahead.

Men were fighting with shovels and axes. The scene was one of horror. There was nothing but gore everywhere. Smoke and darkness tried to envelope the nightmarish scene, but still the killing continued.

When the artillery fired nearby, Taylor could actually hear bones cracking. The sound reminded him of a child snapping match sticks. The canister tore through the bodies. Some men seemed to simply vanish from the face of the earth in a bloody mist.

Taylor crashed into the line of Federals swinging his sword wildly. He was no longer human. Basil stood there in a state of shock as Taylor careened first one way and then another. He cared not for who he struck, whether friend or foe. All the men had given up on surviving and seemed struck with the notion of killing as many of their enemy as possible before their time was up.

****

Uncle Sol sat at the table with Charlie and his parents. He'd brought a long object wrapped in brown paper and kept it at his side at all times.

Sol said, "These some mighty good vittles, ma'am."

"Thank you, Uncle Sol," Charlie's mother winked at the older man. "You're welcome to come eat with us anytime. You don't have to wait for an invitation."

"Thank you, ma'am, but my ma taught me better than that," Sol scooped up another forkful of peas.

Charlie could resist the curiosity no longer. He asked, "What you got in the bag? Is it a baseball bat?"

"Boy, them damned Yankees invented baseball," Sol spoke without thinking. He quickly turned to Charlie's mother and said, "Pardon my language, ma'am."

Helen waved him off with a smile. She looked at Charlie and said, "It's not polite to be so nosey."

"It's just Uncle Sol," Charlie protested.

"It's quite all right, ma'am," Sol spoke up in defense of Charlie. "I'm just like family now."

"So Charlie says you've come here to finish your story?" Thomas asked.

"That's right," Sol paused between bites, "I thought it only fitting that I finish the story for all three of you."

216

"I know Charlie is dying to hear the end," Thomas said, "I have no idea what he'll do when it's over."

"He can still come see his Uncle Sol," Sol said as he shoveled a forkful of okra into his mouth.

Once the meal was finished, Charlie insisted Sol finish the story at the table. He was on the edge of his seat, and Sol noticed that his family seemed just as interested to hear what had their son so worked up.

"Franklin, Tennessee," Sol mumbled. He lowered his head and stared at his plate. "That name will haunt me the rest of my life. It was horrible. Death was everywhere. It was far worse than Spotsylvania or Gettysburg. Shiloh pales in comparison. The dead and dying were strewn indiscriminately across the ground. It was the death cry of a nation."

Sol took a moment to wipe a tear from his eye. He shook his head at a loss for words. It obviously pained him to remember the scene.

"Are you all right, Sol?" Helen asked. She reached out and touched his arm.

"I'll be fine," Sol sniffed and raised his head. "Sorry, ma'am. Silas didn't want Taylor to make the charge at all. He thought Taylor was going down that hill to commit suicide. I still remember hearing Silas telling him he was being dragged to his death by the ghost of a defunct marriage."

****

Taylor had thought the marriage wouldn't be defunct if people would have kept their word. Silas attempted to stand between him and the field ahead. Taylor said, "Silas, don't try and stand in my way. True, life has been bitter for me, but I'm not here to die. I'm at this place to win this war. A brave man only dies once; cowards die many times. Don't you see? We both have to go down there and do our duty. Besides, we shouldn't fear death. Every human being owes God a death in the end."

Silas stepped aside. He felt better now that he knew Taylor wasn't here to commit suicide.

When the order was given, Taylor turned to Basil and said, "It's time to reap the whirlwind. Let's finish this thing."

"Right," Basil smiled. "It's the last charge of Sammy Rodes and his immortals."

Later, during the battle, Silas had just located General Hood and his staff. He glanced down at the envelope and noticed it wasn't even addressed to Hood but to Phoebe. He couldn't believe his eyes. Taylor had hoodwinked him yet again.

The next morning, Silas made his way down to the scene of destruction in search of his cousin. The cries of the wounded would haunt his dreams for the rest of his life. The scene was like nothing he could have ever imagined. One young boy, no more than sixteen, was crying for his mother. His arm was completely blown off by artillery fire. Silas had tears in his eyes as he continued to search among the wreckage. He said aloud, "God forgive me for ever wanting to see a battle."

The dead lay piled four and five deep in places. In the ditch outside the trench, there were so many bodies that some couldn't even fall over. They still remained upright, chins resting on their chests, facing their enemies who'd evacuated to Nashville during the night. Some were shot to pieces and were simply unrecognizable.

Five general officers had been killed. Another was mortally wounded. Patrick Cleburne, the great Stonewall of the West, had been shot in the chest near the cotton gin. His brigadier, Hiram Granbury, was still in the road with his face in his hands, kneeling to the bullet that had taken his life. General Strahl had been hit at least three times, maybe more. General States Rights Gist had been hit twice. General John Adams had been shot seven times. John Carter was lying in a house about a mile from the battlefield, gut shot and suffering from intense pain. He would die within a week.

One man approached Silas with his lower jaw shot away. The man was attempting to talk but was making no sound. Silas shook his head out of pity and moved on past. He saw a wounded man rubbing at his eyes and noticed they were shot out. His face was caked with blood.

There were bodies blown to bits. Another had a pick driven through his temple. Arms and legs protruded from the piles in the ditch in every direction. Silas wondered how anyone had survived this battle. He could barely contemplate what he was witnessing here. He would never think of war as glorious again. Any politician who wanted war needed to witness this battlefield just once to cure him of those thoughts.

As they lifted the dead from the ditch, they found many wounded trapped at the bottom. The ditch contained three inches of blood. The stench was already sickening. Silas looked across the field near the gin and decided that he could walk from one area to another by just stepping on bodies.

He couldn't find anyone he recognized at the main line, so he decided to move on down the road. There were a lot of bodies there also. Some unwounded soldiers sat along the side of the road or against trees with their heads in their hands, unable to contemplate what they'd just survived. Most wondered why they'd been spared at all.

Silas made his way to a brick house with a large amount of battle damage. He saw a man with a shovel scraping brains off the front steps of the home. The outbuildings were full of bullet holes. Silas moved among the bodies in search of someone he knew. He found Basil in the road, staring toward heaven where his spirit had flown. He'd been shot twice in the chest.

Silas took out the letter written to Phoebe and opened it. Taylor had written that Phoebe deserved to be happy and he guaranteed she soon would be. He was going into his final battle and was leaving all things undone between them. He'd understood that his existence was just too painful for her.

****

Sol rubbed at his tear-filled eyes. "I found him just beyond Basil. He'd been shot numerous times. I couldn't bring both bodies home, and therefore, Basil still rests in the Confederate Cemetery in Franklin."

219

"I thought your name was Sol?" Charlie asked. His eyes were bulging from his head with surprise.

"My name is Silas Oliver Lafayette Saunders," Sol looked up, and his watery eyes met Charlie's. "I got the nickname Sol because of my initials."

"Oh," Charlie said.

"I remember him disappearing into the smoke of battle there." Sol pushed the plate away. "I never saw him alive again. Nobody heard his dying words if he had any. Taylor was a hero, fought for his home and his people. I'd like to think he didn't die in vain. I managed to find an old army wagon and mule. I hammered a coffin together out of parts of the old cotton gin and placed his body inside. I rode that wagon out of the war and never looked back. It was about over anyhow. I remember arriving back here in Brick, Mississippi, and we unloaded the coffin in front of the inn. Phoebe came down with her young boy, and I handed her the note. She read the message and knelt down and cried over his coffin. Her tears stained the top of the box. Tom was busy playing with a ball, enjoying himself immensely and not understanding what was taking place. We buried Taylor in the cemetery under a simple sandstone rock. It's the one just inside the cemetery gate. There would be no eulogies for the brave soldier, but it was an honorable death. There was a Federal cavalry regiment occupying the town by this point, and they refused to allow us to have a funeral for no rebel officer. Franklin was not only the death of our nation, but almost the death of our family."

Thomas eyed Sol a long moment. His eyes had begun to tear up as well. He realized that Phoebe was his mother, and now everything about his life began to make sense. The father who refused to be close to him was not his father at all. They'd kept this secret for forty years. He could scarcely believe that had been possible.

Sol said, "I promised Phoebe I would die with this secret, but I just couldn't bring myself to do it. When Charlie arrived at my shack and asked about the war, I knew then that you all deserved to know. You deserve to know that your last name is not Rich, it's Cameron. And you both descended from a great war hero, not

220

some doctor who lacked the courage to fight. You are both truly 'to the manor born.' It weren't Phoebe's fault. The boy she'd married had returned a different person. He'd just seen too much, more than most men would witness if they lived to be a thousand. He'd seen the young boys he commanded killed and maimed and felt responsible as well."

Sol turned to Thomas and said, "Tom, you were playing with that ball. It nearly killed my soul. You had no idea that was your daddy in that box. Your maw has told me a thousand times over the years how she felt responsible for the death of your father. Was she? Who knows. I don't hold her accountable. She may have talked him into staying if she'd just told him she still loved him. Perhaps she was wrong for letting him go. He blamed her for her betrayal."

Tom was shaking his head. Everyone at the table was in tears now. He asked, "What am I to do?"

"I tell you what I want you to do," Sol reached over and unwrapped the package. He pulled out an officer's sword that had been well cared for over the years. "I want you to take this; it's yours now. It belongs to you and the boy. This is the sword he carried throughout that war and killed at least three men, perhaps more at Franklin, who knows. I want you to place a nice marker on his grave also. He's earned that. If there is such a thing as the gallant dead, he is that. We took his personal Confederate flag that flew atop his tent throughout the war and wrapped him inside. It was his shroud—a glorious shroud—and he rests inside it today. Those Yankees laughed and made fun of him as we buried him. They said that he'd gotten what he deserved. I can never forget or forgive them for that, and I hope they get their just reward in the next life."

"I will see that this is done," Thomas said. He wiped at his tears with his napkin. "I'm not sure I can ever forgive my mother."

"Forgive her," Sol answered quickly. "You must forgive her. She did what she thought was right and was only trying to protect you. I still remember the day we laid Taylor in the ground as if it were yesterday. My life has been cold and empty ever since. We all died a little in that war, some more than others. I haven't truly lived since that day. Time distances us from war, but we can never escape the scars. I have a lot of guilt because I survived and others died. Why did I deserve to live? I didn't even see enough action to receive a scratch, and now I question if I'm really a man. I know we'll meet all those who died in that war in heaven when we die. I take solace in that. So, the story ends, I suppose, and now you know it all—or almost all."

Thomas looked up. He didn't know if he could handle any more surprises today. He asked, "What?"

"It wasn't long after the burial that we found the letter," Sol smiled. He watched the family waiting, hanging on his every word. "It was inside Taylor's valise. It too was addressed to Phoebe. It read that, although he was gone, he still loved her and would always be there. He told her that each time she caught movement out of the corner of her eye or felt a breath of air on her neck, it would be his spirit watching over her until they could be together someday the way they were before. He said, 'Life is nothing but a shadow. All will be made right with our death.'"

Tim Kent

Tim has been interested in the Civil War since the age of six. He has been writing for six years and published his first book five years ago. He has just released his second book "Never Smile Again" that covers the Battle of Shiloh. His second book "Die Like Men" covers the Battle of Franklin and is currently available at Books A Million and on Amazon.com. Tim is currently working on his fourth book about Antietam.

Tim enjoys re-enacting and is a first sergeant with the 26th Alabama infantry. He has re-enacted several battles including, Bryce's Crossroads, The Battle of Franklin, Bentonville, Twin Rivers, Resaca, The Battle for Decatur, Winfield and numerous Camps of Instruction. Besides re-enacting Tim enjoys making period clothing for himself and his family, collecting Civil War relics and books and most of all Confederate General autographs.

Tim is also the Lieutenant Commander of his local Sons of Confederate Veterans Camp 898. He has spoken at camp meetings and is a board member of Historical Truth 101. Tim has a personal library of over 400 books on the Civil War. He also uses the internet, other authors and historians and his local library as resources as well.

Tim has assisted other authors in researching material for their books and was involved with Wide Awake Films at Perryville. He has also acted as a guide for numerous family and friends on battlefield tours.

Tim spent 20 years working for Norfolk Southern Railway as an engineer riding the rails of the old Memphis & Charleston Railway, the backbone of the Confederacy.

Also Written by Tim Kent

Die Like Men

In November, 1864 the Civil War is almost over. The Army of Tennessee under its gallant commander John Bell Hood has a chance to reverse the Confederacy's sinking fortunes. With veteran troops, he plans to strike into Tennessee where he will capture Nashville and invade the northern states. General Sherman has taken the best troops with him on his famous 'March to the Sea. George Thomas, the Federal commander is forced to defend Tennessee with scattered forces and green troops.

The Confederate's move into Tennessee almost forty-thousand strong. The Federal's are in a race to concentrate enough men to save Nashville. Die Like Men will take the reader through the invasion from Florence, Alabama to Nashville and provide insight into the colorful personalities of the leading participants. This is a must read for any fan of the American Civil War.

ISBN# 978-1-934610-62-6

Never Smile Again

After the loss of both Kentucky and Tennessee, Confederate
General Albert Sidney Johnston has one last chance to save his
reputation and his nation. He must destroy Federal General
Ulysses S. Grant's army before he is reinforced by General Don
Carlos Buell. Together the two Federal armies will outnumber
Johnston's army by more than two to one. Confederate President
Jefferson Davis has sent General Gustave Toutand Beauregard,
the Hero of the Confederacy, to assist Johnston. Together, they
must stop the Federal invasion before Mississippi and Alabama
also fall to Union control. Never Smile Again takes you on the
campaign from Corinth to Shiloh Church and beyond. This is
the second book in the series by Civil War historian Tim Kent.
A must read for any Civil War enthusiast.

ISBN# 978-1-934610-68-8

Bluewater Publications is a multi-faceted publishing company capable of meeting all of your reading and publishing needs. Our two-fold aim is to:

1) Provide the market with educationally enlightening and inspiring research and reading materials.

2) Make the opportunity of being published available to any author and or researcher who desires to be published.

We are passionate about preserving history; whether through the re-publishing of an out-of-print classic, or by publishing the research of historians and genealogists. Bluewater Publications is the Peoples' Choice Publisher.

For company information or information about how you can be published through Bluewater Publications, please visit:

www.BluewaterPublications.com

Also check Amazon.com to purchase any of the books that we publish.

Confidently Preserving Our Past,

Bluewater Publications.com